Deflowered Lyric

Published in the United States by
Beckham Publications Group, Inc.
P.O. Box 4066, Silver Spring, MD 20914

ISBN: Paperback   978-0-9905904-0-8
Hardover   978-0-9905904-1-5

Library of Congress Cataloging in Publication:

Deflowered
Lyric

A NOVEL

J.J. STAPLES

THE Beckham
PUBLICATIONS GROUP, INC.

Silver Spring

Deflowered Lyric is dedicated to the memory of:

Shania Gray
March 29ᵗʰ, 1996-September 6ᵗʰ, 2012

http://www.huffingtonpost.com/2012/09/10/shania-gray-murder-franklin-davis-testify_n_1871051.html

And to my cousin

Diane Williams
February 2ⁿᵈ, 1955- September 5, 1972
http://en.wikipedia.org/wiki/Freeway_Phantom

"Save Our Children!"

Please

Contents

Foreword

"Every child should have every chance in life, every chance at happiness, and every chance at success. Yet tragically, hundreds of thousands of you Americans shoulder the burden of abuse or neglect."
President Barack Obama

CHILD SEXUAL ABUSE is on the rise. Children are being dehumanized and are the new victims of sexual slavery. Adults are sexually exploiting them. Perhaps it is because they are defenseless to scheming grown-ups or maybe because they are trusting of a society that is to protect, shelter and love them.

According to David Finkelhor the Director of the 'Crimes Against Children Research Center' statistics show that:

- 1 in 5 girls and 1 in 20 boys is a victim of child abuse
- During their lifetime, 28% of the United States Children ages 14-17 will have been sexually victimized
- Children are the most vulnerable to sexual abuse between the ages of 7-13

Modern technology is aiding child sexual abuse. Pedophiles are able to conceal their identity behind the mask of a faceless screen. This is not to say that the Internet has created more pedophiles but rather has provided a way for many to hide from the societal stigma that once kept these perpetrators under control. Unsuspecting children in their quest for acceptance and search for affection are falling victims to their ploys. Many unknowingly become a visual record and victim of child pornography. Others are lured into secret meetings where rape, kidnapping and sometimes even worst, murder occurs. This is known as Internet luring. Thousands of cases are tracked by the National Center for Missing and Exploited Children. The FBI and other law enforcement agencies have established task forces to monitor the repugnant activities on the Internet.

The Child Protective Service in 2010 reported they received 3.3 million reports of children being abused or neglected with 9% being as a result of sexual abuse. They also reported that 34% of victims were younger than 4 years old and with children younger than 1 year old having the highest rate of victimization. These statistics are startling, appalling and unacceptable. If you need more details, Google infant sex abuse for current media cases. You will find this atrocity affects all cultures and cuts across all economic levels. Age, gender, race and economic background are irrelevant. This is a societal issue. Others and I contend that the number of sexual abuse cases among children is much higher then the statistics show. Keep in mind; the above statistics are based on reported cases. What about the unreported cases? Child sexual abuse causes some of the victims, families and/or friends to feel guilt and in many cases responsible. Because of this, there exist a tendency due to pride to hide the assault and pretend it never happened. The family name and reputation becomes more important. These Children are told "what happens in this house stays in this house". Others believe removing the child from the abusive situation is the answer while not stopping to think that the chances the perpetrator will repeat this behavior to another unsuspecting child is not only possible but also probable. Then there is the sexual abuse to infants and toddlers. Because the child is unable to verbalize or understand sexual acts, many are undetected unless it is personally observed by someone, the child is injured or killed, there is documented dramatic behavioral changes or the child contracts a sexually transmitted disease.

The severity and crux of child sexual abuse can best be summed up by understanding every two minutes a child is sexually assaulted and 85% of the time it is by someone known to that child. Perhaps we should consider more emphasis on training and preparing our children on how to deal with people they know since strangers commit only 10% of sexual assaults. 70% were committed by immediate family members or someone very close to the family. Incest also known as incestuous abuse is the most widespread form of sexual abuse. We need to educate ourselves and avail ourselves to every available piece of technology to ensure our children are with trustworthy caretakers. A start is by monitoring their Internet usage and visited sites, hidden nanny cameras, supervise cell phone calls (placed and received) and place location monitors on phones and cars just to name a few tools.

Due diligence by all of society is mandatory! Parents and caretakers cannot afford to use blind trust when it comes to their children. We have to remember there are deceptive people in this world and their intent is to gain the trust of you and your child so they may exploit them. Some are family members including parents, friends, churches members, and school staff . . . This indicates each and every one of us must be vigilant and observant of all children. We have to teach children they can confide anything in us. Parents, caretakers, relatives and friends should create time, an environment and opportunities for one on one time with the children in our lives. We have to put down our cell phones and social media devices to give them our undivided attention. Children are precious and need our protection and discernment. We all have an obligation to protect them whether they are our children or an unknown child in the supermarket.

Deflowered Lyric will reveal scenarios of trusting parents who left their children unintentionally with untrustworthy adults while the parents carried on their daily routines. They believed their child would be protected by the caretakers. This fictional story will also reveal one child whose deflowering was discovered by a trusted adult and how she handled the discovery while yet another child fearful of hurting her mother held her secret sin until it could no longer be denied. Yet, another character did tell of her abuse but her confession cost her to temporarily loose the presence of someone she loved.

This book was written by the author to raise awareness of child sexual abuse with the hopes of stimulating parents, family members, friends and our society to heighten their awareness and educate themselves and children. The stories in this book bear all too real child abduction, rape and murder to the author, as her cousin was one of six children in Washington, DC who shared this unfortunate fate. Diane Williams was only 17 years old when her life was tragically snuffed out by a still unknown perpetrator. The media dubbed the murderer of these six girls, ranging in age of 12 to 18, the Freeway Phantom. Diane was also my sister. The author's goal is to try and prevent other children from being another statistic. After all, it really does take a village to raise a child!

> ESV Matthew 25:40
> *And the King will answer them, "Truly, I say unto you, as you did it to one of the least of these my brothers, you did it to me."*

Lieutenant Patricia L Williams (Retired)
Metropolitan Police Department
Washington, DC

Preface

IN MANY INSTANCES in life, feelings are expressed or acted upon in varying ways. Pain and love although very different both provoke an emotional response. These responses manifest themselves sometimes in positive ways and other times in negative ways. The point is they will not be denied. One way or the other, they will be revealed.

Deflowered: *"To deprive virginity: To take away the prime beauty of."* Lyric knows all too well about pain and love. As a child, she was deflowered. Her prime beauty was stolen from her. On many occasions, she would revisit this time in her life. A sense of loneliness engulfs her as she struggles to understand why she had to endure this sexual abuse. Why her? She questions if it was because of something she did or was it the results of a generational curse? She chooses poetry as her voice to express the pain. Poetry allows her to become aware of her life experiences as she selected words arranging them to create a specific emotional response through the meaning of rhythm and sound. She hears a drum beat only those who have been deflowered can hear.

Lyric in her quest to understand her pain discovers her life's purpose. Her revelation comes from God through a sermon preached by Bishop T D Jakes entitled "Save The Scraps". The words that resonated for her were, "The miracle is not in what you lost but what you have left." Bishop Jakes explains, "That which remains is more valuable then that which was lost." God speaks to Lyric's heart telling her to take her scraps and tackle the secret sins of incest, child molestation and rape. She gets busy doing the work of her heavenly father by first helping to expose her friends and family. Her plea and purpose becomes to 'Save Our Children!'

Acknowledgments and Special Thanks

A SPECIAL THANKS IS extended to my family and friends for supporting me in this endeavor. Having you by my side providing constant encouragement has made it possible to begin this new chapter in my life.

As for my husband, although the road has not always been easy, I appreciate your unwavering support and love.

To my children and grandchildren, I thank God for placing you in my life. You are the reason I fight to expose those who dare to sexually abuse children.

My Father above and master of the Universe, please use me to tackle this enormous feat. Our children are a gift from you. (Psalm 127:3-5)

To Bishop T. D. Jakes, God used you to deliver a message to me that started me on this journey of living and walking in my purpose. I appreciate and thank both you and Sister Jakes for allowing God to use you in the building of his Kingdom.

My family and friends, I love you more!

Finally, I acknowledge every child, man or woman that has ever been deflowered. I pray you will join me as we use our scraps to expose the secret sins and sinners in a collective effort to:

'Save Our Children!'

Life with the Proverbial Wall

HAVE YOU EVER hurt so bad that every part of your being begins to die? Family and friends try to comfort and console you. They tell you everything will be all right. There may even be a quiet voice deep inside of you that whispers, "The storm is passing over." You may even step back and think, "Wow, I survived that crisis!" You desperately hope that maybe, just maybe, you grew up just a little, or maybe you just learned to protect yourself but only for the next time. So begins the building of the "Proverbial Wall."

It's a wall that soon becomes so high that you can't see over it, nor will you allow anyone to see in. Fear becomes your protective barrier and a reason to hide. A brick is laid for every rejection or disappointment that life brings. Your tears become the mortar that seals each brick to another.

Then comes the real fun—you not only are expected to deal with all of these internal problems, but you also have to find a way to protect yourself from the external pressures of life. The news reports five people killed in a car crash. Your friend's brother dropped dead from a heart attack at 38 years old, a crack head shot a woman for $15.00, a 17-year-old girl walking to school was raped and stabbed then thrown beside a dumpster and on and on . . . But you say that's life. Your inner being says that if not by the grace of God, that could have been me. Tragedies seem to be closer and closer to you. You begin to run and run until you collapse from exhaustion.

When you recover, you search and try to surround yourself with the fortress of love—love from your family, love from your friends, and love from your significant other. You rest now, build your strength up because you know it is just a matter of time before a loved one will try to destroy you all in the name of love.

You fight back with relentless self-love: "I love me too much to allow you or anyone else to destroy me." That works for a while (long enough for the smoke to clear). Then what's standing in front of you is old man—guilt. He taps you on your shoulder and says, "I'm your worst nightmare . . . you can run, but you can't hide from me." A friend offers you some well-needed advice. The friend said, "Hey, once you make a decision, don't look back. If you look back, you will go back." You begin to adapt this philosophy, and before you know it, old man Guilt is fast asleep. So . . . you let sleeping dogs lie.

The next stage of progression is that you begin to search around to see if there is someone in this big old world that is like you—someone that understands your unspoken words, someone that would care enough to shine a light through your wall to see the real you inside. The illumination feels so good. Almost magically your wall starts to crumble, brick by brick, until you are standing naked and exposed. Every imperfection is showing. Gratitude overwhelms you. Just as you are about to shout for joy, you see the darkness. At first, you can't figure out why. Then to your amazement, you realize that your savior and knight in shining armor has built his own wall. Their fear has shut you out. Suddenly, that "Proverbial Wall" stands between you and them.

There is absolutely no fight left in you. Your shield and your armor have been stolen. You are no longer victorious. All you can do is muster up enough strength to fall on your knees and cry, "Lord, have mercy. Please, father, have mercy on me!"

CHAPTER 1

Life with the "Proverbial Wall"

IN A LARGE high-end furnished bedroom, with soft lights glowing from the contemporary brass lamp, the sweet aroma of the Cranberry Pear Bellini candle, snuggled in its six-wick crystal container, meanders in the air. Gospel music pours from the wall-mounted 52-inch television, emanating life's direction and purpose. Lyric's 5' 4" body sprawls across her plush king-size bed. Her low melodious voice belts out "The Storm is Passing Over" from an abysmal dark place in her soul, where buckets of pain buried several decades ago took up residence. Salty, rolling liquid runs down her darkened, sun-kissed face. Hidden are the 50-plus years of survival since exiting her mother's womb on a smoldering Friday, the thirteen day of June.

It has been a difficult, drawn-out week, Lyric thought. After working 10 days in a row, she struggles to relax.

"I need a mental break." Her echo responds, ricocheting off the textured walls. Lyric gives her jumbled mind permission to drift. She is all alone with thoughts racing back to a place and a time when a frightened baby girl of four years old played on her grandmother's farm. She fights to escape deep into the soothing, heartfelt music. Ordinarily, spirituals would provide her with comfort and impart feelings of hope while shielding her from the secrets of her past. Only this time, there is a difference. Lyric finds it difficult to slow down the ticker tape inside of her head. Another scent, one of musty cow leather, propels Lyric into her subconscious. Wide-awake, she slips into a daydream of her childhood when she was 4 years old.

Ronald Edward Massey's youngest child—Lyric is running in a front yard that appeared larger than the Cowboy's stadium, goal post to goal post. She imagines going to the springhouse holding a metal cup with red exterior and silver interior paint. Its wide mouth and tall body gives her hands a freezing sensation. She recaptures the sound of water flowing in and out of the magic facility. A shiver starts in her head and ends at her toes as her imagination conjures up the clear and chemical-free frigid liquid. Some believed, but mainly Lyric, that the melting snow must be piped in from the Alaskan tundra into the small country borough of Finleyville, Pennsylvania. The best tasting water in the entire world freely flowed to the Massey family's 300-acre farm. "The crème de la crème and the coldest water I have ever, in all my life, drank and ever will extol," she declared. Lyric's memory replays a scene from her country farm history. Feeling the delectable water slide down her throat and into her stomach, she returns to where her tiny, nippy hands gripped the sweating metal cup as her tongue traces her lips, savoring the flavor. She visualizes her grandmother giving a stern order to her older cousin, ten years Lyric's senior.

"Jason, pay close attention to Lyric and don't let her go into the springhouse alone. The next thing I know she'll be floating like one of those fish in the pond, right to the bottom."

"Yes, Grandmother. Come here, girl. Grandmother said you can't get any more water or you will die."

With a voice of authority, filled with bass while the ending of his words slid up to tenor notes, Jason cracked out his stern instructions, sounding like Lyric's father.

"You're not the boss of me," Lyric mumbled under her breath, but loud enough for Jason to discern.

Jason responded with a forceful backhand blow, producing a sweltering, stinging pain she felt down to her butt.

"I'm telling Momma!" This is the name Lyric used when referring to her grandmother. "You hit me for nothing," she said, quivering.

Jason leaped up, grabbed her, and started shaking Lyric like an old rag doll.

"You better keep your big mouth shut. I am telling grandmother you said she wasn't the boss of you."

Through tears and with her words trembling, Lyric managed to say, "I—I —I did not."

She stutters, looking him straight in his squinting dark brown eyes. She slowly rolls her eyeballs to the back of her head, then shoots Jason an "I will cut you" evil glance.

Jason ignores Lyric by changing the subject. In a nonchalant, calm voice, he says,

"Come on, let's go play."

He grabs her by the hand and pulls her towards the dilapidated graveyard, serving as a four-car garage for dead cars that needed to be crushed and buried a long time ago.

Lyric jumps into one of the old smelly heaps and pretends she is driving to Alaska. She remembers she wanted to go the source of the delicious water.

"Since I can't go to the springhouse, I'm going to Alaska."

Lyric remembers when she answers a question posed by Jason.

"Why don't you fly to Alaska?" Jason asked.

"I can't fly a car," said Lyric, protesting. "Are you stupid?"

"Yes you can."

"How?"

Jason lays down across the seat, stretching his arms wide open, pretending they are a plane's wings.

"Like this. Now who is stupid?"

Lyric recalls lying on the torn leather seats with the stuffing coming out. Something warm, sticky, and wet cascaded down the lower half of her body. As Lyric replays this scene, she cringes at the thought of reliving the details, but is unwilling to step out of her home movie. She continues to view the additional scenes as if she is standing in the distance, out of sight and watching a snippet of her life's story revealed on a huge theater screen.

"Be quiet and do not move. You better not tell anyone either or I am going to tell grandmother what you said."

Lyric closed her eyes tight, squeezing them until black stars danced in her lids, while trying to decipher what Jason was doing to her.

What is that thing spitting on me? she wondered. She wished it would stop. *It stinks in here.* A fishy body odor laced with a musty sweat reached her nose. She did not remember ever smelling this mixture before then, but as an adult, she smelled it many times. Lyric peeks through half-shut, squinting lids. The cloudy air coming from their bodies creates fog on the windows. It reminds her of the way hot steam from her shower blanketed the bathroom mirror. She drifts deeper into this scene of her life. Lyric continues to struggle, attempting to gape out the car's windows.

Startled, she jumps from the abrupt clanking sound of the car door being snatched open, as if someone was trying to pull it off its hinges.

Lyric's grandmother begins screaming in a high-pitched shrill. The deafening noise causes Lyric's bones to shudder.

The sound of her grandmother's voice hollering emerges. "Get off of her! Get off of her! What is wrong with you? Why would you do that to this child? *I'm going to kill you!*"

Even today, when Lyric remembers the gut-wrenching sounds, they conjure the same convulsive effect now as they did then.

Lyric opens her eyes and gazes around her bedroom, convinced she would see her grandmother as well as hear her reprimands and threats to Jason. Realizing she is safe and in the confines of her Texas bedroom, she closes her eyes to return to the final act, where she is crying. Her body is shaking, as if she was having an epileptic seizure. The icky stuff was rolling down her legs.

"I didn't, I didn't, I didn't say you wasn't the boss of me, Momma. I promise to God. Please don't kill me," Lyric howls at the top of her lungs. "Momma, I'm sorry! I am sorry!

Her grandmother ignores her pleas. She yanks Lyric's arm so hard it causes her head to hit the car's roof and abruptly ends Lyric's voyage to Alaska, but not her continued begging and pleading for her life. "I don't want to die!"

Once removed with brute force from the junkie car, Lyric's grandmother cradles her close to her chest. Her hefty arms encircle Lyric, making it difficult to breathe. Although she is physically extracted and feels a sense of safety and protection, Lyric remains quiet as she is carried back to the house. The only noise is that of her grandmother humming and singing in her ear, "Jesus, keep me near the cross."

After that day, Lyric was unsure what her grandmother said to Jason, or for that matter, what she did to him. All she knew is she did not see him until many years later. No one ever mentions the Alaskan excursion. Lyric's first deflowering was hidden under a shroud of secrecy.

The ring of the telephone interrupts Lyric's daydream state. Startled, she springs from the bed, stops to compose herself, and then snatches the receiver. She tries to answer with a perky "I wasn't asleep" tone.

"Hello," Lyric sings in a deep, raspy voice, courtesy of years of smoking abuse.

"Hey, sister. What are you doing?"

"Oh, hello, Angela," Lyric responds to her older sister after taking a few seconds to orient herself.

Angela asks, demanding, "I said what are you doing?"

"Since I'm getting a break from never ending reports, grueling meetings, and tons of email, I'm laying across my bed, resting. I guess I dosed off and drifted back to life on the farm." Deafening silence followed. Lyric checked the connection on the other end of the phone. "You still there?"

"Yeah, I'm here." Angela chastises Lyric saying, "Why do you insist on living in yesterdays? You must not have enough to keep you busy. I chose to forget my childhood."

Soft, low, deliberate, and using a child's voice, Lyric says, "Our farm life was not all bad."

"Correct, but I live in the here and now. Today I am so busy with all the stuff going on in my life, there is little time or energy to waste," Angela snarls.

Lyric retaliates like a rattlesnake striking its prey. "Why would you want to forget? At least you had friends in school. The white kids accepted you. Your features more closely resembled theirs than mine did. You also proved you were quite capable of fighting. Me, they called every color-specific term in the book. My playmates consisted of me, myself, and I."

Angela permits her irritation to show. "What's your point? Hell, I'm not to blame."

A calmer Lyric counters in return. "No point. I guess I concentrated on the bad things and forgot to consider the good times. You're right. How can I hold you accountable for their actions? On a brighter note, do you remember the springhouse? What I would give for a gulp!"

Without a fight and in response to Lyric's positive memory, Angela shares a contrite laugh. "The water was too cold for ice. What about the orchard with apples, peaches, and cherry trees?" Angela yearned to again gorge until her insides hurt. "And the strawberry patch with the 'to die for' huge red berries. Yesterday, I brought some from Giant Eagle. I sentenced those bitter and nasty bunches to the garbage disposal. Fruit in the supermarket does not compare to homegrown. Anytime we wanted high-quality, fresh, sweet, and juicy produce, we picked them from our backyard."

"You are so right. Angela, can you believe our homestead had chickens, pigs, and cows?"

"Well, farming helped make us well-rounded and forced appreciation from whence we came."

"I'm glad my country-living tenure ended while I was still a young child. Our brothers had to get up with the roosters and go to bed with the chickens," Lyric playfully said. "They worked full time without getting a paycheck. They performed manual labor as if they were grown men. Along with their forty hours, they still had to work their part-time job as students." Lyric slid down and snuggled under the comforter. Thinking about their responsibilities exhausted her.

"Everyone except poor little baby Lyric undertook their assigned chores. Grandmother spoiled and treated you like a prima donna. She let you do whatever you wanted."

"I'm sorry, but there is not much contribution a toddler can make." Lyric knew her sister was resentful because of the perceived favoritism, so she hurried to change the subject. "I miss grandmother's large mouth-watering breakfasts. To have some bacon, buttered cheese grits, and her homemade biscuits would hit the spot right now." Lyric sang "my, my, my" as she closed her eyes and began to imagine the strong hickory and yeast smells that greeted her every morning. She drifted further into the delectable aromas. Angela inhaled a deep whiff but did not bother to comment.

Lyric blurted through the silence, "Angela, do you remember when Daddy moved us from the booming metropolis of Buffalo, NY to the not-a-neighbor-in-sight-for-five-miles farm?"

Angela's eyebrows raised as she squinted. She mulls it over, trying to recall the exact day and time the life-changing episode occurred. She replies, releasing the familiar disturbed tone, "Yes, what about it?" Standing up to gaze out her front window and into the night, Angela studies the cars speeding past her rented home. The car turns on Frankstown Avenue in Homewood, an urban fast pace section of Pittsburgh, Pennsylvania. Her conscious state slips into the brink of an unconscious one. Reflecting begins to arouse a physical reaction. Her heart rapidly beats as her temples begin to thump, drum-like. Boom, Boom Boom . . . Speaking as fast as her heartbeat throbs, she continues in a quiet whispered voice and asks her own question: "Do you think I can forget?"

"Well, it's obvious that due to my age I wouldn't remember. I am curious. Exactly how old was I?" Lyric asked.

"I do not have a clue. It happened a long time ago. Do you think I am the family historian? I was a child myself." Angela continues to gaze into the night at an older man with dreads, which fascinates her. The dreads seem to flow down his back like the waves in the springhouse. She snaps back to the conversation. "You were about, hmm, a month old. Let me think about your age." Angela begins to count using her fingers. "If I was seven, then, yeah, that's right." The old man with the dreads disappears from her view. Angela focuses on a new sight: a short dark-skinned person whose legs bow out like two letters C facing each other. The woman high-steps at a rushed speed. She clutches her purse and backpack, heading towards the Port Authority stop. Angela surmises she must be catching the 10:40 p.m. Hill District bus. The sight of the woman causes her to forget about the phone conversation with Lyric. Instead, she reaches far back in the deepest corner of her memory to relive a scene from "Angela's Life; Proverbial Wall," starring Angela Massey-Hughes. The venue is Buffalo, New York around June of 1955. It begins with Lyric; an infant sleeping in a bassinet while Angela is combing her Barbie doll's hair. Roger and Jerald, the older brothers of Angela and Lyric, play on the floor, arguing over a toy car. Ernest, the fourth oldest child, quietly sits in his highchair, observing the rowdy exchange.

The family scene stirs up Angela's suppressed memories of her mother. It causes Angela to press the pause button on her racing mind. She elected to stop and methodically linger on the physical features on her mother. It is as if, in the crevices of her mind, she is gazing at a photograph of a woman. Immense deep chocolate and almond cut marbles decorate the U-shaped brown sugar face. Laced with sadness, the sclera of her eyes appears to be missing. She visualizes the beautiful woman's flawless skin. She sits on a tattered couch staring out a window, just as Angela is currently doing. On Angela's canvas, the colors seem to appear as if Leonardo da Vinci sketches and completes the colossal painting. He creates a set of parentheses for the small waistline. Below them, he drew a pair of saddled thighs. The etch-a-sketch made two perfect half circles bowing below the knees. A round, protruding shelf connects to her small 24-inch waist. The facial features are as keen as the top tip of a surfer's wave. Her thick black hair resembles ribbons on a gift-wrapped box curled with scissors, creating a full head of spiral curls. Leonardo adds a widow's peak, colored as a skunk's fur to the woman's jet-black hair. Still caught in the mother scene from her story, Angela transfixes to circumvent escape. She remains frozen as the artist completes his masterpiece. He illustrates her petite hands. One clutches her heart, endeavoring to protect it from falling out of her chest cavity. He applies the final additions. A low-cut, V-shaped blouse reveals breast cleavage created to provide life-sustaining nourishment to the children she bore.

Angela switches from the artistic masterpiece to the painter. She surveys his face and reactions as he gazes in admiration at his skillful feat. Slowly, he glides his hand to his nature and begins to caress the enlarged pleasure-delivering tool. Once satisfied, he unveils the portrait drawn on the canvas of Angela's mind, divulging none other than Faith Massey, the deceased mother of Angela and her siblings. Lyric realizes that at least five minutes passed since she or her sister said a word. They both were entrenched in their own obsessions. Neither of them cared whether holding a conversation on the phone continued or not. Lyric feared interrupting Angela's thoughts. Something told her to be patient and wait. She hoped the silence meant Angela was spending the time preparing to share additional pieces of the puzzle and answer Lyric's many questions. Meanwhile, Angela remains riveted on Faith and her every move. The sudden screeching of Lyric in her crib moves her mother to lift and hold her baby as a grizzly bear protects its cub. Faith gently kisses her infant. The wailing noise ceases, and Lyric coos and goes back to sleep. Faith returns Lyric to her resting spot, but not before planting another big juicy smack on her lips.

Roger and Jerald calmed down and mutually agreed to share the car. They quietly lay prone on the floor, engrossed in the old-fashioned television with rabbit ears made out of a metal hanger tipped with aluminum foil.

Faith calls to her sons. As each approached her, she gives them a huge momma bear embrace.

Angela feels as if she is a ghost outside her body summoned to witness this scene. Faith reaches to grab Angela. Just as her mother is about to hug her, the pink princess phone rings.

After the first ring, Faith answers. She speaks just above a whisper. Angela overhears her mother declare, "Yes, I'm ready. Can we at least take Lyric?"

"Hey did you fall asleep? Are you still there?" Lyric interrupts Angela.

Angela snaps back from her dream state. She responds with the only defense she can muster up: "Why did you insist on visiting back there?" Her voice starts to rise like the escalators at the Metro stop of the Washington Monument. "I told you I didn't want to talk about this mess. Can't you understand these memories hurt?"

An urgency and desperation consumes Lyric. She refuses to let it go. Hearing her sister express heartache from reminiscing concerns did not stop Lyric. She decides to ignore her pain and further prod for answers. Her instincts say there might never be another opportunity. This fight would go the full ten rounds of serious boxing; Angela would become Manny Pacquiao and Lyric, Floyd Mayweather. This time, their match would happen and could not end in a split decision. Unraveling Lyric's past became a necessity, so a decisive winner must be declared. Lyric prays she will be victorious. She strategically plans her next blow, recognizing the importance that an acceptable comment follows or her sister will throw a knockout punch and shut down, ending their bout.

After a second, Lyric confesses, "Well, sis, I have all these emotions stirred up in me, and I can't seem to bury them back. I need answers." Her voice cracked as she fought to hold the tears back. "I have a right to know the details of my life. As my older sister, you are obligated to help me fill in the blanks."

A defeated Angela asks, "Lyric, what else do you want to know that you don't already know?"

"I want us to have a no-holds-barred conversation . . . " Lyric stops in mid-sentence as at first, she was unable to fathom her sister's agreement. A jolt pushes her off the ropes, as she comprehends that no additional convincing is necessary.

"OK, my first question is an easy one," Lyric began. "Tell me what you were thinking about. You were quiet for at least five minutes."

Angela thought for a few seconds. An OK-you-want-to-know-then-damn-it-I-am-going-to-tell-you attitude appeared in her voice "Are you sure you're ready to hear the details of mom leaving?" Lyric considers the benefit to outweigh the negative. An open dialogue would help them both begin to heal in all their broken places.

Before she could respond, Angela begins to share her rendition. Whispering, Angela says, "I strained to eavesdrop on her phone conversation."

Not understanding Angela's comment, Lyric suspects Angela skipped to where her thoughts left off without any regard to starting from the beginning. "Hear who?"

"Our mother," Angela responds. "I brushed my baby doll's hair and tried to pretend I wasn't paying attention. Mommy's voice changed to high soprano. She asked whoever was on the other end of the phone if she could bring you with them."

"Take me where?" Lyric asked.

Angela kept talking jumbling her thoughts without stopping to answer. "She wanted to know why she couldn't bring you. Daddy was at work. I heard her respond, 'Yes, I love you.' She also told him she wanted to be with him, but she did not want to leave her children. She asked him again if she could at least take you, their baby, with her."

"What baby?" Lyric asked.

Again, oblivious to Lyric and her questions, Angela never stops. She continues, "The next think I knew, Mom emerged from her bedroom and told me to watch you kids while she went to the store for milk. I asked her to bring me some candy back. She said she would." Angela recoiled to her corner. "But she never did."

Lyric sat up in the bed. Frustrated, she banged her fist on the headboard. "She never did what?"

"A week or so later, Daddy moved all five of us to Pennsylvania. We lived on the farm for the next eight years with grandmother and him." Angela began to rub her temples, trying to alleviate the throbbing, which manifested as they neared the ninth round. She let her head plop on the desk and allowed her top lid to kiss her bottom eyelid in an effort to close out the world.

Both Angela and Lyric remained quiet for several minutes as they retreated to their corners to prepare for the tenth and final round.

Lyric swung her legs from the bed, leaped up, and began pacing. She spoke loud and quick. "I remember the first time I recall meeting Mommy. We were at church in Finleyville. Girl, I thought she was so pretty. Just beautiful. I was in awe of her beauty. She smiled at me and then bent down and looked me straight in my eyes. She asked if I knew her. I said no. 'I'm your mother,' she said. I gave her the most confused look and quickly pointed to grandmother, saying, 'That's my mother. Taking the beautiful person by her hand to confront this revelation, I said, 'This woman says she's my mother.' I remember so clearly, as if we first met yesterday. Grandmother's face turned red as a house fire in flames. She told me in the most indignant way that she was not my mother. She said, 'No, she isn't. I am your mother.' I remember feeling sad. The woman was just so pretty and seemed sweet. I wanted her to be my mother. Daddy must have overheard the conversation. He popped up, came over to where we were, and emphatically confirmed the beautiful woman, Faith, was indeed my mother. He pointed to Momma and said, 'That's your grandmother.' From that point on, I stopped calling grandmother 'Momma' and referred to her by her rightful title, 'grandmother.' When this happened, I think I was six years old. Where were you, Angela, when mommy came to church?"

Angela did not entertain Lyric's question. Instead blurted out, "Lyric I'll talk to you later because I told you I didn't want to talk about Daddy, Mommy, or your spoiled ass. This stuff is old history that happened damn near fifty years ago. By the way, she never brought milk or my candy back from the store." For the first time, Lyric realized that her deep-rooted pain and feelings of abandonment, although significant, did not measure to Angela's experience of witnessing life that Lyric was too young to recall. She finally understood why Angela detested focusing on their past. Lyric was the baby her mom wanted to take and not her sister or brothers. Lyric thought, *This must be the catalyst that triggered Angela to build her Proverbial Wall.*

Unable to lift her head, Angela said, "I will talk to you later." She did not give Lyric a chance to respond before slamming down the phone.

The hum of the dial tone blared in Lyric's ear. She continued holding on to the receiver until the annoying voice recording repeated, "If you would like to make a call, please hang up." Lyric retorted to the automated voice, "Yeah, I want to make a call! Give me 1-800-Heaven, and let me speak to my mother. Maybe she can answer some of these damn questions. Who is my real father, and why did she die and leave me again?" She slammed the receiver in the cradle, turned the gospel channel up, rolled over in her bed, and drifted off to Yolanda Adams's rendition of "The Battle is Not Yours, It's the Lord's."

CHAPTER 2

Under The Covers

Now I lay me down to sleep
I pray the Lord my innocence he'd keep

If I be wakened in the dark
deflowered by someone without a heart

And if my childhood he should take
May I forgive before I wake

Unveil his theft for all to see
For you shall judge both him and me

It wasn't my fault or mine to carry
Stealing my innocence was very scary

Help me be an example as you have done
To expose the truth and not run

Saving my scraps, using them for good
It's commanded of me and you said I should

Amen

THE NEXT MORNING, Lyric awoke to the ticking sound of the clock on the wall. A hush and still spirit engulfed her home. A desire to continue living in her past burned inside. Her husband, Johnny, was not at home. He often travelled out of town on business, sometimes staying for several months. This stint was nearing two months. Lyric, although lonely, missed him, but a part of her enjoyed the solitude. She decided awhile back that the next time this opportunity presented itself, she would take full advantage of the isolation. She needed to confront why, at this point in her life, she suffered from feelings of loneliness, as if she was the only person on a subway train during rush hour. This was her second marriage. Her two daughters, conceived during her first nuptial, were grown and independent. The older daughter, Tasha, blessed her with the joy and love only four perfect grandchildren could bring. All lived near Lyric, which permitted her to get plenty of hugs and kisses on a regular basis, except from one granddaughter that lived in Virginia. Growing up, Tasha never gave Lyric a bit of trouble. She thought to herself, *How self-sufficient she is, and what an outstanding job she does raising my grandchildren.* She then drifted to Tianna, her strong-willed Leo child. She, too, mastered self-reliance, but even so, she possessed a fragile side Lyric sensed needed continued monitoring. Although the most loving and affectionate of her children, Tianna enjoys helping others, but she holds a hair trigger. As caring as she is, if you cross her, there will be hell to pay, whether by verbal retort or physical altercation. Whenever cornered, Tianna's response generally resulted in a vehement strike, making her difficult to restrain.

From the outside looking in, Lyric seemed to have a wonderful life. After migrating to Washington, DC, she married an attractive and successful man and birthed two girls. They attained the middle-class dream. After several years, their marriage ended because of Lyric's inability to develop trust in him or their marriage. Her six-figure job from a 35-year career afforded new home ownership in the suburbs of Dallas, Texas, where her money went further than when living in the high rent district of the nation's capital. Here she met her second spouse, Johnny Williams. Married a mere five years, their relationship was deteriorating as the once happily-ever-after relationship started experiencing some rough and rocky roads. As Lyric began to look at her life's accomplishments since rebounding from life's disappointments, she thought to herself, *I take no credit for any of this. Everything I am and all that I ever hope to be—I owe it all to my father, the almighty loving God, Creator of the universe that took his time to create me.* Lyric continued to revel in being spiritually grounded. In spite of it all, she could not deny her cup was half empty, and something was missing. It resembled an irritation you cannot scratch that sometimes bothers you more than at other times. You know the discomfort is there, but if you ignore the sensation the tingling seems to go away. Lyric began thanking God aloud. She could hear in her mind Bishop T. D. Jakes preaching her life changing message two Sundays prior, which spearheaded a desire to dig through her past. His discourse, titled "Save the Scraps," moved Lyric in such a way that she felt compelled to buy the DVD. Repeatedly, she would listen as the word resonated through the clandestine part of her soul.

She first attended The Potter's House one fall Sunday several years ago, after Tianna, who at the time was 15 years old, persuaded her to join their service. Lyric was in search of a new church home to provide spiritual food. For many years, she resisted this church as it appeared too commercial and massive. On this particular Sunday, she prayed and asked God to guide her. After running late and making what first appeared to be a wrong turn, Lyric ended up in front of The Potter's House at 11:15 a.m., just in time for the 11:30 a.m. service. She recalled how Tianna coaxed her to go inside. Lyric's attendance in the bible-based ecclesiastical home for hurting souls prompted every negative preconceived notion to change.

As it turned out, the congregation, although massive in size, was not as large as she once imagined. The church was warm, inviting, and filled with the Holy Ghost. Lyric's soul confirmed God answered her prayers by nourishing her with manna on a regular basis. Bishop Jakes preached the word through every pore in his body. The gospel flowed by way of the perspiration that soaked his clothing, leaving him drenched and wringing wet as he released what "sayeth" the Lord. The one missing piece in Lyric's spiritual walk was Johnny. Although he confessed to believe in God, he did not give credence to organized religion or church attendance. Lyric's profound wish was for her husband to accept his rightful role as the overseer of their family and to accompany her to Sunday services.

Lyric hit the play button on the DVD player. She rolled over and pulled out her Bible, which Lyric referred to as her armor and shield from the bedside table. She began to read the scriptures along with Bishop Jakes. As it had the five previous times she listened to the DVD, Lyric found herself with tears streaming down her face. She lifted her hands up and threw back her head. A sharp nagging pain took over her body. She cried out, "Father, I stretch my hands to Thee, no other help I know. If Thou withdraw Thyself from me, whither shall I go?" Repeatedly, Lyric echoed the lifesaving message until she calmed down while whispering one last time, "Father, I stretch my hands to Thee."

Once ended, silence consumed the remaining spirit in the room. Lyric flopped back on her bed from spiritual intoxication, which did not resemble any other hangover Lyric ever experienced. She emerged in a drunken stupor. She felt as if she just took part in a physical fight rather than a spiritual fight. Her heart began racing as she struggled to catch her breath. All she could manage was enough strength to turn over and drift back to sleep. She slipped into that dark corner of her mind where the nightmares waited on a shelf for her to come and get them. At least three times a week, the imaginings were frequent visitors to Lyric. They were sure beyond any doubt that she would return soon to retrieve them.

Lyric, featured as the main character, slipped into her autobiography. The life story takes place in a time she refers to as "Post Mother Meeting." She was about nine years old and had moved from the farm in Pennsylvania back to Buffalo, New York to live with her mother. Standing hidden in a dark corner, she observes a trembling, timid young girl. Her disheveled braids hang down the small of her back. She is wearing an orange outfit with shorts and a knit top, which reveals perky teen miniature breasts. Lyric recalls the outfit was her favorite and probably the only matching one she owned. She lived in the Fruitbelt section with streets named after fruit, such as Peach, Pear, and Apple. Most of the families, including Lyric's, were on some form of public assistance. Her mother, Faith, worked at the hospital as a cook, making about one dollar an hour. But in spite of the meager wages, she walked five miles daily to and from children's hospital, whether 95 degrees or freezing temperatures, to provide for her children. Faith, a divorced mother of five, acquired a leech and common law spouse, Cedric. At 6'4" tall, he towered over her 5' frame. His skin color glistened dark as midnight without any trace of the moon. He was a professional gambler by trade that either made or lost money shooting dice. He daily consumed Genesee beer as his preferred form of hydration.

Lyric's teenaged sister, Angela, usually hung out with her boyfriend or other friends. Her three older brothers, Roger, Jerald and Ernest, also kept busy, leaving Lyric most times home alone. This particular day during a summer break, Lyric rushed to finish her daily chores. She sat on the porch, anticipating either her mother or Cedric's return so she could exercise her freedom and explore the neighborhood. When the phone rang, Lyric hurried to pick up the receiver. Her mother told Lyric she was going to play bingo. She crushed all hopes of Lyric's escape, instructing her not to leave the porch and that no boys were allowed in the house. Lyric dropped her head in frustration. She resigned herself to an evening on the porch with Lauren, her best friend and neighbor. *Oh well*, she thought. *We can spend our evening laughing and playing games or maybe even go on a scavenger dig in the backyard.* Lauren previously told Lyric a rich man once lived in her house. He buried his money in the yard to hide his wealth from his drunken spouse. Sometimes Lyric and Lauren would find as much as 20 dollars. Because they were best friends, they would split the cash in half. They were so close, they once stuck each other's finger with a needle, rubbed their blood together in a ceremony, and dubbed themselves blood sisters. They vowed they would always be close for the rest of their lives. Lyric's tiny rosebud breasts and small stature clearly indicated she was the younger sister. Lauren was two years older than Lyric, with a body which developed into womanhood early. Her 38 D breasts overflowed from whatever top she wore. Her thick coal black, wavy hair hung down her back, clearly emphasizing her American Indian heritage. Lyric admired her beauty.

The story picks up with Lyric and Lauren playing on the porch. They were hungry and wanted something sweet, but neither of them had money. Lauren suggested they go on a dig expedition. Without hesitation, Lyric agreed. They each dug in different corners of the yard. Lauren shouted, "Found it!"

Lyric rushed to her. She could not wait to see how much money their dig exhibition yielded. Breathing hard and with sweat running down her face, she asked, "How much?" Lauren opened the cotton hanky and pulled out two 10-dollar bills. She handed one to Lyric and kept the other. Lauren shuffled her feet, hung her head, and in a monotone voice said, "Let's go to the store." Without noticing Lauren's sadness, Lyric responded, "I can't. I'm not supposed to leave the porch."

"OK, I'll go," Lauren reluctantly replied. "What do you want? Your usual Nehi Crush grape soda and a bag of Wise potato chips?"

"You know it!" Lyric yelled.

The story then switches to Cedric coming home from his crap game. Lyric is no longer watching from a distance. In the past, when she reached this chapter, she observed her life unfold in third person, but for some reason, this time she was reliving in the present both she and her characters appeared in first person.

The smell of alcohol beat Cedric to the porch and immediately hit my nose. His eyes were fire engine red with a thin slit that provided him a limited hole to peek through for vision. His sway was involuntary and controlled by Bumpy Joe Gin and Mr. Genesee Beer. He stared at Lauren's breast while asking me, "Where's your mother?"

"She went to bingo."

"Who is home with you?" he slurred. Continuing to drink the Nehi grape soda and with a mouthful of chips, I manages to mumble, "No one is here, just Lauren and me."

"Well, get your little self in the house, take a bath, and get ready for bed."

"Aw, why? I don't have school tomorrow and besides, Mommy said I could stay on the porch until she came home."

Once again, Cedric continued staring at my friend's breasts, yet talking to me. "Girl, I said get your butt in the house and take your bath. You can put your pajamas on and come back outside on the porch when you finish. I will stay out here with Lauren and keep her company until you get back."

Lauren and I exchange a glance that only the two of them understand. Lauren looks up to her bedroom window. She stares for several minutes. Hanging her head, she says, "Hurry up, Lyric. I'll wait right here for you, but please make it quick."

Heading for the front door, I say, "I will." I then stop suddenly and turn to Cedric, still looking at Lauren's breast like he wants to bury his head in them and use them for a pillow. Lauren avoids Cedric's gawking by studying the floor of the porch.

"Can Lauren come in with me and wait until I finish my bath?"

Cedric finally stopped staring. He turned to me and began to bargain, as he had done so many times before. Patting his hands on his lap, "How are you supposed to ask me if you want something?"

This meant that I was to sit on his knees and hug his neck as he would say place a wet juicy kiss right on the lips. I hated this because he never wanted me to get off his lap. He would hold me so tight that I felt like I could not breathe. Lauren shot a look that said, "It's OK, you don't have to do that." She and I always had words unspoken, which only the two of us understood. I stared back at her with a look that said, "No, isn't OK." I walked towards Cedric and sat as requested.

"Awww that feels great."

He put his long arms around my waist and pulled me further down. I could almost feel the exact change he had in his pocket, every key on his key ring, and something hard poking me. I tried to get up, but he pulled me back down.

"Where is my tight hug and wet kiss?" I was reluctant to comply. I tried to peck him with the kiss he requested, but he took his huge paws and pushed my head to his face, making the kiss longer and more husband-and-wife-like than one for a child. Startled, I jump up. He pulls me back to his side. Both Lauren and I look down and notice the overwhelming bulge sitting in his lap. He takes his other arm and motions for Lauren to come rest in his other arm. We both flash a panicked look to each other. Lauren glides towards him as if she made an instant decision. She begins to high-step into his arms, staring straight in his bloodshot eyes. She intentionally hides his face in her large breasts. She smothers his head by shaking the fruit of her chest, then grabbing each one and burying his head between them. Once Cedric was fully covered, Lauren gazes at me. I read her eyes, which say, "I am protecting you while sacrificing myself."

Cedric's limp arm drops, releasing me. It is obvious he relishes being captive between the grapefruits of Lauren's bosom. He makes a moaning sound. Lauren steps back and out of his grip. He drops his head, as he loses control of himself. In a slow and deliberate voice, he says, "Lyric, go take your bath." I look at Lauren, and her eyes say, "It is all right now. You can go and take your bath."

She jumped off the porch as if nothing happened. "Lyric I'll be back by the time you finish your bath, or if my bedroom window is open, call me when you finish, and I'll join you."

"OK." Running in the house, up the stairs, and through a bedroom entering the rear bathroom that did not have a door, I start my bathwater and rush to undress as the room begins to fill up with steam. I jump in the tub with the thought of taking a quick bath, but the balmy water takes over my body and senses. I decide to just lie back in the tub and enjoy. The warm soak makes me tingle down there. Thoughts of Lauren's rescue mission play over in my head until the water turns cool. When I remember my promise to Lauren, I rush to dry my body. In my haste, I realize I forgot my nightclothes. Wrapping the towel around me, I head for the bedroom, thinking it's a good thing my mom isn't home. She always fussed that I should not walk through the house in a towel. She told me to wear clothes or my bathrobe. If she was home and saw me with the towel around me, she would say, "How many times do I have to tell you to keep clothed? You are in the house with boys and a man. Little girls need to always stay covered." She would go on and on, repeating her same question and scolding me for being disobedient. I smile to myself as I can hear her in my head. Just as I step out of the bathroom and into the dark bedroom, I see the shadow of someone. Fear causes me to drop my covering.

Cedric says, "It's me. I came to see what was taking you so long."

I begin shaking like a leaf in a windstorm as I bend to grab my towel and attempt to cover myself. He grabs me in his arms and squeezes me tight.

"Don't be scared. I didn't mean to frighten you."

"Cedric, let me go! I need my towel so I can dry myself." He takes the towel from my hand and begins to pat the front of my body while studying me in the same manner he used to gaze at Lauren's breasts. Then he did the unthinkable and cupped my budding strawberry-like breasts with both of his hands, engulfing them. I grabbed my towel, ran into my bedroom, and locked the door. I was so afraid that I sat in the corner of my room and cried. All I could think of was that my mom told me to keep clothes on and how it was my fault for not obeying. Not only did I not have clothes on, but my entire body was exposed because I dropped my covering. I thought, *Mom is going to beat me for disobeying her instructions.*

After several minutes, I heard Cedric at my door. He turned the handle, but the lock protected me from again revealing my naked body. This time, I was glad I listened to my mother. She also told me little girls always lock their bedroom doors so no one can come in their bedroom while they are asleep. I stuttered out, "I can't open the door. I'm not dressed."

He did not respond.

I sit in the corner with my towel around me, listening only to the street hustle outside my bedroom window. Finally, I ease up and tiptoe to place my ear against the wooden barrier. Everything is still and quiet. Relieved and thinking Cedric left, I start the process of clothing myself, but this time with the haste of a cat chasing a mouse. Once finished, I wipe the sweat, dropping like the bathroom leaky faucet down my face. I creep back to the paint-chipped door and listen one final time. I do not hear any sounds coming from outside my room. Trembling, slowly and methodically, I put my hand on the glass knob. My ear is still plastered on the tattered wood. Taking my other hand, I slide the pin lock slider back as it creaks and softly clanks against the metal hinge. The wall light switch to my bedroom, after being clicked off, obscures my presence, which is my intended goal. Inhaling and holding my breath, I slowly count one, two, three, four, five, six, seven, eight, and finally nine. Upon reaching ten, I snatch the door open. My eyes dart around the pitch-black upper hallway, trying to focus. Fortunately, I can make out the downstairs television flicker that casts light on the bottom step. However, the area leading to the steps is hidden from me. I inch out of my dark bedroom and trace the wall with my hands, searching for the light switch as if I was a blind man without my dog or cane. Just as I reach for the stair rail, he grabs me around my waist and lifts me straight up towards the ceiling. Instantly, I knew it is Cedric, even before having the opportunity to smell the stale beer and hard liquor on his breath.

"I gotcha," he slurs. "Where do you think you're going? I am playing hide-and-seek with you. I hid when you got out of the tub. I didn't mean to scare you and make you drop your towel. I was trying to pick it up and give it back to you. I wasn't aware you were not dressed because your mother always tells you to dress before coming out of the bathroom."

As he was holding me high in the air, he kept rattling off one thing after another, planting seeds to explain his actions. "Are you OK?"

"Yeah," I mutter. Cedric turns me around so I am facing him. He looks in my eyes. I drop them down to gaze at his big hands around my waist. He seems taller as he pulls me closer to him and pushes my head down on his shoulder.

"I am so sorry. I did not mean to frighten you. I was only having fun. Will you forgive me?" My mind is like a jumping bean. *Maybe it was an accident. He liked to play hide-and-seek whenever I took a bath. Well, maybe he did not touch my breasts*

on purpose. He was probably tipsy and was grabbing for the towel.
Thought after thought speeded through my head as I attempted
to make excuses for his behavior. "OK, you understand?" he
asked.

"Yeah," I replied as he slowly slides my body down his. My legs
kick, trying to reach the security of the floor. I feel his nature. As
my legs finally reach safety, I try to wriggle away, but Cedric kept
holding me. He starts laughing, then snatches me up and says, "I
got you again," as he carries me back towards my bedroom. He
starts acting as if he was one of my friends playing tag with me.
He flings me on the bed, and as quick as I hit the mattress, he
drops all 200 and whatever pounds on top of me.

"Now you can't get away because I am holding you down." I
lay there, not saying a word. He starts tickling me, at first under
my arms, then my stomach as he continues to hold me in place.
At first, fear keeps me from responding, but I manage to dig up
a fake giggle.

"Stop. Ha, ha. Don't do that," I said.

"Whew, I'm tired," he said as he rolled me over and placed me
on top of him. Although I pretend, I realize what he is doing to me
was not a game of tag, hide-and-go seek or I gotcha. Somehow I
figure if I placate him, he will stop. He slides me up and down his
body, as his nature thing fights, trying to escape from his pants. I
want to holler, "Leave me alone," scream, yell, kick, and get away
from him, but instead, I cooperate and act as if we are playing
one of his twisted games. My mind drifts to another similar time
in my life when Roger also played a so-called game with me.

Cedric begins to kiss me on my neck, as he pushes harder
and faster. I sit on him like a beer can he is lifting, taking a swig,
then placing back on the coaster until it's empty. He groans and
moans, moving quicker. He takes his hands off my waist and
goes under my shirt. This time, he does not cup my breasts, but
gently rubs his hands across my nipples. Although afraid, I also
feel another strange occurrence. My breast nipples become hard

and erect. The same warm wetness I felt many years ago returns, but this time, it is coming from me. I open my eyes and steal a quick peek. His eyes are clinched shut as perspiration rolls from his forehead and drops onto my pillow. His hands slide down and touch my goodness. I tremble all over. He moans one last time, and then the mountain I was sitting on top of melts like snow on a 60-degree day. He lifts me and gently sits me on my bed. He doesn't say a word at first, but as he approaches the door, he turns back to look at me. "Tag, you're it," he says softly, as he closes my door.

Instead of going outside to meet Lauren as promised, I fold my body up in a fetal position, and for an unknown reason, I slide my thumb into my mouth. I think about telling my mother, but I am too afraid. I struggle to understand why I feel guilt for my body responding to the touch of his grown hands fondling me, a child. Deep inside me, I know what he did was wrong, but how can I tell when I didn't try to stop him? But even worse, my body must have wanted his touch; otherwise, why did it respond? I wished my grandmother could have saved me this time too.

I study this younger me sucking her thumb to swallow her hurt, pain, and guilt. My heart breaks for her and me as an additional scene is added and heaped on my scraps.

CHAPTER 3

Are You Who You Say You Are?

Pretending to be someone that you want others to see
Do you portray the person others expect you to be?
Instead of revealing the true you
Has it been so long of you pretending?
The real you has escaped and hidden itself even from you
Are you Doctor Jekyll or Mr. Hyde?
In the daylight, the sun shines for all to see
So you pretend to be someone you're not
But when darkness comes and few can see
You hide your dirt because you're out of sight
Are you who you say you are?

LYRIC AWOKE FROM her dream world and rolled out of bed. She decided it was time to shower and prepare for what was left of the day since she managed to spend most of it in the bed. As she stood, the upward movement snapped her back to reality and signaled her mind, as if part of a ritual, to bury all the memories and nightmares until the next time. She entered the shower and sat on the corner seat. Ready to receive stimulation, she turned on the jets to her newly installed, super-powered shower system. The jets took aim at the front of her body, sending pulsating streams of extremely hot water to massage every area they touched. Lyric soaped her body, scrubbing so hard that if her color were not permanent, it would have rubbed off and rolled down the drain. The bathroom filled with steam, resembling a sauna. Realizing she had been in the shower at least twenty minutes, Lyric acknowledged the time came for her to dress and start the day by tackling her many overdue chores.

First, she put the dishes in the dishwasher as a load of clothes washed. Then she began dusting the family room. She damp-mopped her honey-blonde hardwood floors in both the family room and the dining room. Next, she moved to sweeping and mopping the kitchen. As crazy as it sounds, she liked to mop because of the lavender smell the Fabuloso floor cleaner left in her house. Sweating and completely out of breath, she moved to the last room she planned to clean—the bedroom, her sanctuary and the home of her tender love moments shared with her husband. The safe haven also housed her dungeon, which hosted her nightmare secrets. Changing her bed, she replaced the 1000-count deep purple monogrammed sheets with white ones. She lit her candle, hung up last week's clothes that were thrown over the wing chair, polished the furniture, and ran the sweeper. As Lyric took her last stroke with her Dyson vacuum cleaner, relief and a sense of accomplishment adorned her wet face. After four hours of manual labor, she was finally finished. Spinning quickly around in a circle with her arms wrapped around her body, she collapsed on her bed. Staring at the ceiling while taking a deep breath, she inhaled the clean aroma of her home. She always loved the smells in her house. The sweet lavender violet meshed with the hospital smell of Pine-Sol, bleach, and a hint of the sweet perfume of April seemed to interlock together and create one distinct perfect aroma fit to patent. Marveling in the scents soothed Lyric's mind and her soul. Her friends always told her to pay for a housekeeper. Her standard reply was that cleaning her house is free psychological therapy, besides being a way for her to enjoy her faith and lifesaving music that always played in the background, aiding her therapeutic rehabilitation. She relished over her accomplishments.

"Whew, finally done with that." Thoughts raced like the subway train from Falls Church to the Pentagon. Hang out, go to the movies, stay home, watch a movie, or call Johnny. The ticker tape kept spitting out one idea after another. Finally, Lyric reached for her cell phone, but instead of calling her husband, Johnny, she called her friend, Nicke. After the first ring, Whitney Houston's greatest heartfelt song "I Look to You" ringtone blared through the speaker. Lyric hummed and began to sing along, "After all is said and done, I look to you."

"Hey Lyric," Nicke said.

"What's up?" Lyric asked.

"Nothing, girl, but everything all at the same time."

Lyric realized she probably should have followed her first thought and called her husband instead. She sensed the conversation was going to drain her of what little energy she had left. She could tell from the greeting alone that her friend of 20 plus years sounded lower than a basement in a five-level home. Lyric often wondered if her friend suffered from a undiagnosed case of "woe is me" or maybe was bipolar, a more serious condition. Lyric could not figure out why she was always depressed. She thought Nicke was, by all accounts, gorgeous. She is 5' 8" with honey-colored, silky smooth skin, sister locks that hang just above her round, protruding behind, big legs, and a shape that intimidates coke bottles. She regularly caught the eye of both straight and gay men, gawking for one moment of her attention. Instead, she married Charles, a 5' 5," round, out of shape, and classless man suffering from Napoleon Syndrome. He never ceased trying to make her pay for being beautiful. He projected his negative feelings, insecurities, and verbal insults on her, which the average person would not tolerate. Nicke seemed to feel she owed him to take his abuse. Lyric figured it was because Charles practically raised her daughter, Jada. From the time she was six years old until Jada became a teenage mother at fourteen, Nicke fought the demons of not only emotional abuse from Charles, but also her own alcohol abuse. She became a certified alcoholic from what seemed like the next day after she met Charles. Until that point, she was a loving and nurturing mother to Jada. Once Nicke got involved with Charles, the drinking and partying started. Charles then became Jada's primary caretaker. He combed her hair, bought her school clothes, helped with homework, and even once tried to get custody of Jada.

"Hey, Nicke. What is wrong with you? You sound like you lost your best friend. We know that is not true because Miss Lyric is right here."

"Yes, Lyric, you know I love you too. I would probably be somewhere in a looney pen if it were not for your think positive and your 'what you put out in the universe comes back' speeches."

"Very true, but I keep trying to tell you to let Go and Let God. I told you he would never leave you alone, even if he has to send me as a stand-in to put my foot up your butt to make you get up and walk. You just have to remember after you have done all you can do, stand."

"OK, OK. I get it Lyric. Do not start with that shit. I know you're right, but for now, I need to wallow in self-pity for at least fifteen minutes, if you don't mind."

"I do mind, but hurry up because now you only have fourteen minutes left. So, what is going on with you? On the other hand, do I even have to ask? Does it start with C–H–A–R and end with L–E–S?"

"You know it. Well, it is him, it is Jada, and it is life. I am so tired. I just wish God would just take me home before I have to help him get me out of here. I mean, I have done everything I can to make up for that period when I was too drunk to take care of myself, let alone take care of anyone else."

"Wait, Nicke girl, you have to keep going and see what the end is going to bring. There is going to be rain and sunshine. You cannot give up because life is hard. Stop and deal with each issue. You are responsible for your own happiness. You cannot allow people to keep beating up on you. Eventually you have to stand up, put your big girl panties on, and tell people you have been clean for five years. They and you need to leave the past in the past. I can't tell you to leave your husband or, for that matter, to stay with him, but I can and will tell you that you deserve better."

"I know I do, but every time you turn around, he is accusing me of screwing around on him. Do you know he told me it is my fault Jada became a teen mother? He said if I was a better wife and mother, she would not have gotten pregnant at 14 years old."

"Jada is now 20 years old. She is grown and doing a great job raising Micah. She is a good mother. Lord knows I know it sure was not easy for her, but everybody has his or her own cross to bear. She took lemons and made lemonade."

"Lyric, Jada is just as bitter as Charles. She, too, blames me for her getting pregnant. I tried to explain the birds and the bees to her. It was her choice to open her legs up to some boy. So how is that my fault? Do you know, I went to her apartment today to take Micah some shoes and school supplies. I spent a little over three hundred dollars, and all she said was thanks for nothing. She said she wished when she was going to first grade, I took care of her as I was doing for Micah. She had the nerve to say I was too drunk to protect her and keep her safe."

"Protect her. What did she mean by that?"

"Lyric, I have absolutely no idea. All I could say was I am sorry, but now I am here to help her with Micah, if she would just let me."

Lyric placed her hand on her hip. She hated when both Charles and Jada threw Nicke's past up in her face. "So how did she respond?"

Nicke slowly released words that made the hairs on the back of Lyric's neck stand up.

"She told me she didn't need me anyway and that neither I nor her biological father ever really loved her. She said her Dad, Richard, was a sperm donor and I was the vessel he used. She ranted and raved about what horrible parents we were. The only one who tried to halfway love her was Charles, and he failed too. She said as far as she was concerned, he may not have done right by her, but at least he tried, which was more than me or her father."

"Oh, wow. I am sorry. I know that hurt. Jada uses emotional blackmail the same as Charles is doing to you. They are both trying to make you pay. You lived your life and yes, it could have been different, but like Bishop Jakes says, 'Today you are using your scraps,' trying to help other mothers not make the same mistakes you made. You are the best life-experienced counselor I know. You are saving other families at the New Birth Family Counseling center by telling your story. I say those without sin cast the first stone."

After a moment of silence, Nicke managed to say, "She told me to get out of her apartment, take those damn clothes with me, and don't ever come back." Sobbing from the deepest part of a broken heart, she continued saying, "She also said she hated me, and she said all of this in front of Micah." Nicke cried loud and uncontrollably. Lyric's eyes enlarged with total disbelief. She could not speak for several minutes. She went from having compassion to having her blood boiling, with beads of sweat forming on her forehead. She swallowed to compose herself long enough to say, "She has some unresolved pain. Both you and Jada must work through her anger. Jada is still your daughter, and you cannot give up on her. I know she loves you. She is just enraged. OK, you made some mistakes, but you have changed, and as I said, you are still her mother. No matter what, she does not have the right to disrespect you." Lyric's mind drifted to thoughts of how she would put her foot up Tasha or Tianna's' butts if they ever treated her like Jada did Nicke.

"Then to top it all off, I get home and Charles starts in on me. He accused me of being with another man because I was gone all day. Telling me I gave up alcohol but I did not give up f-ing every Tom, Dick, and Harry. He said I traded in one drug for another. Talking about after all he did for Jada, and this was the way I thanked him." Nicke breathed in slowly through her nose, then exhaled a deep sigh. Her chin fell on her chest to support the weight of her head. Taking her left hand and placing her fingers on her forehead, she supplied additional support for her weighted-down cranium. With her eyes closed she said, "All I did was try to do something good, like buy my grandson's school clothes, and now I am a hoe and an unfit mother. I give up. I quit. Lyric, Charles was so angry; he even pushed me down on the couch and walked out of the house. For a moment, I thought he was going to hit me."

"Wait, Nicke . . . .Did you say he pushed you down on the couch? We ain't taking any domestic abuse even if you were out with some man."

"But I wasn't with any other man."

"Nicke, I know you were not with a man. My point was he had no right to put his hands on you, absolutely no right. This time it was a push. What will happen next time?"

"That fool ain't crazy. I just do not know why he is treating me like this. It is as if he hates me. He treated me better when I was drinking. I think he wants me to go back to being an alcoholic. I get absolutely no support from him or Jada. They seem to have a bond that neither of them want me to be a part of."

"Therefore, Nicke, you cannot continue to live like this. You are doing so well. I want you to stay clean and sober, and what is more important, I want you happy. Have you taken this to God?"

"Girl, I keep praying, but I think God is so tired of me and my problems, he is saying, 'Fix it yourself.'"

"No, girl, not my father. He has told you what to do, but you don't like his answer. You keep praying and asking for your will instead of His will. You know what you have to do, but you don't want to take charge of your life."

Nicke started sobbing again. "I know you are right. Something has to change. The first thing I'm going to do is get Miss Jada straight." Her sobbing began to subside as her voice boomed with authority through the receiver. "She is my daughter, and she will respect me! I am going to go to her apartment, and we are going to have a long talk. I will tell her that I am sorry for allowing alcohol to control me, but I will *not* pay for my mistakes any longer, and she better not ever disrespect again. As for Mr. Charles, he has to get his shit and get out. I am tired. He can go be with the woman he has been with for the last year or so anyway. No wonder he is accusing me. I know who is the one out there messing around. I smell her scent on him, but I keep my mouth shut, but no more. I am through."

"Nicke, wait a second. Slow down. I agree you need to confront both Jada and Charles, but I do not think you need to do it in anger. Have you thought about getting some family counseling or about talking with your pastor?"

"No, Lyric. I have to get this straight now before I go crazy."

"Girl, what are you going to do?"

"I am going back to Jada's apartment."

"Nicke, it is almost 11:00 p.m. I think you should wait until the morning. This will give you time to cool down and allow you to go in peace, not anger."

"Lyric, I cannot wait. I have to go now. I am about to explode or have a drink. One of the two of them will happen if I do not get this handled."

Lyric considered Nicke's last response. She did not want her friend to throw away her sobriety. "Do you want me to go with you to help mediate?"

"I couldn't ask you to do that for me."

"You did not ask. I offered. Actually, I am on my way. I will pick you up. You are much too upset to get behind the wheel of a car."

"I got this, Lyric. I appreciate your willingness to assist. Thanks anyway." Nicke rushed to end their conversation. "Good night. I'll call you tomorrow and let you know what happened." Without waiting for her friend to respond, she placed the receiver in the cradle.

As Lyric put the phone down, her stomach started doing flips. Her palms began to sweat. Her gut told her Nicke was going to need help, but her instincts tried to convince her it may be better to wait for Nicke's call tomorrow. Lyric decided to listen to her gut. She began to throw on clothes while grabbing her keys and purse all at the same time. She was going to meet Nicke just in case. After all, that was what friends did for each other. *Being there in a time of need is called sacrifice*, Lyric thought.

She pushed the start button on her 2010 Lexus, backed from her garage, then weaved through her neighborhood and turned left out of the gated community. Before she knew it, she was taking the exit and turning into Jada's complex, parking right next to her friend, Nicke. Lyric jumped out the car when she realized Nicke had already exited her vehicle and appeared to be walking in a stupor. She did not even notice Lyric. She shouted to Nicke once, then a second time.

Nicke took at least ten steps before noticing Lyric. She glanced at Lyric as if she was expecting to see her. "Well, I guess I will get two for the price of one tonight," Nicke mumbled.

Lyric surveyed the parking lot, then stared dumbfounded at Nicke, trying to comprehend. She studied the entire building complex and parking lot. She looked left, right, up, and down.

They both stopped. Judging by the few lit apartments, it appeared there were many available rentals or that most folks were asleep or out for the evening. Lyric caught a glimpse of Nicke's eyes in the moonlight. They appeared glazed over, as if she was carrying the weight of the world on her shoulders. She also noticed Nicke's shallow breathing, as if she was engaged in a yoga exercise. She was inhaling, holding for approximately a 30-second count, then breathing out for 30 seconds. Lyric, although uncomfortable, remained silent. She rationalized Nicke's behavior as her practicing a stress technique she learned from Alcoholics Anonymous.

Nicke pointed her finger to the southwest corner of the parking lot. "I wonder why Charles's car is over here this late." Her voice had a suspicious edge, but it was also wrapped in fear.

Turning in reverse, Nicke headed back towards her car. Lyric followed. Once Nicke reached her Cadillac, the beep of the doors unlocking resonated. She opened the passenger door and took something out of her glove box. Lyric was standing behind Nicke and could not tell what she retrieved. Nicke's plump rear, which tooted up, blocked Lyric's vision as she leaned down into the car. However, she was aware Nicke travelled with a gun.

The thought of firepower caused Lyric's heart to work in high gear and beat as if the organ was going to pop out of her chest. A sickening anticipation caused her blood to rush to her head. Fear jumped in her spirit. It was apparent that she had to end the silence and take control. She could not shake the thought of her witnessing a scene that had the potential to be the morning news. Lyric stopped walking and shook her finger in Nicke's face.

"What are you about to do, and what did you get out of your glove box?"

Nicke, while examining Lyric's eyes, responded in a matter-of-fact tone. "I just got Jada's spare key and, of course, my little friend. Just in case she's not at home or someone tries to attack us in this parking lot, I'll have what we need." She continued to stare into Lyric's eyes, attempting to scrutinize her thoughts. She wanted Lyric to provide plausible answers to why her daughter had been so mean, why her husband was angry enough to push her, and why his car was in her daughter's parking lot this late.

Lyric instinctively took the nonverbal cue from Nicke. She blurted out, "Charles is probably babysitting while Jada is out with her new man friend, David, and blowing off some steam."

Nicke stopped and looked up towards her daughter's apartment. She thought about what Lyric said. For the first time tonight, something seemed to make sense. They were plausible answers to some of her questions. She prayed Lyric was correct.

The moon cast a bright glow, which allowed Lyric to see her friend's frown lines dissipate, resembling an ice cream cone left in the heat. Nicke was considering the possibility of her explanations, and they appeared to somewhat calm her down. Nicke took a deep breath and exhaled as she continued walking towards Jada's apartment. Lyric marched behind her, assuming the role of Nicke's protector.

As they approached, both Lyric and Nicke inhaled at the same time. They looked into each other's eyes, and in their minds, prayed, "Lord, please be with us tonight."

Nicke stopped in front of the door and put her ear to the door, listening for any sounds coming from the apartment.

Lyric leaned forward too. Nicke did not knock, but instead pulled the key out. She entered like a burglar, tiptoeing into the dimly lit apartment. Lyric hesitated at the threshold, frozen in place. She surveyed the apartment, looking for any signs of life or movement. She glimpsed Nicke walk down the hall and turn the door handle to Jada's bedroom. Her friend started firing questions like a machine gun.

"Charles, what are you doing here and why are you laying across Jada's bed? Where is Micah?"

Lyric stepped into the apartment and closed the door. She eased down on the love seat conveniently facing Jada's bedroom door. She could see Nicke standing with her hands on her hips, grilling Charles. Charles started asking some questions of his own.

"What are you doing here? Who let you in? How did you get here?"

There was silence for the next 60 seconds as Nicke stood motionless in the doorway. She closed the bedroom door, turned, walked out of the bedroom and into the family room, and sat across from Lyric on Jada's flower print couch. She put her hands to her face and began holding her head, as if she was trying to keep her brain's house attached to her veined neck.

After about five minutes, Charles exited the bedroom with one arm in his shirt and the other fumbling, trying to find the left sleeve. He looked like a kid that was caught with his hands in the cookie jar. Without noticing Lyric, he started stammering and explaining how he came by to visit, and the babysitter had to go, so he sent her home, and he got tired of waiting for Jada, so he laid down in her bed because his back was hurting and that Micah left with Jada's male friend. He took a short breather. Charles looked at Nicke, still supporting her head, then continued a series of questions. "How did you know I was here? Why? What did you think I was doing at Jada's house?" His voice changed from a little boy's questioning voice to a grown pissed-off man's voice. He and his anger headed towards Nicke as if he was about to physically assault her when, out of the corner of his eye, he glimpsed Lyric. He stopped abruptly and flung around to Lyric.

"What are you doing here, Lyric?"

Before Lyric could respond, Nicke blurted out, "She is here to keep me from hurting somebody tonight!"

"Hurting someone?" Charles repeated. "Why would you want to hurt Jada or me? Haven't you done enough?" Then Charles threw a verbal sucker punch intended to hit below the belt. As nasty as he could say, his venom discharged: "It is not our fault you loved the bottle more than us." He followed up with another poisonous strike. "Jada never had to question my love for her."

He continued talking about how much they loved each other and how neither of them needed Nicke. He spewed as if he was describing a love affair rather than a stepdad and stepdaughter relationship.

Without lifting her head or making eye contact, Nicke said, "Charles, my suggestion is you make haste, get your shit, and get out now. As a matter-of-fact, leave *my daughter's* apartment and stay out of our lives forever. I would also suggest you take everything you want or need out of my house before I get there!" Nicke frothed as she lifted her head and slowly stood up. She placed her hand in her pocket, fingering her concealed equalizer. "I am about 10 seconds from killing you dead right here where you stand."

Charles felt the same goosebumps Lyric experienced climbing her arms. He hung his head, tucked his tail, and strutted out the door. Nicke slumped back down on the couch like a limp dishrag. Both Lyric and Nicke sat quietly in a daze.

Ten additional minutes passed when Jada emerged from her bedroom. She was wearing a sexy red, strapless nightie. She exhibited the same sheepish guise Charles displayed. She could not look her mother or Lyric in the eye. She stood with her head hung down.

At that moment, Lyric realized what she was witnessing. Sorrow consumed her as she saw the tears streaming down Nicke's face, conveying the same pain displayed from the death of losing a love one. Lyric's heart broke as she observed her friend begin to emotionally crumble right in front of her. Lyric walked over and knelt down on her knees, facing Nicke.

Without a word and right on cue, Nicke 's head dropped onto Lyric's shoulder.

Jada slid down the wall and folded to the floor. Her dignity got up and walked away from her. Her legs gapped open, and through either disregard or unknowingly, her v-jay-jay appeared from under her Victoria Secret's negligee. The room remained quiet. The silence was so deafening that it brought the uncertainty of an irreparable mute button in their stereo of life.

At last, Nicke raised her head and beheld in disgust Jada sitting on the floor with her legs still open. She stood slowly, swaying forward, trying to catch her balance as she headed for the exit. Before leaving, she turned to Jada and said what had been replaying in her head.

"I guess you really do hate me. Now I know why. I am so sorry for everything I did to you. My drinking exposed you to more harm than I ever realized. You were right. I didn't protect you." Nicke wanted to die right there. She prayed in her heart, asking God to spare her from the hurt and pain of her failure and grant her immediate death. Jada never raised her head. She remained in a silent stupor, thinking. She wanted to tell her mother how she really hated Charles and how much she loved her. She wished she could run to her mother and beg for her protection, but she just could not expose Charles for fear of crushing her mother even more.

Lyric followed Nicke out the door. She was unable to look at Jada. In her mind, she wanted to say something to her, but a voice of reason whispered to keep her mouth shut. Nicke walked to the car, dragging the weight of pain around her neck. She shuffled her feet because she lacked the strength to lift them. She was dejected and, like older folks said, down trodden and beaten.

Lyric, aware Nicke was not in any condition to drive, walked to her Lexus with her arm looped in Nicke's arm, hoping to shore her up. "Nicke, I'll take you home. We can come back tomorrow when you're feeling better to pick up your car."

Nicke did not protest. She flopped her weighted body and weary soul into Lyric's car.

On the ride home, each tried to process what they just observed and heard. Lyric rolled Nicke's window down so she could get some fresh air. She pushed in a gospel CD and turned the volume on low in the event Nicke wanted to talk. She told herself it was late, and she needed to be sure to comply with the speed limit. She was afraid the police would stop her. Lyric feared Nicke having a gun in her pocket would get them in trouble and did not know if she possessed a concealed gun license. She made a mental note to ask Nicke at another time.

As Lyric approached the intersection of MacArthur and Beltline roads, the stoplight turned yellow. She considered continuing but remembered the traffic camera, so she punched her brakes, screeching to a sudden halt. The jolt caused Nicke to bolt forward in her seat. Lryic glanced in her rearview mirror and saw a police car behind them. It also squealed to a sudden stop. She watched the officer through her sideview mirror, terrified he was going to pull her over. She held her breath in anticipation. The light changed to green. She slowly accelerated, hoping to not draw any more unwanted attention from the officer. She noticed the officer was still behind her. She surmised he must have been calling in her tags. Lyric tensed up and held the steering wheel tight. Under her breath, she mouthed, "Lord, please do not let this man pull me over."

Nicke remained oblivious to it all. She was lost deep in thought, struggling to find a light to guide her back to reality. She continued repeating in her head, *She really hates me. How could Jada do this to me, her mother? How could she?*

Lyric noticed the officer pull around her and enter the left lane. He slowly passed her, but not before peering into her driver's window. She glanced at him while keeping her eyes on the road. She sighed a sense of relief as the officer sped away and out of sight. She put her signal on and turned into Nicke's middle-class, well-manicured neighborhood. She continued driving slowly until she pulled in front of Nicke's house and parked.

Nicke did not attempt to get out of the car. She stared at the house that once held all of her dreams. *My futile attempts to make the house a home were all for naught,* she thought. It was just a house with brick and mortar, which failed to shelter both her and

Jada from the storms of life. As she continued to study her house, she noticed the foundation cracks and thought, *The structure is crumbling right before my eyes.* Tears began to race down her face. She decided because of the severely damaged bricks and mortar, neither she nor Charles would be able to inhabit house number 214. The shelter and security with an irretrievable structure must be sold, demolished, divorced, and forgotten.

Lyric exited and walked to Nicke's side of the car. She opened her door and gently pulled Lyric to her feet. She hit the key lock and listened for the beep. Afraid Nicke may fall, Lyric held her up as she helped Nicke up the front steps, then pushed the unlock code on the exterior mahogany wood-paneled door. While reaching to turn on the foyer light with one hand and hold Nicke up with the other hand, she kicked the front door open with her foot.

Nicke appeared to gain her strength back. She walked in front of Lyric, leading her to the master bedroom. She turned on the floor lamp. Nicke scanned the room, spotting Charles's belongings still in her house. She wanted to gather them all up and start a bonfire, as any distraught spouse would do at a time such as this, but she concluded she did not have the energy. She then strolled over to her unmade bed. At first, she just stood there, until finally plopping down on the bed and kicking off her shoes. She fell back onto the bed with her arms extended and wide open.

Lyric told Nicke she was going to spend the night with her and would sleep in the guest room. "If you need anything at all, call me. Good night, Nicke," she said as she walked out of Nicke's bedroom. She opened the guest bedroom door and flung her exhausted body on the bed. She could not fathom the tragedies of her night. As she lay there, she thought about Johnny. She was not sure if he had called. She reached for her cell phone and did not notice any missed calls. Lyric turned to the small grandfather clock on the bedside table. The hands read 12:12 a.m. She calculated the hour difference in Central Standard Time and Eastern Standard Time. She thought the hour is 1:12 a.m. in New York. I know Johnny is sleeping, but I really need to decompress. She dialed his number. After the third ring, the phone went to Johnny's voicemail.

"Johnny, I am sorry to call you so late, but I really needed to talk. I am staying at Nicke's house tonight. Call me in the morning. I love you." She pushed the end button on her cell phone. "It is probably just as well," she said aloud. She laid back on the bed and closed her eyes, drifting off into a deep sleep that provided her mind and body some much-needed rest.

Lyric was awakened by her cell phone blaring the ringtone she had copied from Nicke, "I look to you. After all is said and done, I look to you." She was so mesmerized by the song that she did not bother to answer and let her voicemail take the message. She looked around the room, and the memories of the previous night came flooding back Hurricane-Katrina style. As Lyric continued her recall, a sad feeling inched through her body. Tears began to form on her face. She tried very hard to prevent anyone or anything from stirring up her own raw hurtful emotions by opening the gates of hell to her past. Quickly, terror replaced the sad distress that overtook her mind. She struggled to climb back to focus on her friend. Questions flooded her mind: Where is Nicke? Did she get any sleep? Is she in her bed? Did Charles come home? Then other fearful concerns surfaced, such as: Is she alive? Did she kill herself? Maybe she took sleeping pills to escape. Lyric could not shake the possible scenarios clouding her mind. She decided she had to get up and go check. Even though her thoughts almost paralyzed her, she managed to crawl out of the bed. She sat on the edge for a while to steady her balance. Whispering a silent prayer, then hesitating to listen for any sounds of life, she exited the guest bedroom into the hallway. To her amazement and delight, her nose sensed the first sign of life. The aroma of a freshly brewed pot of hazelnut coffee reached her nose. Her ears picked up the low thumping music coming from Nicke's kitchen. Lyric headed towards the sound. Her eyes observed a disheveled woman still shouldering the heavy weights.

Nicke appeared lost in the cup of coffee she was stirring. She glared through the milky surface, searching the bottom of the mug as if trying to determine where her next moves were hidden.

"Good morning, Nicke. Did you get any sleep last night?"

Nicke looked up with red, slightly closed, and puffy eyes. Without any voice tone inflection, she whispered, "No, I am too destroyed to sleep. I tried but all I managed to do was toss and turn, so I just got up and made a pot of coffee." She motioned towards another cup on the table she poured, "That's for you."

"Thanks. I really need this java and probably a few shots of the strongest alcohol in the house." Just as those words rolled from Lyric's mouth, she wished she could reach and grab every one of them back. She thought to herself, *How could I say something so stupid to a recovering alcoholic facing the infidelity of not only her husband, but the lowest of all betrayals? His unfaithfulness was with her daughter.*

Recognizing Lyric's now-that-was-stupid moment, Nicke responded, "I know what you mean. I have been fighting the craving of pouring me a cup of some strong alcohol minus the coffee. Don't worry. I made it through last night, and now I'm taking one second at a time."

Without pausing, resting, using a comma or a period, Nicke flowed into a subject that shocked Lyric beyond disbelief and caused her to choke on her coffee.

"Micah is his child," she proclaimed. "That no good son of a b had sex with Jada when she was only 14 years old. She was just a child. He is the culprit who impregnated my teenage daughter." She spewed out matter-of-factly.

Lyric coughed to clear her throat. With amazement and skepticism, she asked, "Nicke, are you sure?"

"Yes, I am sure. I feel sick at my stomach to say this, but I suspected something was wrong with the way he took care of my daughter. To be honest, I remember once when I was drinking and had been out on one of my binges, I stumbled into Jada's bedroom just as that sick man was leaving her room. She was crying. When I asked that bastard what was wrong with Jada, he gave me a song and dance about how she woke up crying for me, and he was trying to console her. He said she would not stop crying because she wanted me. From that night to this one was the last time I had a drink. I knew in my heart I needed to be sober to take care of my baby. I suspected him, but my mind would not allow me to believe he could do such a thing."

"Nicke, OK, but why do you say Micah is his baby?"

"When I got home last night and after you went to bed, I called Jada and I asked her."

"What did she say?"

"She did not say anything."

Looking perplexed, Lyric responded. "That does not mean he is the father of Jada's son."

"Jada's silence told me I was right. When I came home, even though I was drunk, something in my soul told me, but as I said, I fought hard to disbelieve my intuition. Maybe it was the way Jada's eyes looked at me the next morning. They seemed to be saying, 'Save me mommy.'" Nicke's voice cracked as the tears overflowed and dropped into her coffee. "So you see, Lyric, this is my fault. I did not protect my baby girl from a sick and deranged dog. I let him ravish my baby girl like a pit bull would do to a rag doll. It's all my fault," she sobbed.

"This may not be the right time to mention this," Lyric hesitated, "but, Nicke, if you are right, what he did was against the law. She was a 14-year-old child when he got her pregnant." Lyric stopped to absorb what she said. "So what are you going to do about his sexual abuse to a minor?"

Nicke scanned the room, studying every piece of furniture, paper, or any other object in her vision. She stopped for a second and just like a tornado without warning, she jumped up and started whirling any and everything in her path. She flung them in the air, on the floor, or anywhere else they happened to land. First, her coffee cup, and then came all the papers on the table. She was spinning completely out of control, just as Dorothy's house did in the *Wizard of Oz*. Her eyes glazed over, as if possessed by demons. Things were flying, then shattering when they collided with a hard surface or landed on the ceramic floor. Lyric was stunned. She remained seated and tried to wrap her head around what was happening.

She leaped up and subdued Nicke in a tight bear hug. She calmly repeated, "I got you, Nicke. I will be right here with you every step of the way. I love you. You will get through this. It is OK. Let it out." Lyric felt Nicke begin to wilt and collapse into her arms. They both slid down the wall to the floor. Lyric gently pushed Nicke's head on her lap and stroked her fingers through Nicke's locs. Starting at the scalp and down to the budded ends, she fingered her hair while rocking Nicke, just as she did when Tasha and Tianna were babies. Her tears overran as she tried to imagine how she would feel if Johnny had violated one of her daughters, not to mention impregnated one of them.

Nicke sat on the floor while Lyric continued consoling her. Time passed by while the two of them each escaped to their own despair. Neither of them intended to move from this moment of being comforted or comforting until the ringing of Lyric's phone snapped them back to the present reality.

With one hand wrapped around Nicke, Lyric reached on the table and grabbed her purse. She dug until she clasped her iPhone. "Hello." She whispered.

"Lyric, where are you? Are you OK? I have been calling you. I know you haven't been at the casino all night," her husband fired with a voice of concern tainted with anger.

Realizing she did try to call Johnny and left a voicemail telling him where she was, Lyric questioned his anger or concern. She continued in her whispered voice, "I am sorry, baby. I was with Nicke and spent the night at her house. I called you last night, but you did not answer. I left you a message." Turning the tables on Johnny, Lyric asked, "So where were you?"

Johnny remained quiet, as he did not want to address Lyric's question, so he waited for more details.

Lyric hesitated as she tried to get her thoughts together on what she was going to say next. She knew she could not tell her husband all the details of the evening, at least not now. She feared Nicke might not be able to handle having her family business discussed in front of her or within earshot.

Just then, Nicke began to crawl off her lap. She was still pulling the heavy weight of pain attached to her waist. She eventually managed to crawl from the kitchen to the family room and collapsed, lying prone on the floor.

Lyric took advantage of her release and lifted herself from the floor. She snatched her clove cigars and headed for the garage.

"Lyric, are you there? What is going on?" Johnny's voice lost all of its concern and clearly became irritated as he hollered, "Lyric, are you still there?"

"Hold on a second," Lyric snarled back. "I'm trying to answer but I need a second!" She opened the door to the garage, and then gently closed it behind her. Still not saying a word, she lit her cigar and took a deep inhale, causing her to cough rather violently for a few seconds.

With a somewhat calmer voice, Johnny asked, "Just tell me you are OK? I worried that something was wrong. Is Nicke all right? Don't tell me, she fell off the wagon."

"No Johnny, I am fine and Nicke did not start drinking again. I wish it was that simple." She took another drag, pulling the smoke deeper inside her lungs.

"Well, what is it?"

"Johnny, Charles is having an affair with Jada."

"With who?"

"You heard me."

In an exasperated voice, Johnny stuttered out, "Jada, his stepdaughter?" Sill in disbelief, Johnny asked Lyric again to be sure he heard correctly. "Charles, Nicke's husband? I mean that is his daughter for all intents and purposes. Wow. How long has this been going on? What kind of mess is this?" Johnny stated loudly, "Is Nicke OK?"

Lyric thumped her ashes. With sorrow from her core and repulsed, she managed to get out, "No, she is not doing good at all."

"Wow. That is some deep shit!" Johnny hesitated as he tried to decipher what he heard. "I'm stunned. I do not know what to say. I guess some men like young girls."

Lyric shocked by her husband's comment replayed it in her head. Unable to control her anger, she shouted at Johnny. "What did you just say?"

Johnny instantly recognized Lyric's anger but refused to acknowledge it or recant what he had said. Instead, he chose to ignore her and abruptly ended his conversation. "Call me later. I have to work late tonight. Lyric, you need to be with Nicke. She needs you now more than ever. Give her my love."

Lyric pushed the "end" button without even saying good-bye. She smashed the clove cigar butt in the ashtray and rushed back into the house. She decided her and Johnny would revisit his callous statement, but for now, she could not put another thing in her brain. Johnny had reminded her she could not leave Nicke alone. She pulled the garage door open and immediately noticed Nicke was not on the floor where she had left her. She searched the room but did not see Nicke. Her heart began to thump rapidly.

Carefully, she stepped over the papers, glass, and fruit slung on the floor from Nicke's prior outburst. Lyric reached for the master bedroom door handle with anticipation, not sure of what she was going to find. Her eyes converged on the steam coming from the master bathroom. She heard the water running but realized she had to check to be sure Nicke was showering. Lyric pushed opened the partially closed door and saw Nicke completely clothed sitting on the floor, allowing the water to saturate her from head to toe. Without saying a word, Lyric slid off her Michael Kors pumps and joined Nicke in the shower. She pulled Nicke's head to her shoulder as the two of them allowed the water to bathe them and wash away the filth of Charles's sin.

After about fifteen minutes, Lyric shut off the shower. She stepped out of the shower, holding Nicke's hand. She removed the large guest towel and began wiping Nicke's clothes and body. Once dry enough, she removed Nicke's wet garments. Nicke, still not saying a word, allowed her best friend in the world to rescue her from the misery she was experiencing. Lyric ushered Nicke back to her bedroom and gently laid her naked body on the bed. She took the lotion from the oak dresser and began applying the substance over her friend's body, as if she was a baby fresh from a morning bath. Lyric found a cotton nightgown in the drawer. She slipped Nicke under the covering then laid her down and pulled up the comforter. Lyric closed the floor length curtains to darken the midmorning sun. Before exiting the bedroom, she turned the radio on to a soothing jazz station and allowed music to play softly in the background. She took Nicke's fuzzy, floor-length bathrobe and tiptoed out of the room, while shutting the door behind her. Lyric removed her wet clothes and snuggled in the robe on the couch. She turned the television on for sound to mask the silence. *What a night, and now what a morning,* she thought to herself. Real drama. She decided to try to push all thoughts out of her mind and try to catch up on her missed sleep. Lyric dozed off, as she, too, needed to escape, if only for a few hours.

CHAPTER 4

Friend

First you must find someone who allows you to be who you are
Rather than judge you or tell you what you ought to do
Intelligently she suggests a way to rethink the situation
Eagerly she supports you
Never forgetting to pray with you or for you
Diligently, she is always there.

LYRIC WAS AWAKENED by Nicke's phone ringing. She looked around for the cordless, thinking, *Let me hurry up and answer this before it wakes Nicke.* She reached for the handset just as she saw the caller identification on the television read the call was from Jada.

"Hello," Lyric said. There was silence on the other end. "Jada, is that you? It's Lyric."

"Hi, Aunt Lyric." Jada's voice cascaded.

Lyric and Nicke's children referred to each of them as their aunt even though they were not blood related. They recognized their relationship and love for each other as being representative of two blood sisters.

"Hey Jada. How are you?"

"I'm cool. I called to check on my mom."

"She is sleeping right now, and I don't think it's a good idea to wake her."

With hesitation, Jada asked, "Did this make her take a drink?"

"No, Jada. Your mother is very strong. She understands what one drink will do, however, she is extremely hurt."

In a tear-filled voice, Jada responded, "I know. I know how I hurt her, and I am so sorry. Aunt Lyric, I don't know what to do. I really love my mother, and I wish I could take her pain away. I made the biggest mistake of my life, and I'm sure she will never forgive me. I know she is going to disown me, but I hope she will stay in Micah's life. All I tried to do was to be sure Micah had what I did not have—his biological father in his life. I wanted Charles to confess and tell everyone he was Micah's father. Repeatedly, I told Charles I did not want a relationship with him, but he said the only way he would be in Micah's life was if he could have me. He was aware I never intended to hurt my mother like that."

Lyric stood up from the couch. It took her a few seconds to comprehend that Jada just admitted Charles was Micah's father. She gulped as she took a deep breath to calm her nerves. Lyric knew she had to handle this delicately. In her calmest voice, she asked, "Jada, do you realize you were 14 years old when you got pregnant with Micah?"

"Yes, I do know, but Charles said he loved me. He took care of me when my mom was unable or too drunk to fulfill her role."

"You are right, Jada, but Charles did not love you. He took advantage of a child. At that age, you were a child, incapable of understanding the consequences of yours actions and his. He was a grown man, and adults should not, under any circumstances, touch children. He was and is sick. He took your innocence by convincing you it was love. Baby, that was and is not love. That was lust."

Jada remained quiet. She cried out loud.

Her sobs reminded Lyric of the same pain she witnessed Nicke let out earlier that morning. "Jada, listen to me. This is not your fault. You were a child that trusted Charles. He is to blame. Now I can understand why he wanted to keep your mom drunk. He talked about her drinking, but he continually brought alcohol for her. I even remember when he tried to convince Nicke she could keep drinking because she was not an alcoholic. His encouragement all makes sense now. Even after she was sober, he kept trying to antagonize her into drinking again. Jada, Charles is sick. I think both you and your mother need counseling. You need to find out why today, at 20 years old, you still believe it was love with him and not him taking advantage of a child. What he did was wrong!"

Jada continued to sob while listening to Lyric. She travelled back in her mind to the first time Charles touched her. She remembered it was a night that Charles had taken her mother out for their anniversary. She recalled how her mom and Charles argued that night about Jada being permitted to go to Lyric's house. Charles told her mom that she was old enough to stay home alone. She remembered him telling her he thought Lyric's daughters were fast and that they snuck boys in her house. He kept asking her mother if she wanted her to get pregnant. Jada was reminiscing about how afraid she was to be left home alone. She was only 12 years old. She also remembered when her mother left the house, she had not been drinking. The memories came flooding back. She hid these memories for so long, so she was amazed how real they were. As she pondered her deflowering, she became 12 years old again. She saw her mother and Charles as they came home. Charles was holding up her drunken mother. He was ranting and raving about how Nicke had gotten drunk and how embarrassed he was. She recalled he told her to clean her mother up and put her to bed. In Jada's mind, after all of these years, she could still smell the stale cigarette smoke as well as the alcohol emanating from her mother's pores.

After she put her mother to bed, Charles told her to sit on his lap. She reflected on how uncomfortable she was, but how she did it anyway. He began holding her tight and breathing very hard. He then kissed her on the mouth and told her to go to bed. He said he would be in her room later to watch television with her after he took his shower. She recalled how she thought that was a strange thing for him to do, but she wanted to make him feel better about his terrible evening. In her head, she heard him say, "Since your mom was too drunk to commemorate our anniversary, you and I can celebrate." He asked her to pop the jiffy popcorn for their movie date. She watched the popcorn pop in the covered aluminum pan with the foil enclosure.

Lyric interrupted her thoughts as if she had been in her head, listening to her replaying the night her innocence was stolen by someone she loved. "Jada, would you like to talk about how this all started?" Lyric asked in the most caring way that only an aunt could ask her niece.

Jada relayed to Lyric the journey and the first night that the thief came to steal, kill, and deflower her innocence. She picked up from the popcorn movie night.

"Aunt Lyric," she continued, "I remember I felt so embarrassed about my mom being drunk enough to pee on herself. I really did feel bad for Dad, I mean Charles. This was the first time he told me he loved me not like a daughter, but as a woman."

"Woman!" Lyric interrupted, as she was unable to contain her anger and disgust. "You were 12 years old!" Realizing the anger in her voice, Lyric took a deep breath and, with a more calm voice, told Jada to continue.

"Well, we never did watch TV or eat the popcorn. I remember he sat on my bed and began to cry. My heart went out to him. He started telling me he tried to love my mother, but she was so selfish. He told me how she had been sleeping with other men and how he could not take it anymore. He asked if he could lie in my bed and just hold me because he was hurting so bad. I didn't respond. I just let him lay on top of me. It hurt so bad that I started to cry and kept telling him how he was hurting me. He replied by telling me love hurts. When he finished, he kissed me on the mouth and told me how much he loved me and how I saved his life. When he left my room, I saw blood on my sheets. I thought my insides came out. I managed to take the sheets off my bed and hide them in my closet. I was afraid my mother would see them, and I would be in big trouble for messing up her white sheets."

Jada and Lyric both remained silent for several seconds since both were absorbing Jada's confession.

Jada finally broke the silence. "After that night, he came into my room on a regular basis. Truthfully Aunt Lyric, even though a part of me knew it was wrong, I began to try to do what I thought my mother should do for him. Mom was drunk every day. When Charles was not at home, my mother would physically abuse me for no reason. She was so mean to me. I remember one time just because I would not ask Charles for some money so she could go to the liquor store, she fought me like I was a woman in the street. She kicked me in my ribs and broke one of them. When Charles came home, he saw the pain I was in and took me to the hospital. He made me tell him what happened. He promised me he would never let my mother hit me again. After that time, she never did strike me again. That's when the doctor told Charles that not only did I have a cracked rib, but that I was three months pregnant. I remembered I freaked out. I started crying uncontrollably. Charles kept telling me things would work out fine. I remember being so scared."

Lyric gasped. She could feel her stomach turning. She thought she was going to throw up the cup of coffee she consumed earlier.

Jada continued, "On the ride home from the hospital, Charles asked me who I had sex with. I remember how much his question stunned me. At first, I could not answer. I think it was at that moment, I realized I could never let anyone know I got pregnant by my stepfather. It was like I didn't even want him to know. I made up a lie. I told him I slept with Kevin, the boy who once lived next door to us. Charles started talking to me like he was suddenly my stepfather again. He told me not to worry about being pregnant because he would help me. He also said I had nothing to be ashamed of and that I just made a mistake."

Unable to control her anger any longer, Lyric screamed out. "He did what? He knew he was having sex with you and did not even admit to you he was the father. He blamed you. That no-good, sorry bastard!" Lyric managed to compose herself again, but this time, she gagged out loud. She felt the coffee she drank earlier run up her throat and into her mouth. She swallowed the vomit back down. Thankful the puke was not too much, Lyric gulped the remaining saliva, which built in her mouth.

Jada continued explaining to her choking aunt, "After I got pregnant, I did not allow Charles to touch me again. I slept with a bat in case I needed to fend him off of me.

Lyric could not help feeling perplexed. Even though her strategy was not to ask Jada questions but rather listen to what she felt comfortable sharing, Lyric wanted an explanation for what she and Nicke witnessed last night at Jada's apartment. From all appearances, it seemed as if something more was going on between Charles and Jada. "So, what was Charles doing in your bedroom with his shirt off and you in a negligee, if you don't mind me asking?"

Taking a deep breath, Jada continued, saying, "I was out on a date with my friend, David. We have been seeing each other for about six months, and I really like him. After the date, I invited David in and was in the process of entertaining him. I changed my clothes to entice him because he refused to make any sexual attempts towards me. Aunt Lyric, David is the first man that did not try to have sex with me as soon as he could. In fact, he told me how he respected me and that he was a Christian practicing celibacy. He even asked me to change into something that was not so revealing." With amazement in her voice, Jada continued, "Can you believe he said he respected me? When I was about to change, that is when Charles knocked on my door. I tried not to answer it, but I did," Jada asserted. "I told him I had company, but he barged inside anyway. He seemed very distraught to the point where it scared me. I thought something had happened to Mom. I immediately felt guilty because earlier in the day, I was really mean to my mother. I intended to call her the next morning and apologize. I had a rough day at work and took my frustration out on her."

Lyric now listened more attentively as she recalled Nicke sharing how mean Jada treated her. She told Jada to continue.

"Charles told me that he had to speak to me in private and that what he had to say was extremely important. His face was red and he was pacing , with sweat rolling down his face, so I did not know what to expect. Like I said, I thought something had happened to my mom. He even said it was 'a matter of life and death.' I excused myself from my company, and Charles and I went into my bedroom to talk and that was all, I swear, Aunt Lyric. David knocked on my bedroom door and told me he was leaving. He, too, thought whatever Charles wanted must be very serious. He offered to take Micah to his house and said I could pick him up in the morning. David whispered to me that he understood and that for real he needed to go take a cold shower to calm down." Jada giggled. "Well, when David left, Charles started tripping. He told me he was outside my apartment watching me, and he wanted to know how I could let another man touch me. He went into this rampage about how much he loved me and how he waited after I got pregnant. He said he only stopped having sex with me until I was old enough for us to be together. He also said he was going to divorce my mom in order be a father to Micah. He talked about how him, Micah, and me could finally be a family. I tried to tell him he was sick and that I would never hurt my mother again."

"Oh my God, Jada. I am sorry, but Charles is crazy." Lyric continued, "I bet he did not tell you that he argued with your mother and even put his hands on her!"

Jada hesitated, and then she slowly asked her aunt, "Did you say he put his hands on her?"

"Yes, Jada, he did. Your mother and I came to your apartment because she wanted to talk to you about how disrespectful you treated her. She was hurt when you told her to get out of yours and Micah's lives."

Jada sadly said, "I really didn't mean what I said. Someone at work found out about my teenage pregnancy and started spreading the news in my office. Because I was angry, I left work early. So when mom showed up, I blamed her for allowing Charles to touch me in the first place."

"Wait one second, Jada. Your mother did not allow Charles to do that to you. Yes, she was an alcoholic, but she never gave Charles permission to ever touch you."

"Yeah, you are right," Jada said as she began to cry. Through her tears, she managed to get out, "He really is crazy. When I told him I did not love him and did not want him, he really lost it. He finally admitted to me that he knew when the doctor told him I was pregnant that it was his child. I told him that I would never forgive him for what he did to me and that my son would never know the circumstances in which he was conceived. That's when he snapped. He said it was all right for me not to admit to anyone about him being Micah's father but for our next child, everyone would know. He said this could be our secret. He said he would always take care of both Micah and me, but I could not tell anyone or I would never get a dime from him. He threw me on the bed and pulled my underclothing off. He told me no other man would ever make love to me. He said if I told, he was going to tell my mother that I came on to him and how much I always wanted him. That is when you and mom came in and rescued me before he could rape me."

"Jada, you have to tell your mother this whole story. She deserves to know, and I am sure she will believe you."

"Aunt Lyric, I don't think I can. I am so angry with her and Charles. I was a child, and both of them abused me."

"I know, baby, but your mom had a disease, and she has turned all of that around. She is trying to make up for not being there for you. Baby girl, this battle is not yours, it belongs to the Lord. You did not do anything wrong."

"You don't understand." This time Jada burst into a loud overwhelming cry, making it difficult to understand her heart-wrenching words.

Lyric managed to make out what Jada was saying.

"I did not stop him nor did I tell anyone but Tianna what he was doing to me. After a while, I just accepted it and didn't even try to stop him. I would just lie there and let him do his business, then cry for mommy, hoping she would help me. Don't you understand, Aunt Lyric? It is all my fault!" She cried out from deep within her broken life with such pain, that tears began to roll down Lyric's face as she identified with Jada and relived her own abuse.

Collecting herself, Lyric managed to get out in a whispered, compassionate voice, "No, baby, it was not your fault. Charles is the monster here. He was supposed to be the adult, not to mention he pretented to love you and your mother. That was not love, baby, that was the devil inflicting a sickness, which is the lowest of lows." Clenching her teeth and twirling her tongue, Lyric sucked the saliva in her mouth and gathered it in her jaws so she could swallow to lubricate her parched throat. She was just about to continue reassuring Jada that it was not her fault, when there was a pronounced click that came from the bedroom phone extension. The sound made it apparent to both Jada and Lyric; Nicke was listening on the other end of the phone. Neither Jada nor Lyric were sure just when she picked up the phone. At first, neither of them said another word.

Lyric then heard muffled crying and the most sincere plea coming from Jada, "Dear God, please have mercy," just as the call ended, leaving nothing but the sound of the dial tone. Lyric held on for several additional seconds while she composed herself. She tried to understand the twisted way Charles had stolen Jada's innocence and deposited his seed into the womb of a child, causing another child to be born and shattering the dreams of one of God's chosen.

Her mind drifted to a Bible verse she recalled from Matthew: "Truly, I say to you, as you did it to one of the least of these my brothers, you did it to me. Then he will say to those on his left, depart from me, you are cursed into the eternal fire prepared for the devil and his angels." Lyric then heard the annoying recording, "If you would like to make a call, please hang up," to which she complied and cradled the receiver down. She became convicted as she recalled her biblical teachings that raced through her mind, giving her a warning to judge not.

Lyric realized she still needed to address Nicke's temperament. After she eavesdropped on Jada's bone chilling confessions of how a fleshly Satan abused one of God's little angles, Lyric was uncertain of how she would respond. As she entered Nicke's bedroom, she found her sitting on the side of the bed with one leg tucked securely under her.

Nicke raised her head and gazed at Lyric. There was a negative spirit permeating from her that levitated a smoke image of Nicke's body and caused Lyric to shiver. The atmosphere was as if Nicke was possessed and at any second her head was going to do an exorcist 360-degree turn around her body. Nicke blurted, "I am going to kill Charles. He hurt my baby, and he is going to pay. I promise you that worthless, no good son-of- a- bee will not see tomorrow." She lowered her head down as if she had just declared she was going to the store. Her voiced lacked any inflection.

For the first time since Lyric left the security of her home, she felt inadequate and unable to assist her friend. She realized she needed to get some professional help for everyone. She admitted there was a possibility she may be summoned to court to testify against her friend, as she was a witness to Nicke's premeditated murder statement. She hoped in her heart that Nicke was making an idle threat, but she realized the magnitude of the warning. Every fiber in her body was certain that if Charles walked in the door right then, Nicke would kill him. The thought of this scene made Lyric shake even more than thinking of Nicke taking a drink. Lyric tried to search her storage box for a memory that would assist her with what she could or should do to prevent this scenario from happening. She failed to come up with anything that prepared her for this moment. Her mind did a 100-meter dash in nine seconds, beating Usain Bolt's record, as she raced through the files of her life. She felt the desperation of finding an immediate solution designed to snap her friend back to reality. Lyric understood that the stress of the last 48 hours had taken its toll on her friend. She worried if this time her fear of Nicke having an emotional breakdown was more real than she ever could have imagined.

Instinctively, Lyric slowly exited the bedroom and went into the living room. Picking up the receiver, she dialed 911.

"What is your emergency?" Lyric heard the woman ask. Hesitating and trying to figure out how she would explain what help she needed, she quietly said. "I have to report a crime against a child." The 911 operator started firing questions, asking what, when, and where. Lyric gave as much detail as she could, but insisted that a police officer and an ambulance be dispatched now. Lyric hung up the phone. She turned around and saw Nicke holding a gun and standing behind her, which startled Lyric.

Lyric's heart started racing. Her fears were real and manifesting right in front of her. She slowly approached Nicke with her hand out, quivering, "Nicke, give me the gun before you hurt yourself."

"If I was not drunk, he never would have touched my baby or gotten her pregnant. What kind of mother am I? It is my fault, all my fault. I allowed him to hurt my baby."

In a calm voice with a slight tremble, Lyric pleaded, "Nicke, give me the gun. Please. Your daughter needs you. If you hurt yourself, you won't be able to protect Jada from Charles. She needs you. I need you." To Lyric, Nicke appeared as if her body was there, but her soul had flown out of her body. Nicke's eyes seemed as if they were hollow, and her eyeballs had sunken an inch back into her head. She continued to plead. "Nicke, please don't. Give it to me."

Slowly reaching for the powerful 380 Smith and Wesson semiautomatic gun, Nicke released the gun without a fight. Lyric gently slid the life-taking metal object from Nicke's hands. They both slumped down on the couch. With one arm wrapped around Nicke's neck, Lyric took her other hand and slid the gun over to the glass end table on the other side of the couch. Lyric accepted that this was only a temporary, out-of-sight hiding place. She planned to put the gun in the Nicke's safety box on the top of the bedroom closet. She then noticed the real weapon they both needed. Lyric picked up the Bible and turned to Proverbs. She began reading to Nicke from Proverbs 24:1-22:

Be not envious of evil men, nor desire to be with them, for their hearts devise violence, and their lips talk of trouble. By wisdom a house is built, and by understanding it is established; by knowledge the rooms are filled with all precious and pleasant riches. A wise man is full of strength, and a man of knowledge enhances his might, for by wise guidance you can wage your war, and in abundance of counselors there is victory. Wisdom is too high for a fool; in the gate he does not open his mouth. Whoever plans to do evil will be called a schemer. The devising of folly is sin, and the scoffer is an abomination to mankind. If you faint in the day of adversity, your strength is small. Rescue those who are being taken away to death; hold back those who are stumbling to the slaughter. If you say, "Behold, we did not know this," does not he who weighs the heart perceive it? Does not he who keeps watch over your soul know it, and will he not repay man according to his work? My son, eat honey, for it is good, and the drippings of the honeycomb are sweet to your taste. Know that wisdom is such to your soul; if you find it, there will be a future, and your hope will not be cut off. Lie not in wait as a wicked man against the dwelling of the righteous; do no violence to his home; for the righteous falls seven times and rises again, but the wicked stumble in times of calamity. Do not rejoice when your enemy falls, and let not your heart be glad when he stumbles, lest the Lord see it and be displeased, and turn away his anger from him. Fret not yourself because of evildoers, and be not envious of the wicked, for the evil man has no future; the lamp of the wicked will be put out. My son, fear the Lord and the king, and do not join with those who do otherwise, and for disaster will arise suddenly from them, and who knows the ruin that will come from them both?

As Lyric concluded reading the last word of the verse, she felt a personal relief as the word meant to minister to Nicke had given her a sense of understanding and soothed her soul. She hoped, as they both sat quietly, that it had done the same for Nicke, but somehow she felt doubtful. Her friend was in such excruciating pain. Lyric discerned that all she could do was wait for help to arrive. She realized with certainty that she was not equipped or prepared for this type of psychological intervention. This would take the help of someone with the title of doctor in front of his or her name and a practice that had seen it all and done it all. Better yet, she knew only divine intercession and Jesus Christ himself could save her friend from the depths of betrayal and degradation. Lyric was reassured by the fact that she called both the police and the ambulance because Nicke's behavior was deteriorating and her flashing a gun made it apparent both would be needed.

As they both quietly sat, Lyric was startled by the sound of the door off from the kitchen opening. She could not see who was coming in but prayed it was Jada. She thought she remembered Jada hinting at coming over to talk to her mother. She even asked what Lyric thought about it; at least Lyric hoped she had said that. If not, Lyric meant to suggest for her to come over. Lyric honestly could not remember. She began to pray, "Please be Jada." She thought that whoever it was, he or she was taking a long time to come into the living room. Lyric began to hold on to Nicke's shoulder and held her limp body closer while she held her breath. Nicke never flinched or moved. Lyric hoped Nicke had not heard the noise of the door as it squeaked open. She toyed with whether she should get up to go see who was in the kitchen or just wait for Jada to enter the living room. All her questions and indecisive thoughts became clear to her, as the shadow followed by the silhouette of Charles darted across the living room's threshold.

Suddenly, Lyric pushed Nicke off her as she jumped up and headed for the kitchen to prevent Nicke from seeing his face. She knew there was about to be some real drama—the kinds of drama movies were made from after hitting the morning news. Without saying a word, she rushed in the kitchen, grabbed Charles's arm, and pulled as hard as she could to remove him from the house. She managed to yank him into the mudroom off from the kitchen at the threshold of the garage, but not out of the house.

Whispering, she snarled at Charles. "Charles, what the hell are you doing here?"

Taking his signal from Lyric, Charles whispered, "Because I live here."

Lyric was not sure how to respond to Charles as it shocked her that he had the gall to think after what he did, Nicke was going to forgive him and take him back. *What arrogance*, she thought.

Charles looked into Lyric's eyes as if he was searching to see if Lyric knew. His searching clearly revealed the answer. He saw Lyric's eyes squinting closed, only revealing fire flames that radiated from them. He clearly understood he had been discovered.

Without responding to Charles's statement, Lyric maneuvered him from the mudroom into the garage. She was still being careful not to speak too loudly for fear that Nicke would hear her talking. But what was more important, she would hear Charles, which definitely would not be a good thing.

After she maneuvered Charles out and shut the door, she looked into his eyes with the most loathing glare that she could conjure up. "How could you, Charles? How could you do that to Jada?"

Appearing uncomfortable and shuffling his feet, Charles hung his head and searched for something to say. He shifted from one foot to the other, wringing his hands in guilt.

At least, that was how Lyric read his body language, as she waited for Charles's attempts to provide an answer to her question. Lyric stood with her hands on her hips, demanding Charles explain what type of stepfather sexually abuses his stepchild.

Charles held his head up slowly and looked Lyric in her eyes, as if he had not heard what she asked. He refused to shelter any blame. Instead, he flipped to denial mode, exercising the true form of his character. "What are you talking about? I was a good stepfather to Jada."

Lyric gulped and tried to maintain the anger, which about to erupt like lava from a volcano. She no longer saw Charles standing in front of her. She pictured her cousin, Jason and her mother's boyfriend, Cedric. She saw every man who had ever sexually abused her and anyone else who hurt her. Their faces flashed in front of her one by one, as if she was viewing a slideshow. Some faces she quickly recognized, and others she did not. They were passing one after the other, then repeating the sequence. Lyric lashed out at Charles as if he was one of her abusers. Her voice rose as she spit out a hatred that lacked any form of Christ. "You sorry, no good pedophile. You are the scum of the earth. You took that child's innocence for your own pleasure, impregnated her, denied fathering Micah, and to make matters worse, you attempted to rape the woman she became in spite of your manipulative behavior. Now you have the balls to stand here and say you were a good stepfather. Are you serious? Who the hell abused you when you were a child to make you think you had the right to molest Jada? You are going straight to hell without passing go or collecting 200 dollars." Foam soared from Lyric's mouth, leaving a white substance around the corners of her lips as she spit out the pain that consumed her for over 50 years. For the first time, she was getting the chance to tell all those who hurt her what she thought of them and how much hate she still harbored in her heart, mind, and body. Lyric tried to forgive because she was taught if she wanted to go to heaven, she must. What she had not been taught is how to forgive. She comprehended she would never be able to forgive until she was able to release the poison eating away at her. At that second, her mind reflected back on Bishop Jakes's message, "Save Your Scraps." She realized she could finally save her scraps because, at last, she identified them. Not only did she understand how to save her scraps, but also she now realized how to use her scraps to help someone else through what she endured and survived. She heard Bishop say, "If God will bring you to it, he will bring you through it."

Charles stood, watching her, as if he could read her mind. He lay back against the door to the garage. He stopped shuffling his feet and wringing his hands. He appeared to be observing Lyric, as if he could tell she, too, had been abused.

Lyric wasn't sure, but she thought she saw his arrogance and his cocky entitlement melt away. She struggled to regain her composure, as she did not intend for anyone to know her story. She thought her abuse stories died with her abusers. She took solace in the fact her Father would judge them accordingly.

Interrupting her thoughts, Lyric heard Charles say, "It was my uncle."

"What?" Lyric asked as Charles turned to walk away from her, heading further into the garage. Lyric hoped he was preparing to leave. At the same time, Nicke emerged from the mudroom, snatching open the door. She looked like a stark crazy woman. Her eyes were glassy, and her hair was all over her head. She pointed her gun at Charles. She assumed the defensive stance, with her legs slightly spread apart and both arms extended, as she pointed the barrel of the gun straight at Charles's head.

Lyric froze, as did Charles. For a few seconds, no one said anything.

Lyric was standing to the left of Nicke. She was close enough that she could reach Nicke's arms, but the way Nicke had locked them and the grip she had on the gun suggested it would not be a good idea and could cause an accidental shooting. Lyric did not say a word. She stood, observing Charles.

Charles started sweating and shaking as fear encircled his entire body. All of a sudden, he seemed to be three feet tall. Again, he stood humbled and riddled with guilt. His head hung down so low it looked as if it was going to touch his knees. His cockiness dissipated.

Nicke was the first to speak. "So you enjoy having sex with children, and my child at that? I used to wonder why you would not sleep with me. At first, I thought it was because I was an alcoholic. So I got clean. Then I thought it was because you fell out of love with me. I even thought, perhaps, you had another woman. Charles, I spent years trying to make up to you. I allowed you to mentally and physically abuse me. I blamed myself and thought I deserved for you to treat me like shit. I thought, *This man stuck by you while you were a drunk,* so I needed to just shut up and take whatever came my way." With a chuckle in her voice, she continued, "Little did I know that your not wanting me was for none of those reasons. It was because," Nicke's voice changed from a chuckle to trembling, tearful pain. "It was because you wanted a child. *My* child. Tell me, Charles, how did you justify doing what you were doing? Please don't tell me you were in love with a 14-year-old child." Nicke stopped, as if she was thinking. She changed her stance to be more relaxed and held the gun to her own head as if the weapon was going to help her think more clearly. Flipping back to the sarcastic chuckle, Nicke took a few steps closer to Charles as she asked him, full of all the sincerity of an inquisitive mind asking a hypothetical question. "So, Charles, how old was my baby when you first touched her?"

Charles flashed a quick pleading look towards Lyric, as if he wanted to say, "Please help me." Lyric caught the glare of Charles but remained quiet. Her eyes remained on Nicke while her heart raced out of control. She gulped and her eyes were wide open, as if she was scared to blink.

"Charles, I asked you a question. What is wrong? Was it that long ago that you have to count it up in your head?" Nicke lowered the gun from her head and pointed it back at Charles, as she took another step towards him.

Charles, still visibly shaking, did not respond. He continued to plead to Lyric with his eyes, search the floor, and then back to Lyric. He was very careful not to look at Nicke or the gun.

Nicke then turned her cross-examination towards Lyric. "Lyric, why do you think this Mr. Charles is not answering my questions? He usually has so much to say. He is always hammering on about what a bad mother I am, and how my alcoholism hurt my daughter, and on and on."

Trying to speak as calmly and unemotionally as she could, Lyric responded with the only thing she prayed would help, which was to not answer Nicke's line of questioning, but rather to deflect to what she hoped would defuse the situation. "Nicke, think about Jada and Micah. Let the police deal with Charles. He has to answer to the courts and God. Jada and Micah need you now more than they have ever needed you." Just as Lyric got her last word out, the sound of the front door opened, and the security chimed. A mechanical voice announcement followed the noise, "Front door opened."

Lyric froze as she remembered she called 911 and had demanded the police and an ambulance be sent to the Smith's home. She began regretting her decision. She wondered about them walking in with Nicke holding a gun aimed at Charles, and if that sight would cause them to react and ask questions later. Lyric was snapped back by a sweet, low familiar female voice. For a second, it sounded like music to Lyric.

"Aunt Lyric, where are you?" The sound of Jada's voice seemed to bring everyone back to the moment. Jada continued. "Aunt Lyric, where are you? Where is my mom? The police and an ambulance are outside. What is going on?"

After hearing what Lyric thought was music to her ears, she heard the heavy, harsh voice of an unknown male. "It's the police." There was no doubt the song was going to be sung, even if it was out of tune.

Lyric realized, as she heard the steps getting louder and closer to the mudroom that she had to prepare the police and Jada for the scene they were about to walk into. "Jada, please don't come in here. Your mother has a gun pointed at Charles," Lyric shouted just as the officer touched the door handle to the garage.

The officer pushed Jada back with one hand, and with the other hand, he grabbed his gun, pulling it from his holster and aiming it at the closed door. Motioning to his partner, the officer again forcefully shoved Jada, but this time, into the arms of his partner. "Get her out of here." He covered them both while they exited the house. Once the officer with Jada was out, he returned to his squad car, opening the door to use it as a shield. He grabbed his radio and called in for backup.

For safety reasons, the other officer went to several neighbors' houses and ordered them to leave. Additional police cars roared down the middle-class streets with their sirens blaring. They surrounded the house and set up a semicircle perimeter in the cul-de-sac and alley encompassing Nicke's four-bedroom brick home.

The officer took Jada to his car, bombarding her with a series of questions. Who is Charles? What is your Aunt's name? Why does your mother have a gun on Charles? Who else is in the house? How many people live in the house? Finally, the officer stopped his rapid line of questioning. He peered deep into Jada's face, noticing she was either in shock or had not heard any of his questions, not to mention that she did not even attempt to answer any of them.

A female officer walked up to Jada and put her arms around Jada, asking, "Is that your mother that lives here?"

Jada broke down in tears and sunk into the female officer's arms. She managed to pull herself together enough to answer the officer's questions, but not before accepting the complete and total blame for the situation. "It's my fault, all my fault," she said, as she relayed her life story to the kind, nurturing policewoman and confessed the sins of her abuser.

"Jada, I need to talk to your mother," the officer began, as if she were talking to a little girl. "Do you think you can call her so we can let her know we are going to help you and her?"

Jada reached for her cell phone and scrolled to the word "Mom." She pushed the talk button. The officer reached over and gingerly took the phone from Jada's hand. The cell phone went immediately to voicemail with a once bright, cheery voice: "You have reached the cell phone voicemail of Nicke. Can't take your call. At the tone, leave a message and remember, make it a great day because you control your own destiny." Beep

"This is officer Judith Nelson, Mrs. Smith, please call your daughter. She needs you." As the officer made her last statement, Jada looked in her eyes with renewed determination and strength. She continued watching the officer as she dialed the home number. The officer reached for the phone, but this time, Jada pulled away from her. She turned her back, which did not allow Officer Nelson a chance to retrieve the phone.

Jada pleaded, "Mom, Aunt Lyric, somebody answer the phone! Please pick up. Somebody please pick up the phone!" Jada's pleas were answered.

"Jada, this is your Aunt Lyric."

"Oh thank God." Jada shouted.

Realizing contact had been reached in the house, the kind, considerate police officer snatched the phone from Jada's grip, only this time, there was no compassion or kindness, only the urgency of life and death.

"Lyric, this is Officer Judith Nelson. Do you think I may be able to speak with Mrs. Smith?"

"I am not sure she will come to the phone. She has been through a lot, and I think the stress of it all has taken its toll."

"Lyric, yes I certainly understand. Jada has told me what she has been through, but we need to prevent someone from getting hurt. Where are Charles and Mrs. Smith?"

"Nicke and Charles are in the garage."

"Where are you?" Officer Nelson asked.

"I am on the kitchen phone."

"Do you think you can take the phone to Nicke?"

"I can try. I am not sure she will talk though."

"If not, put the phone on speaker so at least she can hear me."

Lyric took the phone into the garage, moving very slowly and making sure she did not do anything to spook Nicke.

"Nicke, the police want to speak with you."

Nicke slid down the wall and was sitting on the garage floor with the gun resting on her knees, but still aimed at Charles.

Neither of them was saying a word. Charles's head was still hanging down. Nicke did not seem fazed by what he was feeling. She seemed to be rehearsing different plans for Charles, playing each scenario through her mind, while she was trying to figure out which one she would execute.

In the same compassionate and friendly voice, Officer Nelson greeted Nicke. "Hello, Nicke, I have been speaking with Jada, and she told me why you are so upset. I understand how you must feel because I have a daughter too. We just need you to let the police handle this situation."

"You said you understand how I feel and that you have a daughter," Nicke replied. "OK. Then tell me what you would do to your husband if you found out he deflowered your 14-year-old daughter, took her innocence, and got her pregnant."

"Nicke, if he did that to Jada, he will be punished. You have to let the police and the courts handle this."

"*If* he did this?" Nicke shouted. "My grandson, or should I say stepson, is living proof. Officer Nelson, I asked you a question. What would you do to your husband?"

"Nicke, I know you are upset, but please let the police handle this."

"Lady, you are avoiding my question. I want to know what you would do!" Nicke shouted.

"Please let me come in the house, and we can talk," Officer Nelson stated in a firm voice. "No one has to get hurt. We are trained to handle this. We will arrest him, and he will get his day in court. We don't want you to go to jail too. Who is going to help your daughter raise your grandson?" Officer Nelson turned to an officer standing nearby as she muted the phone. "Get her daughter over here now," she commanded.

As Jada exited the police car and walked towards Officer Nelson, Officer Nelson unmuted the line, putting the phone on speaker so Jada could also hear the conversation. She whispered to Jada, "Ask her to put the gun down and come out of the house."

She then went back to the phone line. "Nicke, Jada wants to talk to you. Would that be all right?" She handed Jada the phone without waiting for an answer from Nicke.

Jada began to cry. "Mom, I am so sorry. Please put the gun down so no one will get hurt. I love you, Mommy, I need you. Please don't hurt anyone. It's not Charles's fault. It's my fault," she cried.

Nicke stood up and assumed her I-am-going-to-shoot-his-ass stance.

Charles raised his head. His life flashed before him. A part of him was sorry for what he did, but another part convinced him that he was in love with Jada, thereby justified her deflowering. He resigned to himself that if he could not have Jada, he did not want to live.

Lyric jumped up from the chair and yelled, "Nicke don't do it! He's not worth it." She wanted to walk over to Nicke, but she was afraid she would scare Nicke.

"Jada," Nicke began with a bit calmer tone. "Baby, it is not your fault." She pointed the gun at Charles, saying, "This bastard is to blame. He is at fault, and he is going to pay."

Officer Nelson snatched the phone from Jada's moistened hands, sliding it to her ear. "Nicke you are right. It is not Jada's fault. She was a child. I can tell how much you love her and how much you want to protect her." Officer Nelson, aware that the situation was beginning to get out of control, realized she had to do something, and she had to do it fast. "I am coming in the house, Nicke. I want to be the one who puts the cuffs on Charles, and I want to be the officer to take him into custody."

Nicke interrupted in a calmer voice, saying, "No, please don't come in." She turned to face Lyric. Her voice seemed to change to a high-pitched, childlike tone. "Lyric, thanks for all of your help. This is between Charles and me. You need to leave, and go outside with Jada. She sounds like she is very upset, and she needs you. I love you, my friend. Thank you for being the best friend in the world."

For the first time since this ordeal began, Lyric realized that Nicke was capable of killing Charles. Not only was she capable, but Lyric also felt in her spirit that Nicke wasn't just trying to scare him but intended to murder him right there in cold blood. Lyric's eyes quickly flashed over to Charles, and what was once shame in Charles's eyes had obviously been replaced by the fear of dying. Charles stopped with the "woe is me" attitude and became a pitiful person ready to die.

Lyric knew she had to prevent anyone from shooting. Things moved from desperate to critical. She was sensing Nicke's change from victim to villain. Lyric did the first thing that came to mind. If she had more time, this probably would have been her last choice. With her body shaking, she walked over to Charles and placed her hand on Charles' shoulder.

Charles looked up at Lyric with large dilated eyes. His eyes said what Lyric thought his mouth wanted to say, "Help me. Don't let her kill me."

Nicke angrily blurted at Lyric. "Get away from him and get out of my house now, Lyric!"

Lyric's brain quickly tried to think of a way to stall Nicke and how to remain in the house. Without looking at Nicke, Lyric tried to use the calmest voice she could. "Nicke, if you are going to kill Charles, I need to pray with and for him. He needs to repent for his sins first. You can't deny him the right to pray and ask for forgiveness."

Nicke slowly processed Lyric's request. Something in her from the many church services she heard rationalized the request. She nodded in agreement to allow Lyric to pray. "Lyric, I am going to need you to make it quick though."

Officer Nelson, still listening on the phone, heard the entire conversation. She continued to use her hostage training and immediately ordered a sharpshooter. She wrestled with whether to do this because she repeatedly heard Nicke's voice in her head, asking her what would she do. She tried hard to block this thought from her mind because her innermost feelings were telling her she would probably do just what Nicke was doing. Her police training was telling her everyone is innocent until proven guilty. It was her duty to make sure this happened, as she had taken an oath almost 20 years ago to uphold everyone's inalienable rights.

With all the activity going on, Officer Nelson thought she would give Jada one more try. She figured this time, she would give Jada some things to say to her mother. Officer Nelson turned to look for Jada, but she was not in sight. "What happened to her daughter? I want to give her one more chance before we move in."

Jada could not be found, and none of the officers knew where she went.

Officer Nelson realized she was out of time and options. She had no choice but to put the sniper in place. She spoke to the sniper on the radio. "Don't do anything until I give you the word." She headed for Nicke's front door. "Nicke, this is Officer Nelson. I am coming in."

To Officer Nelson's surprise, as she entered, she saw her missing option inside the house. Officer Nelson stopped in her tracks, as if she was not sure what to do next.

Jada had quietly slipped away and entered the house through her old bedroom window. She used this escape method as a teenager when she was trying to avoid Charles. Jada cautiously walked into the garage, attempting to enter quietly.

Charles was the first one to speak. "Jada, don't let your mother kill me. She doesn't understand. I love you, and I never meant to hurt you. We have a child together, and Micah needs his father."

Jada felt a strength she never encountered before. She whipped her head around to face Charles, and for the first time, she looked at him not as a victim, but as a survivor. "Charles, you don't love me. You are a sick individual. What you did to me was not love. You made me hide this from my mother because you knew how much I loved her and how I never wanted to hurt her. You used that to keep me quiet. I fell for it hook, line, and sinker." Jada was standing straight, tall and erect. She was looking straight into Charles's eyes. All of her timid nature evaporated and was replaced with a stern verbal attack on Charles. "You need help," she shouted. "I am going to tell the world what you did to me. For so many years, I was so ashamed of myself and angry with everyone. You not only took my virginity, but you stole my dreams. I will never forgive you. What you feel for me was never love. It was your twisted mind playing out the damage someone did to you. You used love to justify what you did to me. You call it love. No, Charles. Love is why I couldn't tell anyone the man my mother married got me pregnant. You told me not to tell anyone, and I didn't, but the reason I never told wasn't because you told me not to. I didn't tell because I loved my mother. Now that's what love is. This cycle is broken today! Right now. It is going to start with me. You were supposed to be my stepfather. You were to fill the role my biological father could not or would not fill."

Tears fell from Charles's face. He hung his head much lower. He did not say a word, but wondered how Jada knew about his secret. He had not told anyone. He thought no one would ever find out how he was abused by his uncle that died several years ago. Jada's words appeared to pierce him deep within his own world of do not tell. It was hard for everyone to distinguish if he was reacting to guilt from what he had done to Jada or guilt because his own life's secret was exposed. It was difficult for even Charles to know. There stood a man who once tried to convince anyone he met or knew that he had taken care of Jada like her real father while her mother was a drunk. At this moment, Charles, in his own eyes, stood less than three feet tall and had loss his status of being called a man. He flunked manhood and was, by choice, repeating boyhood again.

The room was quiet for a moment. Both Lyric and Nicke just witnessed a side of Jada neither of them had ever seen. She typically was either childlike angry or very introverted. Seeing her explode in a controlled adult way shocked them all—most of all, Charles.

Nicke, being proud of her daughter standing up to Charles, felt her own independence. She took her turn exploding at Charles. She turned to him and lowered her head as if she wanted to try to make eye contact with him. Her voice was controlled but full of disappointment. "You blamed me and my alcoholism for your desire to be with a child, my child. For years, you beat me up with how well you took care of my daughter and what a bad mother I was." But before Nicke could finish her ranting and attack on Charles, Jada turned to her mother and spilled years of pain and neglect on her.

She wheeled around and admonished her mother. "Mom, it was not because you were drunk that you did not know what was going on. It was because I knew if I told you, you would kill Charles. So that is why I didn't tell you. I was trying to protect you from going to jail. Look at you now," she yelled. "You are doing just what I was afraid you would do for all those years. My silence will not be in vain." Jada sounded like she was the mother, and Nicke was the child. She ordered her mother to put the gun down right at that moment. "I need you! We need you." She let go and shouted, losing all control of her emotions. Spit built up in her mouth and came flying out with each word she spoke. She began to hyperventilate. She stopped long enough to try to catch her breath while still managing to get out, "It's not your fault, Mom." She spun around on her heels, turned and pointed at Charles, "It's his fault and his alone. I was a child. He was the adult. He was supposed to be my dad." Just as Jada got out the word "dad," she grabbed her face with her hands and buried all the years of tears in the cup of her hands. For the first time, she realized she had stopped blaming her mother for what Charles did to her. What is more important, for the first time, she forgave herself by putting the blame where it should be. She ran across the room like she was a baby again, falling into Nicke's waiting arms and heart.

Lyric, without being prompted to do so, walked over to Nicke and gently took the gun from Nicke's now limp hand, which was draped around Jada's neck. Lyric, in one fluid motion, opened the door and handed the gun to Officer Nelson.

Officer Nelson took the gun and made sure it was disengaged. Several other officers rushed past Lyric and headed into the garage. Their guns were drawn. They were prepared for a battle or self-protection.

Officer Nelson walked over to Jada and Nicke and joined in the group hug, as if she was personally identifying with the plight of their pain.

Her fellow officers headed straight to Charles. Without being told, Charles assumed the arrest position by placing his hands behind his back. The officers secured handcuffs on them, preparing him for his ride to jail also known as a facility for caged animals. One of the officers intentionally gave an extra push when tightening the cuffs around Charles' hands, meant to purposely cause pain and make the restraints uncomfortable.

A detective then approached the group hug. He gave Officer Nelson a look, showing his disapproval of her partaking in this action. Officer Nelson, realizing she had lost her professionalism, pulled away quickly and tried to regain her poise.

In a very insensitive but businesslike manner, the detective pulled out his notebook and began questioning Nicke. Pointing to Charles, "How do you know this man? How do you know he had sex with your daughter?"

Stunned by his line of questioning, Nicke's arms dropped from around Jada like a wet noodle. Her mind said, "What the hell do you mean," but her mouth could not get the words out. It became apparent to everyone in the room that the stress had finally taken over Nicke. Her eyes were glazed, and they rolled back in her head. Her body slumped to the floor, as it appeared she had fainted or passed out when her head hit against the garage wall.

Jada tried to grab her mother and break some of her impact, but was unable to keep her from the unexpected fall and collapsing on the garage floor.

The paramedics, which were notified when the police were called, as if they had been cued, either heard the noise or saw the fall and entered the two-car garage just as Nicke's head slammed to the floor. They were carrying a stretcher. It was as if they knew Nicke was going to need them right at the second of their arrival.

Lyric assisted Jada and ushered her from the commotion and out of the way of the professionals attending to Nicke.

They lifted Nicke's limp shapely body. Gently, but in sync, they placed her body on the stretcher. One of the medics placed smelling salt under Nicke's nose while the other one placed a blood pressure cup on Nicke's already extended arm. Nicke's entire body jumped with a quick flinch as her nose sniffed the smelling salt that immediately went to her brain. Her eyes bucked open, then slowly closed. Both the paramedics looked at each other, as they seemed to realize this was not going to be a classic case of a woman fainting, but rather a more serious medical condition. They both began to move at a faster pace. One placed an oxygen mask on Nicke's face. The other medic attempted to leave the garage in a quick rush to return to the waiting ambulance. Fortunately, it had been moved directly outside of the closed garage.

Lyric, seeing him rushing towards the closed door, moved with the same haste. She pushed the garage door opener button. The door slowly opened, humming at the same pace it did time after time, unaware and incapable of understanding the haste the situation called for. The medic, not waiting for it to completely open, ducked and exited as soon as he was able. Revealed outside the door were the waiting ambulance and a gathering of Nicke's neighbors, rubbernecking and trying to see what the drama was in their typically quiet neighborhood. All that was missing from the attention they were showing were lawn chairs and popcorn.

The rude and insensitive detective turned his attention to Lyric. Without even asking who Lyric was or, for that matter, what her role was, he spouted out, "Tell me what happened here?"

Although Lyric felt a twinge of embarrassment for her and the entire Smith family, her blood began to boil. She was about to create some additional drama directed at the cold, unfeeling detective but thought better of that approach. Instead, she responded indignantly, "Excuse me?"

Officer Nelson, who was much more composed and sensed Lyric's obvious disapproval of the detective's abrupt approach, quickly intervened, saying, "Ma'am. Lyric, right?"

Lyric responded in a calmer tone, saying, "Yes, that is my name."

After glaring at the insensitive detective, Officer Nelson took over the questioning. She was being very careful to remain kind and sensitive to both Lyric and Jada. They responded more favorably but were still preoccupied, as neither of them could hide their worry and concern for Nicke.

At one point, Officer Nelson asked Jada if she would be willing to accompany her to the police station to file charges. They all stopped suddenly when they overheard one of the paramedics relaying to the hospital that Nicke had slipped into a coma. They reported that Nicke's blood pressure was at hypertensive crisis, 200/190, and they were bringing her in stat. Nicke lost control of her bodily functions. Lyric saw a puddle of what appeared to be urine drip to the floor from the stretcher.

Jada managed to respond to Officer Nelson with a quick but simple, "No" as she hitched a ride, climbing into the back of the ambulance just before the rear door closed going to wherever they were taking her mother.

As the ambulance speed out of Nicke's neighborhood with its loud siren echoing get out of my way, Lyric remained with Officer Nelson, giving as much information as she could on what occurred over the last 24 hours, up to and including 14-year-old Jada's pregnancy by her stepfather.

Officer Nelson sent several other policemen on their way, telling them she would finish up the investigation. She assisted Lyric into Nicke's house. Both had a seat at Nicke's disheveled kitchen table. Lyric tried to pick up the objects that Nicke had thrown. She asked Officer Nelson if she wanted a cup of coffee or a glass of water. Officer Nelson declined; stating she knew Lyric would want to get to the hospital to check on her friend.

After finishing her questioning and explaining to Lyric what the next steps would be, she thanked Lyric for being a friend to Nicke and Jada. She told her if it were not for her, things might have turned out differently.

Lyric thanked Officer Nelson for her understanding as they both shared a glance only someone who had been sexually abused would or could share. It was a silent glance Officer Nelson and Lyric exchanged indicating I know how you, Nicke and Jada feel basically meaning, I've been there and got a T-shirt to hide my scars to prove it.

After sharing their unspoken words, Officer Nelson asked Lyric if she needed a ride to the hospital.

Turning to walk Officer Nelson to the door, she said, "Thanks, Officer Nelson, but no thanks. I will need to bring Jada back home, so we will need a car at the hospital." Just as Lyric was about to say good-bye to Officer Nelson, her cell phone began ringing. Both stopped in their tracks, as if they instinctively knew the ringing of the cell phone represented bad news. Lyric motioned to Officer Nelson not to leave yet as she hesitantly answered her phone. "Yes, Jada," she slowly began, with her eyes fixed straight into Officer Nelson's eyes.

Officer Nelson closed the door, deciding not to leave. She could tell by Lyric's intent listening that things must not be good for Nicke.

"Coma? Intensive care? What do you mean? What happened!" Lyric shouted. "Jada, calm down. I am on my way. Officer Nelson was just leaving. What made her brain bleed? Are they saying it is an aneurism?"

Officer Nelson sat back down at the kitchen table. She was hanging on to every word Lyric was saying. From the one-sided conversation, she was able to gather the stress of Nicke's ordeal adversely affected not only her mentally, but now it was having an effect on her physical health. Officer Nelson surmised from the conversation that Nicke must have had a brain hemorrhage or possibly a stroke. Chances are that given either diagnosis, the increased blood pressure was the culprit, no doubt triggered on by stress.

Lyric continued to secure details from Jada and kept repeating her account, wanting to be sure Officer Nelson was aware of the news as Jada was relaying it.

"No, I do not think she took her blood pressure pills. In fact, I am sure she did not. I could not even get her to eat or rest. Jada, call your mother's sisters and let them know they should get to the hospital as soon as possible. I will be there soon. Yes, Jada, I will." Lyric stopped to look at her cell phone before pushing the end key. She sighed and looked at Officer Nelson for some possible relief.

Officer Nelson could see how upset Lyric was by the expression on her face. She reached over and gently cupped Lyric's hand in hers. "Lyric, you also need to be careful. You have been through an awful lot yourself. You have to take care of your body and mind or you can end up like Nicke. Please take a moment to rest or you will not be able to help Jada."

Lyric did not respond. Knowing what Officer Nelson was telling her was right, she struggled to conjure up the energy she needed to keep moving. She could feel her body and mind crying out to her subconscious for rest and a break. She had been at this for over 24 hours, operating on less than six hours of sleep.

Officer Nelson interrupted Lyric's recount of how much rest she had with an attempt to offer assistance to Lyric. "Is there anyone else who can go be with Jada, allowing you to go home and sleep for a couple hours?"

Lyric, without stopping to think, started to say, "Charles," then caught herself before she could completely finish saying his name. She forgot Charles was not an option, as he was in jail. Lyric could not help but put the blame on Charles. He was the perpetrator and the sole cause of her best friend laying in the hospital in intensive care, fighting for her life. Responding to Officer Nelson's question, "No, Nicke has other family, but all of them are out of town and could not get to Texas for at least a few days. I need to get it together and go to the hospital to be with Jada. I am certain she is scared to death."

Officer Nelson gave Lyric one last warning along with an additional pat on her hand to convey her understanding. "Take care of yourself, Lyric, and be careful. My prayers are with Nicke. I will stop by the hospital later, but officially. I will need to get a statement from Jada."

As Lyric grabbed her keys off the countertop, she thanked Officer Nelson. They both left Nicke's house. This time, there were not any neighbors hanging around, trying to see what was happening in the Smith residence. In fact, everyone resumed their own lives and was probably getting caught up in their own drama.

CHAPTER 5

Storms of Life

A flower has withered from the storms of life
Downpours of rain have caused misery and strife
Winds have blown its petals to the ground
Sinking in floodwaters, trying not to drown.
Its stems are dying, injured by hail
Bent and broken down
Although it's too early to tell
The flower's roots have been damaged
From a lightning strike . . . deep in their home
Igniting a fire . . . burning its way to the bone
A flower has withered from the storms of life
Bent over and broken, as if cut with a knife.

ALMOST 12 HOURS later was the first time since last night that Jada had thought about her son. A blind distress took over her body. She realized that she truly did not know David or his secrets. She permitted her son to spend the night with him. Tears flowed from her eyes like a cup that runneth over. Jada now understood how easily a person could put a child in potential harm and not realize it or mean to expose them. She wondered if her mother trusted Charles just as she had faith in David. She asked herself, "Why would I leave my son with a man

I've only known for six months?" However, in the back of her mind, a part of her said she could have confidence in David. She then wondered if her mother was ever conflicted when she left her with Charles.

Jada took out her cell phone and called David. She took a deep breath and said a quick silent prayer before David answered: "God, please let David be trustworthy. Let my son be OK."

David answered the phone on the first ring. "Jada, where are you? I have been calling you. I started to worry. Micah and I went out to breakfast. After that, I took him to the gym, and we played basketball. We then ate dinner. All day, I tried calling you. We even drove by your apartment, but I did not see your car in the parking lot. Are you all right?"

At first, Jada was unable to talk. She struggled to subdue her tears. A part of her appeared grateful because David took care of Micah, yet another part wanted to scream for him to bring her child to her now. But the part she chose to express was vulnerability: "David, I need you. Please come and bring Micah to Baylor Hospital. It is my mother. She may not survive." Jada cried inconsolably before ending the call.

David heard the agony in her voice and realized whatever was wrong with Jada's mother must be serious. He hung the phone up and rushed to the garage as he pulled Micah's coat over his stiffening shoulders. He fastened the seatbelt around him, then quickly started his brand new blue 760 BMW Li.

Before backing out, David glanced over at Micah. He knew by Micah's body language that the young boy sensed something was wrong. He understood he needed to say something to prepare Micah, even though he did not know if he himself was ready. All he knew was Jada needed him, and she said it was bad. David felt a slight warmth hearing that Jada needed him. She always appeared to be independent, and it sometimes seemed she preferred to take David or leave him. He detected that for some reason, Jada placed a proverbial wall around her heart to protect her from vulnerability.

Although he had faith that eventually Jada would let him get close to her, he accepted that it was going to take hard work and time.

David pulled into the visitor's lot of Baylor Hospital. He was about to exit his car when it hit him—he did not know her mother's last name. He was sure they did not have the same last name since Jada's mother remarried. Grabbing Micah's hand, he decided to call Jada.

Micah studied David with concern in his eyes. David acknowledged his feelings as he reached in his rear seat to secure his Bible. "Everything is going to be fine, little man. We are going to see your mom. Your grandmother is sick, but we are going to pray she will get well soon."

Micah turned away and did not say a word. He clenched David's hand tighter.

The emergency room sliding doors opened wide as they both entered, not knowing what they were going to face. David pulled his cell phone from his shirt pocket. He surveyed himself, wondering if his appearance was up to standards, thinking he did not want to embarrass Jada. After all, this would be his first time meeting with what he hoped would someday be his mother-in-law.

"Micah, Micah!" a familiar voice known to Micah hollered.

Micah turned around, quickly dropping David's hand, as he ran towards the voice of his grandmother's best friend, Aunt Lyric. He jumped into her waiting arms and hugged her neck so tight that Lyric gasped to breathe.

David stood quietly, watching their embrace.

Lyric stood up and extended her hand. "You must be David," she blurted out with somewhat of a sly smile.

David nodded and returned a cunning grin as he extended his chest outward because he was thinking Jada must have told her about him, which was a good sign.

"Yes, I am David. And you are?"

Lyric interrupted him, saying, "I am Lyric. Jada's mom and me go way back. I am so glad you are here. Jada is going to need you."

There go those same words again. *Jada needs me. This is good for me, but things must be bad for Jada*, he thought. He hoped he owned the strength she was sure to need. "I will do my best. How is her mother?" David hesitantly asked.

Lyric reached down and cupped her hands around Micah's ears. "She is in serious condition and is in intensive care. We are going to need to pray hard," she said as she spotted David's hand holding his Bible. Dropping her hands from Micah's ears, she pushed the elevator button.

Micah took his tiny hand and slid it back into David's while, once again, looking up at David with the concerned plea of "please protect me, and help my mom."

David, sensing Micah's anxiety, smiled with hope into his big brown concerned eyes. Then feeling like Micah may need more than a smile, he handed his Bible to Lyric and picked up five-year-old Micah.

Micah showed his approval with a smile that lit up not only his eyes and his entire face, but also the elevator. Most times, Micah felt he was too big to be picked up, but this time, he was willing. He wrapped his legs around David's waist and his arms around his neck.

Watching this exchange of care, Lyric thought, *Jada finally has a man capable of loving her and Micah.* Judging by him carrying his Bible, she surmised he was also a Christian that prayed to a miraculous, healing God. She considered his appearance from head to toe and thought, *He is also attractive and extremely pleasant on the eyes.* Jada just may have hit the jackpot. God knows she is going to need both of them to make it through the storms that are raging in her life. Lyric stepped off the elevator and onto the intensive care ward. She scanned until she located the family waiting room. Lyric took the lead and hastened her steps. When she entered the door, Jada jumped up and ran towards her.

Jada's eyes were swollen almost shut, appearing as if she lost a recent fistfight. Her hair was smashed flat on one side, and white salt left a trail from her bottom eyelid down below her chin. Her form-fitting dress hugged her shapely body. The black knit revealed every curve, although it managed to become hiked up on the sides. As Jada ran to her aunt, her eyes caught the sight of her knight in shining armor holding her most precious gift in the entire world. She stepped past Lyric towards the arms she prayed would offer her comfort. She stopped for a second to straighten up her dress and try to fluff her hair, but she was unable to do anything about the dried tear tracks. She reached around Micah and David with open arms that wrapped them both with all the love she had in her heart.

David stared at her, noticing the pain she was carrying revealed in every fiber of her body. For the first time, he was witnessing vulnerability in a woman he once thought never existed. She always seemed so composed and strong that she kept her feelings locked somewhere deep inside.

Lyric, feeling a little put out with Jada pushing her out the way, reached for Micah to allow the couple a complete and unobstructed embrace.

Micah, sensing his mother needed the same type hug he received, did not protest, but rather fell into the waiting arms of Lyric.

Once Jada was locked into David's empty arms, she let go and cried a river on his chest. She was unable to stop crying or trembling.

David held her so close, giving Jada what she needed most: a sense of security and protection. He lifted her from the ground, allowing her body to sink fully into his body and his heart. His eyes were tightly closed. At that nanosecond, he vowed to himself and God that he would protect her and never let her go. He felt a love for Jada that he had never experienced for any other woman. He was certain that between him and God, they both would help Jada lug the heavy cross she carried.

Just then, the door to the waiting room opened, and standing there was a short white man clothed in green scrubs with a mask hanging around his neck. Looking at Jada resting in David's arms, he asked, "Are you the family of Nicke Smith?"

Lyric answered for Jada. "Yes we are? How is she doing?"

The doctor tried carefully not to alarm the family any more than necessary. He asked them all to have a seat. Looking at Jada, he asked, "You are the daughter, right?"

Jada responded with a slow, fearful, "Yes."

"Well," the doctor began as he placed his hand on the seat, motioning for Jada to sit near him.

David stood behind Jada's chair and wrapped his arms around her neck. He was not sure if he would need to embrace Jada if the doctor said her mother would not or did not survive, but positioned himself in case.

"Things are touch and go and will be for the next 48 hours. Mrs. Smith is still unconscious. We have her on a ventilator," the Doctor said.

Hearing the word "ventilator" made Jada begin to cry again.

The Doctor continued with Nicke's prognosis. "We have her on the ventilator so we can assist her breathing. We have to be careful we do not overstress any of her other organs. We have placed her in a medically induced coma. We need to try to get her blood pressure down, then we will know if there was any damage done from the strokes."

"Strokes?" Jada cried out.

"Yes, your mother has suffered several mini strokes. We are not sure what nerve damage has been done or if there has been any other injuries. She also had a few seizures since being admitted. We have to wait until the swelling in her brain subsides before we will be able to assess the impairment. Everyone needs to keep their fingers crossed for the next 48 hours."

"Can I see her?" Jada sheepishly asked.

"Yes," the doctor replied as he surveyed the room. "Is that your son?" he asked pointing to Micah.

"Yes, it is."

"Well, I would suggest that you let your mom build her strength up more before allowing the little fellow to see her. There are many tubes everywhere, and they may frighten him. Also, no more than two people are allowed in the room at any one time, and they may stay for no more than 10 minutes. It is extremely important she gets proper rest."

Jada nodded and turned to her aunt, whom she had almost completely ignored since she first laid eyes on David. "Would you like to go in with me?"

Lyric stopping to think for a moment, then said, "No, I will stay here with Micah. Why don't you and David go?"

Jada was so relieved because her desire was for David to accompany her. After all, this may be the last time he sees her mother alive. Jada stood up. David wrapped his arm around her waist and escorted her out of the room.

The door to the waiting room closed. Jada and David exited and walked down the hall. They entered the room with all the machines beeping and leads hooked to the woman who gave birth to Jada.

Lyric put Micah on her lap. She knew Micah was feeling the stress because he had not said one word. This was so unlike him. Most times, Nicke would be telling him to go sit down somewhere. She would tell him he was going to fall flat on his face from so much ripping and running. She would also say to

Lyric that Micah was the most inquisitive child she ever knew, stating that all of Micah's questions begin and end with the word "why." Nicke would complain about how Micah needed a sedative to stop his mind and body from racing, but not this time. He was very quiet. His eyes moved from one person to the next until he lie in Lyric's arms and fell fast asleep.

Again the waiting room door squeaked open, revealing the next chapter. There stood Officer Nelson dressed in full uniform. Lyric's keen awareness alerted her that this was official business.

Officer Nelson still managed to produce a warm and inviting smile. She greeted Lyric in a low soft voice, being careful not to awaken the child sleeping on her lap. She was not sure, but assumed the child must be the grandson of Nicke and the alleged son of Charles Smith.

"How is Nicke doing, Lyric?" Officer Nelson's deep bass voice asked.

After taking a gulp and a deep sigh, Lyric responded, "It is still touch and go for the next 48 hours."

"Is Jada visiting with her now?"

"Yes, she and her male friend, David, are in the room with Nicke. The doctor has asked that we limit our visits to 10 minutes and no more than two visitors at a time. So she should be out shortly." Lyric, knowing the answer to her own question, decided she would pose it to Officer Nelson in statement form. "So this is not purely a social call, but an official business one."

Officer Nelson peered up and rather timidly stated, "Yes, Lyric, that is correct. I need to complete my report before tomorrow morning. Charles goes before the judge for arraignment. Do you think Jada is up to answering questions?"

"Yes, I believe she is but I am not sure David is aware of the situation. I am unclear if she will want to talk in front of him. But, if you do not mind, I would like to be there when you question her. I may need to give her some moral support. That young woman has shouldered a lot in her 20 years of life. I am sure if Nicke were able to, she would be right beside her. Since she cannot, I would like to be there."

Officer Nelson responded affirmatively with only a nod as the door to the waiting room swung open.

Jada took one step in, and then noticed Officer Nelson. She stopped abruptly, causing David to run into the back of her. Jada also realized Officer Nelson must be at the hospital to speak with her. She entered and sat next to Lyric.

David spied the couch on the opposite side of the room. He glided his 6′, 210-pound body towards the sofa, with his Bible grasped tightly in both his hands. The ladies gawked at him walking down the hall and so did those sitting in the waiting room. They lionized him as they admired his stride. His walk exuded a confidence, which made him sexier than his finely tuned and chiseled body. David was unaware of the attention his stature commanded.

Officer Nelson examined him so intently, thinking to herself, *I wonder if he has an older brother and is he single? If he is married, thank your mom and dad for me because their egg and sperm created a handsome young man. If your brother is single, give him my card and tell him to give me a call.*

As David sat on the couch, he examined Jada and gave her a half smile. He hoped she comprehended he was there to offer any support she desired. He wished Jada had sat beside him, but he understood she needed the comfort of her aunt. In his mind, he hoped she would let go and depend on him. He perceived she constructed a wall and was only allowing him to glimpse inside. She did not seem ready to tear her shelter down and trust him.

Jada's thoughts were, *Wow, David is so damn fine and quite the gentleman. I sure hope he will still want me once he hears the truth.* She returned a half smile to him.

Officer Nelson was the first to break the silence of secret admiration and adoration. She cleared her throat as she walked over to Jada with her pen and paper in hand. "Jada, I would like to ask you a few questions. Would you and Lyric like to find a more private area?"

Hesitating but looking straight into David's eyes, Jada told Officer Nelson, "If Aunt Lyric and David don't mind, I would like for them both to be present. I am going to need them to help me through this." Jada never broke eye contact with David.

David understood her pleading eyes. He said a quick silent prayer, "God, help me be the support Jada needs. Remove me, the man, and replace me with the love and understanding of Jesus." His heart also said its own silent prayer, "Baby, I got you, and thanks for dropping your wall. He thought, *Girl, with your fine, sexy self, I am trying to make you my lady. I want you to be my wife and baby's momma."* David felt a twinge of guilt for allowing his heart to revert to the man in him. He dismissed his sexual thoughts of Jada and returned control to his head. Without responding and only recognizing Jada's captivating green eyes that were now red and starting to overflow, David closed his Bible and walked towards her without breaking eye contact. He knelt in front of her and put his arms tightly and securely around her small waistline that connected her pear-shaped butt to her full perfectly rounded hips. He pulled her up from her chair. They both stood with his muscular arms invincibly encased around her.

Officer Nelson and Lyric watched the love scene play out in front of them. They both expected David to plant a big wet slobber to Jada's mouth.

David wanted to kiss Jada's delicious full lips that were slightly elevated at the corners. Instead of kissing her on her mouth, he placed his lips on her forehead and delivered an extended sensuous loving peck. He wrapped his toast-colored arms around her waist while gently laying Jada's head on his hard rounded shoulder. He then began to pat her as if she was a baby in his arms that he was trying to make burp.

Jada was unable to hold her emotions together any longer. David offered her a safe haven in his arms and his heart. She was unable to fight any longer. She collapsed and began to cry a weep that said, "I am broken and I cannot do this alone." Her mind raced with the fear of David and the world knowing her true story, to her mother possibly dying, and then to the most bizarre thought of all: sorrow for Charles in jail. She knew he was wrong and he had to pay, but a part of her felt pity for him.

David said, "Officer, if you don't mind I would like to say a prayer before you begin." He did not wait for an answer from Officer Nelson. He began praying. "My father. Father of all fathers and master of the universe, I come now as a fleshly man of God asking for you to step into this hospital and touch the body of Miss Nicke. Lord, you know what she needs for her body to have a miraculous healing. I ask, Lord, if it be thy will that you please heal her body."

Jada began to sob out loud. Her tears wet the front of David's shirt. She responded to David's prayer with, "Lord, please, heal my mother. I'm so sorry for my sins. Please, Lord, do not punish her for my sins."

Lyric, with her head bowed and her own tears running from under the lids of her closed eyes, joined in the prayer with an occasional "Lord, have mercy." She was rocking back and forth as she held sleeping Micah in her lap.

Officer Nelson's head also lowered, but her eyes remained open, staring at the blue tightly woven carpet on the floor. She whispered "Please, Jesus." several times. She wanted to cry as her demons came back to haunt her, but she fought to keep it together; after all, this was official business.

David continued praying through the prayer interjections, encouraging comments and an occasional "amen" from each one in the room, as they responded to different parts of his prayer. His prayer then focused on Jada. He prayed God would give her strength to handle his will. He asked God to protect her and keep her from all hurt, harm, and danger. Next, he shocked the room when he prayed and asked God to open Jada's heart to accept his love and support. He continued his prayer, asking God to help him be the man for Jada that he believed he was created to be.

David's prayer ending surprised Jada so much that her tears instantly dried up. She lifted her head, opened her eyes, and checked out David's demeanor. She forgot she was supposed to still be praying. Her mind drifted to his comment that God would open her heart to accept love from him. She wanted nothing more than for David to love her and eventually take her as his wife. She began to doubt herself for agreeing to allow David to be present for Officer Nelson's questions. She wondered if once David found out about her having sex with Charles, if he would leave her now and save her from being hurt in the future. Tensing up, she laid her head back on David's shoulder in time for the prayer's final amen.

"In Jesus's name we pray. Amen." David opened his eyes and ushered Jada back to her seat. He knelt down beside her as he gave a nonverbal cue to Officer Nelson, indicating it was now permissible for her to begin her questioning. He encased Jada's hand inside his.

Officer Nelson responded and moved closer to Jada. She took out her pen and small pocket pad. She clicked the top of her pen and placed it on the paper. She again asked Jada if she was sure she didn't want to discuss this in private.

All eyes were now on Jada, waiting intently for her reply. Jada took several seconds before she responded. She told Officer Nelson, "It is all going to be public knowledge one day, especially when Charles goes to court." She stared at the same blue carpet on the floor in which Officer Nelson previously found solace. She fought to avoid eye contact with David or Lyric. Her hands begun to sweat as she loosened the grip of David's hand.

Officer Nelson broke the silence. "Jada, I just need enough information to file charges against Charles. We can get a more detailed statement later."

Jada hesitated, then it was if a surge of electricity shocked her body. She dropped her hand from David's and stood. Without blinking an eye, she clearly and distinctly stated, "Charles molested me from the time I was 12 years old until I turned 14 years old."

The room was completely silent. The only sounds were the ticking from the big-faced clock on the wall and the deep breaths Micah took as he laid on Lyric's lap sleeping, oblivious to everything.

David stood up and put his arms around Jada's waist. He stood behind her but his gesture indicated that he would stand beside Jada and would certainly catch her if she fell.

This symbolism was clear to Lyric and Officer Nelson.

It even made Lyric smile as she watched and admired the obvious love this man possessed for Jada.

Officer Nelson peered up over her reading glasses, continuing to write without looking down at her paper. "Jada, do you have any proof this occurred?"

Stunned by Officer Nelson's question, Jada took a deep breath, holding the air in her diaphragm. She swallowed the saliva that pooled in her mouth. Just as she was about to answer, her knight took the lead.

Pulling Jada even closer in his arms and placing his cheek next to hers, David began in a soft but matter of fact way. "Her proof is because she said it happened. Jada does not need to prove she is telling the truth. He needs to prove she is lying."

Officer Nelson paused to think about what David said. She glanced towards Jada, waiting for her response. She then turned her attention back to her pad of paper and continued writing.

Jada slid even further into David's arms. Her heart began to sing a love song as she replayed David's words in her head. She shut her eyes for a second and reveled in the safety of his arms. She did not remember ever feeling safe in any man's presence, let alone their arms. She never wanted her sanctuary to end, but she knew she had to get the interrogation completed to again check on her mother. "Officer Nelson, the proof I have is my son. Micah was the only good that came out of having sex with Charles."

Officer Nelson continued taking Jada's statement, but momentarily succumbed to the urge to observe David's reaction. She tried to steal a quick look at David, but when she looked, David's eyes were shut. He was holding onto Jada for dear life, with his face still pressed against hers. Officer Nelson saw tears rolling down David's face and dropping onto Jada's. For a second, she was not sure from whom the teardrops came. They seemed to have found their way to each other, intertwining together and forming one stream. She looked behind the couple and caught the eye of Lyric. Once more, they both flashed a glance of understanding Jada and of each other's plight for yesterday and today. Officer Nelson turned her attention back to Jada. "Jada, we will need to swab Micah's mouth to perform a conclusive DNA test. Would that be OK with you?" she asked.

Jada opened her eyes and turned around, facing David and scooting her entire body into his arms. She looked over her shoulder and nodded to Officer Nelson before giving a verbal response of, "I guess that would be OK. Do you want to do it now?"

Officer Nelson responded, "That is up to you."

Jada questioned Lyric with her eyes, asking what she should do.

Lyric immediately read Jada's concern and responded. "Now is a good time, Jada."

Jada turned towards Officer Nelson and nodded in agreement. She then buried her head in David's chest. She placed her hands on either side of her face, sheltering it from everyone in the room.

This made David hold her closer. He wrapped her with a vow and a veil of protection.

Officer Nelson opened her kit as she brushed past Jada and David. She knelt down and gingerly placed the swab into the sleeping child's mouth. She rubbed the swab inside of Micah's cheeks. One, two, three; she was finished.

Micah did not even stir. He laid in Lyric's arms in the deepest of deep sleep.

Officer Nelson remaining stooped down over Micah and carefully placed the swab in a plastic kit. She labeled it with a black marker. She then placed the specimen in a plastic black compartment bag. Standing up, she turned to Jada as if to say, "You are next." Jada stepped away from David, walked to the other side of the room, and took a seat. She used her hand and the chair's arm to prop her head. Looking as if she was going to buckle and topple to the floor, Jada sat and waited for her mouth to be swabbed.

David, suspecting Jada may need a moment to regroup, sat beside Lyric. He reached and took Micah from Lyric. He was careful not to awaken the honey-skinned boy that was conceived from an appalling act into the love of a teenage mother. David held Micah just as he had previously cradled Jada. From all appearances, he was also sheltering and protecting Micah. His huge muscular arms around Micah resembled a grizzly bear surrounding his cub. However, when they were wrapped around Jada, they were equivalent to the lion, king of the jungle, ready for battle to save his lioness.

Micah squirmed and opened his eyes, looking at David. He closed them back, securely resting in the arms of his protector.

Lyric watched in complete amazement of the attentiveness David was showing both Jada and Micah. She marveled at how right he seemed for Jada. She silently wished Nicke were able to witness how David stood in the gap for her, protecting and praying for both her and Jada. Lyric, watching the display of love and affection, was reminded that she needed to call her husband. He would be shocked when he found out all that happened in the last several hours. She pulled out her cell phone. She was amazed at the eight missed calls and three messages left by Johnny. She listened to the voicemails while watching Officer Nelson swab Jada's mouth. As she watched Jada, she saw her strength dissipate. She seemed to return to being a 14-year-old child. The empty stare struck Lyric as she recalled seeing the same sadness in Jada's eyes as a teenager. She remembered a time she once dismissed this as the effects of Jada having an alcoholic mother. She wondered how she could have been so stupid and missed the lifeless, hollow refection. She noticed the same hurt in Officer Nelson eyes, and she was sure Officer Nelson observed it in her eyes.

"Lyric, where are you?" Johnny asked. "The last time I spoke to you, you were going to call me back. How are Nicke and Jada? Call me." Lyric advanced to the next message. Johnny said, "I guess you are asleep. Call me." Lyric replayed this message. She heard a woman's voice in the background. She strained to listen clearly, but the sound was muffled. After listening to the message for the third time, she chalked up the voice to perhaps someone in a restaurant. Feeling somewhat relieved, she forwarded to her last message from Johnny. "Lyric, call me in the morning. I am going to sleep. It has been a long day, and I am tired. I hope everybody is doing better."

Lyric checked to see the time the last call was made. It was time stamped 12:13 a.m. She flipped her arm over and read her black Movado watch. The short hand was kissing the diamond on the number twelve and the long hand rested the number three. The time was 12:15 a.m. CST and 1:15 a.m. EST. She figured she just missed her husband's call by two minutes. While she reviewed her messages, Officer Nelson finished her official business and was saying good-bye to Jada and David. She waved good-bye to Lyric, not wanting to interrupt. Lyric waved back as she replayed message number two again. Officer Nelson closed the door softly behind her to prevent waking Micah.

Jada walked over and planted a thank-you kiss on David's mouth.

He smiled and mumbled to her about how proud he was of her. He told her what she did took strength.

Jada shot him a nod of confidence as she left the room to visit her mother. She felt strong. She wished she held the fortitude to share with David that her strength came not only from God but also from his acceptance. She smiled to herself as she strutted with her head held high. Harboring a sense of freedom, she complimented herself because she stopped accepting responsibility for Charles's lust. Before today, she always accepted blame.

Lyric left the room just after Jada. She thought she would walk down the hall for some privacy to call Johnny back.

Johnny's phone rang four times, and on the fourth ring, Johnny answered. He sounded out of breath, but Lyric dismissed the thought, as she was so glad to finally speak with him. She had so much to tell him.

Lyric began her tale. "Hey, baby. I'm sorry I missed your calls, but so much has happened. Nicke tried to kill Charles, and the police came. They arrested him, and Nicke's in the hospital fighting for her life." Lyric continued rambling the last twenty-four hours to her husband without stopping to take a break. "Johnny, are you there? Hello? Hello? Johnny!"

"Lyric, I'm here, and I'm listening." Johnny spoke just above a whisper.

"Johnny, why are you whispering?"

"We must have a bad connection. Lyric, let me call you back in about 10 minutes." Without waiting for an answer, Johnny hung up.

Lyric checked out the phone screen in disbelief. "What is up with that?" she muttered. Johnny sounded strange, but whatever, she needed to check on Nicke. Although still perplexed by her conversation with Johnny, Lyric managed to put it out of her mind as she slowly pushed open the hospital door to Nicke's room.

Jada was standing at the head of her mother's bedside, holding her hand. Lyric examined the many machines and tubes hooked up to her best friend. She studied the tube inserted in Nicke's throat and knew the apparatus was meant to help her breathe. She also noticed Nicke's hands were tied to the bed rails. "Why do they have her tied down?" she asked Jada in a concerned tone.

"That's to keep her from pulling the ventilator out." Jada responded in such a knowledgeable and caring voice.

Lyric walked closer to her friend. She approached Nicke's bed in a slow timid way. Tears began to fill up in the wells of her eyes as she realized for the first time that her friend may not live. She took Nicke's other hand and began to rub it softly. She leaned down and whispered in Nicke's ear. "Nicke, hang on. We need you. Please don't stop fighting." She asked Nicke to squeeze her hand if she heard her command. Nicke did not respond. "Nicke, please squeeze my hand," she begged.

This time, Nicke responded with a slight squeeze of both Nicke and Jada's hands.

"She did it. She did it!" Jada announced with jubilation. "Mom, you can hear us? Please get better, Mom. Fight, Mom, fight," Jada cried out to her mother. She laid her head on her mother's chest. "I love you, Mom."

The door to the hospital room opened and in walked another doctor. He was holding Nicke's chart in his hands. His head was down as he read the chart. He glanced up when he realized his patient had visitors. "How's my patient doing?" he asked, startled by their presence.

Jada struggled waiting to share the news. She excitedly reported, "My aunt requested my mother squeeze her hand if she was able to hear us, and she squeezed both of our hands. That's a good sign, right, doctor?"

In an unimpressed tone, the doctor responded, "I hope so, but she has a long way to go. We need to be sure she does not have any neurological damage from the cerebral hemorrhage. We will not know for sure until we get a little further into treatment. Some of my patients recover completely but because there is evidence your mother had several strokes, we won't know if there is any loss of brain function. There is also the possibility of her having side effects from the medication or treatment. We have to try to see what works and what does not." The doctor stopped speaking for a moment and surveyed Jada and Lyric's faces. He checked for their understanding. He took a deep gulp. I must tell you though, her condition is serious. We can do all we can, and death may still occur. It can happen quickly."

Jada, through her sobbing, said in a positive, convincing voice, "My God will determine the outcome. I just ask you to do all you can, and God will do the rest." She turned to her mother, "Mom, we are praying for your healing, and we need you to pray too."

Lyric said, "Doctor, I'm sorry we have not met. I am Lyric Brooks, a close friend of the family, and this is my niece and Nicke's daughter, Jada."

The doctor extended his hand for a warm handshake as he introduced himself to Lyric. "I am Dr. Maxey. It is a pleasure to meet you all." He held onto Lyric's hand as he gazed upon her beauty.

Lyric also found it hard not to notice the distinguished, built, and well-put-together doctor. She tried not to stare, but her failed attempt caused her to get lost in his light brown eyes. His hair was cut close to his scalp, accentuating the wavy pattern of each salt and pepper strand resting neatly on his head. Lyric had to strain her neck to investigate the face of 6' Doctor Maxey. His skin was smooth as silk, free of all blemishes, and the color of dark brown sugar. Lyric wondered if he indulged in regular high priced facials. He had a confident aura that emanated a sense of compassion and professionalism. Lyric realized that the two of them stopped talking and reverted to checking out each other. Trying to hide her embarrassment, she lowered her head and asked Dr. Maxey, in a pretentious tone meant to conceal the smitten exchange she gave the gorgeous doctor, saying, "What is your prognosis?"

Dr. Maxey quickly dropped her hand and returned to his physician role, answering, but also stuttering, "Well," as he tried to compose himself. "It is still too premature for me to give a prognosis. We need to wait to see how she does over the next couple of days. We all need to pray, just as Jada suggested."

A smile came over Lyric's face as she thought, *Educated, fine, and a Christian. Now, that is sexy, Two men in one night fitting every woman's ideal man description. It is a good thing I am married.* She said a quick "Lord, forgive me for the lust I feel" as she giggled to herself. She also thought, *Lord, after all, I'm only human, and you shouldn't have made him so handsome if you did not want me to admire his beauty.* She smiled.

Interrupting Lyric's thoughts of esteem, Dr. Maxey said, "I think I need to examine our patient, so I can give God all the facts." He chuckled and gave a short wink to Lyric.

Lyric blushed but did not miss the opportunity to comment on the Doctor's last statement. In a dignified way, she responded, "Doc, God don't need no help. He knows all." She twirled, flashing a flirtatious smile as she sashayed from her friend's room. "Doctor Maxey, I'll see you later."

Jada watched in amazement as her holy, sanctified, and quite married aunt flirted with the doctor. She knew if her mom witnessed the scene between Lyric and Dr. Maxey, she would crack up laughing and tease Lyric. She would also threaten Lyric with telling her husband, Johnny. Lyric would play dumb and deny doing anything.

Jada slid away from her mother as she watched the doctor warm the stethoscope on his white jacket before listening to her mother's heartbeat. She quietly watched Dr. Maxey complete his examination as if she was a bodyguard dispatched to protect her mother from everyone, even her doctors.

Dr. Maxey completed his examination. He reached across Nicke and held his hand out to Jada.

Jada responded and grabbed the doctor's hand. She watched as the doctor lowered his head and began to pray. A warm sensation started at the top of her head and slowly entered her body. A sensation infiltrated through her entire being as if she had sipped a cup of hot coffee. For the first time since the ordeal began, her fears for her mother's full recovery seemed to lessen. She paid attention to Dr. Maxey asking God to guide his decisions so he could treat his patient to the best of his ability. He ended the prayer the same way David ended his conversation with God: by asking God that his will be done, in Jesus's name.

After the prayer, Dr. Maxey collected Nicke's chart, nodded good-bye to Jada, and left the room.

Jada told her mother to hang in there. She told her everyone was praying, including her doctor. She then told her mom she would be back because she needed to go check on Micah. She kissed her mom on the check and headed to the waiting room.

Jada turned the door handle. As she entered the room, David stood up and greeted her, securely holding her close to his body.

Jada pushed back slightly and asked, "Where is Micah?"

David told her Lyric took him to her house. "She said we could pick him up tomorrow."

Jada sighed a slight relief because she wanted Micah to get some much-needed rest. She fell back into David's arm. "David, thank you for your support. You will never know how much having you stand by me meant. Baby, I know you are tired. Why don't you go home and get some sleep? I'm going to spend the night here at the hospital with my mother."

Stroking his hands through Jada's hair, David told her, "I'm going to stay with you tonight, if you don't mind. I would like for your mother to know how much I care about her daughter."

Jada started to protest but decided to listen to her heart, which told her she wanted David to stay. She moved out of his arms and slid her hand into his hand. They held hands as she led him back to her mother's room. As they walked down the hall, she smiled as she looked up at David. With a playful giggle, she said. "OK, but my mom is hard on any man that wants to date her daughter. She may even come out of her coma and start asking you a thousand questions."

David jokingly responded, "That is fine with me. I'll tell her my intentions are pure. I'll also tell her she should hurry and get well because I want to take her and her daughter on a tropical vacation."

Jada smiled as she reached the door. She continued to pull David towards her mother's bedside. She introduced them to each other. "Mom, this is a special person to me. His name is David." Turning to David, "David, this is my strong mother."

David silently wondered why Jada used the word "strong" to describe her mother. Of all the other possible words she could have chosen, why that adjective to describe her? David shrugged it off. "Hi, Mrs. Smith. It's a pleasure to meet you. I hope you get better soon because I'm falling in love with your daughter."

Jada snapped her head up quickly and looked at David. Her face, head, and eyes made one of those gestures Gary Coleman used to make when he would say, "What's you talking about, Willis?"

David ogled Jada, then turned away. He was embarrassed because he admitted to falling in love with Jada. He tried to keep his feelings in check and using the "love" word this quickly in their relationship was against his dating principles. He remembered he promised himself the next relationship he entered into, he would take it slow.

Nicke's close eyes fluttered, as if she had heard David.

Both Jada and David gazed at Nicke. They thought she was about to awaken from her coma. Her body shook as if a chill went through her body.

Jada approached her mother's bedside, "Mommy, its Jada. Squeeze my hand if you can hear me." She could not contain the overwhelming excitement consuming her intense optimism.

Nicke squeezed Jada's hand just as Jada requested. Her eyes remained closed.

Jada celebrated in the hopeful response and bowed with grateful expectations. Again, it was confirmation for Jada that her mother did not have brain damage. She was so elated; she laid her head on her mother's chest and cried tears of joy.

David joined Jada at Nicke's bedside. Opening his Bible, he read Proverbs 4:5 aloud.

CHAPTER 6

It Cost To Be Me

That's the part you can't see
Pennies for pride
I paid before I could begin life's complex ride
Quarters for quality,
Once I figured out it wasn't about
how much or the total quantity.
Dollars for dignity
Hundreds for humility
Thousands for tenacity
Millions for maturity
Billions for brains
You'll never know how much I paid when
my body was taken from me
It left me thinking that's the way it was supposed to be
I even bought courage from abandonment and neglect
Just imagine what that did. It left a lasting effect.
There were even times I had no pennies so I had no pride
Those were the times when no one was around.

It cost to be me, that's the part you can't see

I allowed men to play me and hide behind love

When all they really wanted was my body
since I was giving it away for free.
At other times I had no quarters, no quality could I find
Taken on an emotional roller coaster ride.
I thought I would lose my mind.
I thought I was capable of saving them all but when it was over,
All that was left was my bankrupted heart
and the realization I had sold my soul.
Out of dollars for dignity, I found my destiny.
Refusing to accept another blank or bounced check.
I found my Black American Express.
From now on, it's cash and carry. No more layaways allowed.
Today I am rich. I'm finally a millionaire but not before I paid:
Pennies for pride.
Quarters for quality.
Hundreds for humility.
Thousands for tenacity.
Millions for maturity
Billions for brains.

Yes, it cost to be me
That's the part you can't see.

*H*OME AT LAST, she thought. Lyric pulled into the garage. For several seconds, she rested her head on the steering wheel. She marveled that she finally reached her own space. She quietly exited her car, being careful not to awaken Micah. She gently carried Micah to her bedroom. As she strolled through her house, she basked in the wonderful aroma of a clean home. All the products used when she labored over 24 hours ago smacked her in the face. She took a deep breath, inhaling the fragrances with delight. They seemed to instantly provide relaxation.

Micah's exhaustion prohibited him from stirring. She laid him on the chaise lounge and tucked him in snugly to create an ambiance of safety and comfort. Lyric's mind thought of what would happen if Micah wakes up. *He might be frightened in his new surroundings,* she thought, so she placed a night-light in the socket nearby.

After laying Micah down, Lyric reflected on the escapades of her day and night. She slid into her nightgown and climbed into bed. She sprawled across her California King without folding back the white silk duvet down comforter. She adjusted her pillows behind her back, propping herself upright. Still considering the unbelievable occurrences, she failed to comprehend the amount of excruciating pain taking over her body, mind, heart, and feet. She prayed aloud, asking God for strength and mercy. As Lyric attempted to come to grips with everything, she jumped as she remembered she needed to call Johnny. "Wait one minute; hold on a half a second," she mumbled out loud. "He said he would call me." She attempted to dismiss her disbelief about Johnny working late, which hid inside her insecurities. Oh well, the hour may be late, but we need to finish our conversation and find out what he meant by such a crazy remark. Lyric picked up her cell phone while looking at the blue light illuminated by her alarm clock, which read 2:45 a.m. As Lyric dialed Johnny, she felt a twinge of guilt for calling so late. The phone rang four times. When Lyric considered hanging up, the sleepy voice of her husband emerged.

"Hey, baby, it's me." Lyric used her sexy, sultry tone as she softened her deep voice to a whisper.

Changing her pitch must have worked because Johnny replied, "Who is this?"

She responded in a surprised, slightly angered, voice. "What do you mean who is this? Who else calls this late?"

Hearing the edge in Lyric's voice, Johnny's voice changed from groggy to instantly wide awake. "Oh, I'm sorry. I didn't catch your voice."

Lyric, realizing Johnny's initial response sounded plausible and probably a likely one from someone awaken by a late night call or, in this case, early morning call, calmly apologized for waking Johnny.

"Don't worry about waking me, Lyric. How is Nicke doing?"

"Unfortunately, she is still unconscious, and her condition is the same. The doctor said the status of her recovery is going to be touch and go for the next 48 hours, but my God is able."

Lyric faintly heard Johnny's television in the background. A deep growl with a clutching sound followed by deep breathing rang through. "Johnny, are you awake?"

Johnny answered in a startled but somewhat irritated voice. "Yes, Lyric, I am aware of what you said."

Lyric made a hissing sound. She decided she would challenge Johnny. "OK, what did I say?"

Johnny pushed and pulled air through his nostrils as if he was a bull and Lyric the bullfighter. He snapped back at Lyric. "Look, Lyric, the time is late, and I am tired. Did you call to argue or what?"

Lyric, still perturbed about Johnny's statement from when they last spoke, wrestled to understand why Johnny would trivialize what Charles did to Jada by saying he guessed he liked young girls. She also did not comprehend why lately, each time they spoke, both insisted on throwing jabs towards each other. She thought their verbal warfare was so out of character. This time, she decided to take the road of least resistance. "I understand you are tired baby, but a chill is in the air between us. I just thought we needed to straighten out the conflict before our fighting gets out of hand. Are you upset with me about last night? I did call once and left a message concerning my whereabouts. It's just things moved so quickly with Jada and Nicke. I got caught up with helping them. I'm sorry. I love you and did not mean to neglect or worry you." She cowered down and decided this was not a good time to discuss his comment. "I'm sorry, Johnny. I am crabby because we haven't spoken in a while, and I'm also tired and extremely worried about Nicke."

"I understand, Lyric. You have been through a lot. I should be a little bit more sensitive. By the way, I guess I did doze off. I'm not sure what you said." Johnny took Lyric's lead and softened his tone. He sat up in the bed and slung his legs over the edge. "Hold on, let me go to the bathroom, then we can talk for a few."

"OK," Lyric responded. She held on the phone, waiting for Johnny's return. As she listened to the background noise, an infomercial for fish oil said the omega supplement would cure any aliment. She wondered if the miracle drug had the capacity to heal Nicke. Next, she detected a door clicking. She listened to someone opening and shutting a door. Nausea settled in the pit of her stomach, but she swallowed and pushed the sensation away. The demon of jealousy raised his ugly head. Lyric recognized him immediately, but made the decision to avoid the nagging anxieties that plagued her mind over the last month or so.

Johnny returned to the phone. "OK, I'm back." This time his voice rang through with life, as if 9:00 a.m. snuck up on him.

Lyric hesitated for a few seconds as she tried to compose herself. She fought to gain her control before asking, "Johnny, when are you coming home?"

Johnny answered, "Not sure."

"I miss you and would like to see my husband. You have something here in need of a tune up," she said as she licked her lips and closed her eyes. "So what are you going to do?"

Johnny ignored Lyric's attempt to turn their conversation X-rated. "What am I going do about what?"

Lyric knew he understood, but threw out another worm to bait Johnny. "I need you to come home and release some of this stress in both you and me."

Once again, Johnny overlooked Lyric's advances and refused to entertain them. His demeanor changed from sweet to downright nasty. In fact, he told Lyric, "I have to get some sleep. I'll call you tomorrow." He attempted to end their call without either of them saying good-bye.

Lyric held on the phone line as Johnny did not fully disconnect their call as intended. She pushed the mute button to drown out any of her background noise and continued to listen. It soon became clear as glass why Johnny tried to rush Lyric off the phone. She overheard Johnny say, "Donna, I told you I'll handle it."

A woman's voice responded, "I thought you told her. I am sick of being your secret."

The phone then disconnected. Lyric studied the face of her cell phone in disbelief as her suspicions were realized. The only remaining factor was for her to believe her own ears. She knew if she discussed the results of eavesdropping with Johnny, he was prone to deny any of the conversation took place. Johnny would blame the television and attempt to convince Lyric she possessed an extra hole in her head.

Before she could try to figure out Johnny's bizarre behavior or decide who she was going to believe, Micah squirmed in his sleep. He sat up and observed his surroundings.

"Micah, you are OK. You're at Auntie Lyric's house. Do you want to go to the bathroom?"

While rubbing his eyes, Micah shook his head from left to right. He climbed down off the chaise and staggered over to Lyric. His nonverbal cue from his eyes spoke, saying that his original sleeping place did not provide the security he needed.

Lyric reached down and lifted all 52 pounds of God's little angel. She hugged him tight and patted his back while rocking him.

Micah enjoyed the comfort Lyric provided. He pulled away from Lyric and laid in her bed, resting his head on her king-size memory foam pillow. He wiggled until he nudged against Lyric's warm body.

Lyric continued to gently pat him on his back, as if he were a baby she tried to keep from fully awakening.

Micah groggily said, "Good night, Auntie Lyric," as he assumed the fetal position.

"Go back to sleep, baby. Everything is going to be fine. "She kissed Micah on the cheek while rubbing his small muscular shoulders. Once she was sure Micah had returned to a deep sleep, she hit the talk button on her cell phone, calling Johnny back.

After four rings, Johnny answered his phone. "Hello"

Lyric acted as if unaware that Johnny had abruptly ended their call or that another woman wanted Lyric to learn of their obvious affair.

"Baby, did we get disconnected?"

"No, I told you I would call you tomorrow."

"No good-byes or I love you," Lyric tauntingly asked.

Knowing he omitted to say good-bye, Johnny lied and said, "I did say good-bye."

Sarcastically, Lyric responded, "You must have said that after you hung up the phone, or I mean, assumed our call ended."

Johnny responded with a simple, "OK."

By this point, Lyric was livid. She hurled a pillow on the floor. "All right, Johnny, what is going on?" She refused to stop the ugly monster from making his appearance. "Johnny, are you alone?"

Johnny did not chance his voice inflection. In a whispered voice, he asked Lyric, "What do you mean?"

Lyric popped back at him with an edge of anger. "Which part of my question did you not understand? The Johnny part or the alone part?"

Johnny chose not to respond. Instead he said, "Lyric it is late, and I am tired. Can we talk about this tomorrow?"

Unwilling to relent, Lyric continued, saying, "Will we talk before or after your female guest leaves?"

Still refusing to address any of Lyric's accusations, Johnny thought it best to remain cool and end the call before Lyric or

Donna revealed a truth he fought so hard to hide. "Lyric, for the last time, good night."

After hearing Johnny's response and his obvious avoidance to answer her question, Lyric's anger barometer jumped from zero to ten in a matter of two seconds. She quickly pushed the end button the same way Johnny did with her. Her gut and her ears confirmed no matter how hard she tried to discredit her woman's intuition for the last several months, Johnny was indeed indulging in an affair. She thought back on all the signs she tried to ignore. Now she had confirmation. She uncovered the other woman's existence and voice. Tears rolled from her eyes and down her cheeks. In the past, the man known to her and the one she married would never hang up without saying he loved her. In fact, Lyric recalled how Johnny was always trying to initiate phone sex. He told her phone sex kept him honest. She concluded his refusal to entertain her sexual advancements meant his honesty flew out the window and spelled trouble for their marriage.

Lyric slid down in the bed, snuggling next to Micah. She said a prayer and asked God to give her strength. She refused to take on another item or situation requiring additional brain juices or a further tax on her energy. Her focus, for now, remained on her friend, Nicke, fighting for her life. Lyric wondered why crises seemed to gather in bunches. They seemed to occur either by feast or famine. She thought when things were good, they were really good, but when they were bad, they were really bad. She recalled a sermon Bishop Jakes preached about holding on and not fainting. He said, "Instead of feeling battered, hold on and have faith. God is positioning you for courage, exposure, and knowledge." He also said, "Setbacks are set ups for God's purpose." Lyric whispered to the universe, "I can do all things through Christ who strengthens me."

Although Lyric remained unsure of what to do about her marriage, how to stop worrying about Nicke, or how to address

Jada's mental well-being, she rested in the faith of her own sagacity. She repeated and mediated on her declaration until the meaning took up residence deep inside her wounded heart and empty soul.

She reached for the remote to her Bose six-disc CD player and hit play, but not before repeating again, "I can do all things through Christ who strengthens me." Unknowingly, Yolanda Adams brought Lyric the word from God's angel, who escaped through the speakers and over to her bed with the song "Open My Heart." The song brought Lyric crashing down to a spiral low as she listened to her life and testimony sung: "Alone in a room. It's just you and me. I feel so lost. 'Cause I don't know what to do. Now what if I chose the wrong thing to do. I'm so afraid, afraid of disappointing you. So I need to talk to you and ask you for your guidance, especially today when my mind feels so cloudy."

When Yolanda sang the most compelling part of the song and the part that coincided to what Lyric now experienced—"My hopes and dreams are fading fast. I'm all burnt out and I don't think my strength's going to last,"—the tears flooded her eyes and rushed down her face. She was sure at that moment that there was a hairline crack in her heart. The pain flowed out of her like a faucet. She knew Yolanda was bringing her a word from God himself. She sensed he heard her pain and saw her tears, so he sent the answer in song. She wondered if Yolanda envisioned just how many people like her would identify with the words of this song. She even wondered if Yolanda understood her ministry was so far-reaching and capable of saving someone's life. Lyric stopped thinking momentarily about the problems she was facing just to thank God for the gift he gave Yolanda. She clearly recognized Yolanda's song was God's way of talking to her and others in need. He was answering Lyric's prayers at this exact moment. The solution was to open up her heart to the only one that held the power to help and save her.

"So show me how to do things your way. Don't let me make the same mistakes over and over again."

Lyric hit the repeat button. She wanted to be certain the words permeated every cell in her body. She was in a fight with the devil himself. He was trying to steal her joy.

Lyric closed her eyes and finally drifted into a peaceful sleep, believing her father held the authority to redress the disquiet in her life.

CHAPTER 7

Me

You're a piece of my dream
An intricate part
Like life is to death
or blood to my heart.
You're a portion of my happiness
A serving for three
Like an affair is to a marriage
or the blessed Trinity.
You're a segment of me
A detailed piece
Like water is to coffee
or sugar is to tea.
The piece is the portion
The segment makes three
Together they form
The complete circle of
Me

THE NEXT MORNING, David stood from his cramped sitting position on the hard hospital chair. Rolling his head in a circular motion, he attempted to stretch the sore muscles in his neck He glimpsed Jada curled up on the small uncomfortable Symmetry recliner. She appeared to be in a deep sleep, letting out slight snorts that resembled more deep aspiration then snoring. Next, he monitored Nicke. She peacefully rested with the lifesaving machines still connected. He studied Nicke a little closer, confirming she was breathing. Once satisfied that Nicke survived through the night, he gingerly pulled a blanket over Jada, being careful not to awaken her. He tiptoed to Nicke's bedside, laid his hand on her shoulder, and said a silent prayer. Quietly, he slipped out of the room. David continued down the hallway, headed towards the cafeteria for two cups of coffee.

As David passed the ICU workstation, the on-duty nurses and a female doctor all stopped to leer at the attractive male specimen with a swagger equivalent to President Obama's. They admired him from a distance with their lust-filled eyes.

Just as David entered the open elevator and was about to push the button for the first floor, he saw Jada scurrying towards him. He stepped back out, letting the door close without him. He wondered if he had awakened Jada. He smiled as she approached.

One of the registered caretakers from the station peeped into the corridor to be nosy and snoop on the handsome couple's embrace.

"Jada, I tried to be quiet and let you sleep. I was on my way to the cafeteria to get us some coffee but since you are here, we can both go grab breakfast."

Jada said, "Please. I am starved, and no worries, you did not wake me. The nurse came in and asked me to step out of the room while she took mom's vital signs and prepared for a new shift. I spotted you, but I didn't want to yell. I also enjoyed watching the ladies paying visual homage to my man."

The blood rose in David's face, revealing a red tint to his light brown complexion. His eyes sparkled from delight as he bathed in Jada's comment. He pushed the button again without making a remark. He cradled Jada's hand as he intertwined his fingers through hers.

Jada held on tight, adding a swinging motion to their arms.

The elevator stopped on the first floor. They followed the signs to the cafeteria. As they entered, David asked Jada what she would like to eat.

Studying the menu intently, Jada responded, "I think I will have an egg, cheese, and turkey sausage sandwich."

David thought for a moment as he also reviewed the selection. "I agree. I'll have the same."

Jada surveyed the room, looking for the coffee station. She spotted it on the opposite side.

"I'll get our coffee. How do you take yours?"

With a sly smile, David responded, "Black and sweet, just the way I like my lady."

Jada let out a giggle as she headed towards the serving area. Pouring their coffee into two takeout cups, Jada fixed David's as he requested, all the while being amused and flattered by his comment. After completing her self-assigned duty, she turned to join David. Out of the corner of her eye, she spotted him engaged in a conversation with a tall, slim employee with flowing hair tailored around her strikingly featured face. Jada hesitated a few seconds as she studied the beautiful young woman with curve-fitting green scrubs. She caught sight of a similar hug shared by them. Jada, unsure if she should approach or allow them their privacy, decided to take her time to prepare their coffee. An obvious bond between David and whom Jada surmised was a female doctor existed, perhaps a little more than a casual acquaintance. She also noted David's friend did not fit the profile of the women he stated he preferred. Jada compared the Miss Caramel Cream to herself, Miss Sweet and Black.

Strutting with her head held high, Jada gathered her confidence as she traipsed towards the mystery person and David. Before she could reach them, the individual walked away. She passed by Jada, but not before studying Jada and giving her an x-ray with her eyes. She flashed a fake semi-smile to Jada along with a tad bit of eye rolling, suggesting she had a past with David.

Just as Jada reached David, the cook handed him their food. David said, "Man, I hope you didn't do anything to my sandwiches because I maintain the Redskins will whop those sorry Cowboys."

The man threw his hands up as if saying I am innocent. "Dave, why do you like to give your money to me every year? Da Boys always beat on them Dead Skins, and you make me a rich man."

Both men laughed. Jada realized they also had a history and seemed to be acquainted with each other. She approached David and placed their coffee on the tray David had secured.

David introduced him to Jada as his man, Jones. "We grew up and played basketball together over the years, but he has a Cowboy sickness and it's terminal."

They all laughed.

Jones gave Jada a beholding once-over with a devilish smile on his face. He flashed in the direction of the caramel cream lady. He made eye contact with David, giving him the glare of a cat that swallowed a canary.

Jada responded, "Nice to meet you, Jones. I hope you feel better soon."

Jones turned his attention back to Jada. His fat stomach shook up and down as he laughed out loud. "Not you, too? You can't be a dead skins fan, can you?"

Before Jada had an opportunity to respond, David responded for her. "Not yet. She is a Steelers Nation junkie, but I am working on a conversion."

"Well, as pretty as she is, I can tell she is intelligent enough to make the right decision and pick a winning team." Jones shot one final up and down gawk at Jada. "My pleasure to meet you also

Miss Jada—a pretty name for a beautiful woman. I hope your mom gets better soon."

Jada, touched by his concern, realized David must have told him the reason for being at the hospital. "Thank you, Jones." She turned, picking up their food, and headed towards the check- out register.

David followed behind her. He reached around her and took the tray as if saying, "I got this." As they approached, David pulled out a fresh 20-dollar bill to pay the person.

"How are you doing, Dave? I haven't seen you in a long time," the cashier said as she cut her eyes towards Jada.

"I'm good, Carol. Much better," David responded as he motioned towards Jada while collecting his change.

Jada wondered how he became familiar with so many of the employees at the hospital. She dismissed the thought as she decided if David, or Dave as they called him, wanted to share the reason for his popularity, he would have to volunteer the information. She determined she would not ask him any questions, although she did pick up that he seemed uncomfortable.

At first, David fumbled with his napkin and silverware. He then held Jada's hand and said grace over their food. Nervously, he tried to engage in small talk about things that did not seem to interest him or Jada.

Jada smiled but remained speechless. She recognized David's stall tactics as he waited for her to question him. Her mind raced from one negative thought to another. She resigned herself to prepare for the worse while praying for the best. A part of her feared David may not be all that she hoped. She kept bracing for bs, wondering if David would reveal his dark side in due time.

David scrutinized Jada's face and noted that her mind held an overflow of questions. He decided not to address any answers, so he was glad she chose to bypass them for now. He slowly ate his food and sipped his coffee. It had been several months since being in the company of his ex-girlfriend, Candy. He prayed many nights for God to remove the love he carried for her from his heart. David endured pain inflicted by her because Candy played between David, her baby's father, and any other man she desired. She went back and forth to each of them like a ping-pong ball, the men being the paddles. She became the catalyst and primary reason he exercised celibacy. He understood that in order for their relationship to end, he had to stop sleeping with her. Candy used sex to control him and grew savvy enough to seduce him into forgiving her whenever she fancied. David would take her back each time. Finally, he got tired and decided to cut the strings. Usually, Candy found it quite easy to manipulate him. Part of her stronghold concluded when David stopped blaming her and snatched his power, returning it to its rightful owner. He abruptly refused all communications with her until he gained the strength to dismiss any sexual advance she made towards him. It took almost a year to detach from Candy. Until today, he thought he was completely over her, but now he had to admit he was feeling some kind of way—one he was not sure how to describe nor was he ready to try to figure out.

Jada, knowing David seemed preoccupied and deep in thought, searched for an escape. She understood if she sat there much longer, the questions would spill out and she preferred not to ask him anything. David had to realize he was able to share with her as she did by exposing her life. But he needed to figure this out on his own. Jada searched her cup as she continuously stirred, trying not to show her concern but rather appear busy preparing her drink for consumption. As she lifted her head, she spotted the Miss Caramel Cream headed towards them. David's back faced the unwanted visitor.

Hastily, Jada told David she needed to check on her mother. "I'd like to catch the doctor," she said, placing her purse on her shoulder and neared seconds from walking away.

David pulled her down to him and planted a surprise sensual kiss on her mouth. Jada, trying to escape, looked straight into the eyes of Miss Caramel Cream. She immediately read her disapproval. At first, Jada thought the young lady aggressively approached with intentions of striking her.

David restrained her from leaving. "Baby, I owe you an explanation, and I will discuss everything with you later. You have too much going on right now. I do not want to burden you with my problems."

Jada tried to wiggle free as Miss Caramel Cream reached their table.

"Hey, Dave. I thought I would check back with you to find who you are visiting in the hospital. I hope it is not any family members. I spoke to your mom yesterday, and she didn't tell me about anyone being sick."

Jada caught the slur and recognized this woman played the "I know his mother card." She instantly thought, *She is messy and trying to start some crap.* Jada took a deep breath as she fought to regroup. She refused to partake, She thought, *Silly rabbit, tricks are for kids.*

Jada did not wait for David to introduce her to Miss Caramel Cream. She extended her hand stating, "I am Jada, and my mother is in the hospital."

Miss Caramel Cream refused to accept Jada's greeting nor did she bother to state her name. In fact, she dismissed Jada and turned to face David.

"Dave, your mom says she hasn't talked to you in several days. What's up with that?"

Jada fought to avoid blowing a gasket and to remain calm. Whoever this no-name Miss Caramel Cream was, she seemed determined to cause a scene. Jada thought if this low-class girl is who "Dave" wants, more power to him and her.

David grabbed Jada stopping her as he stood wrapping his arm around her neck. "Jada this is an ex-girlfriend, Candy. Candy this is my girlfriend, Jada. Candy, please do me a favor," David said in an exasperated voice as he slightly pushed Candy out of his way. "In the future, do not *ever* disrespect Jada again!" David stepped around Candy and walked past her, holding Jada closer.

Jada smiled to herself for a moment. *Silly Miss Caramel Cream*, she thought, replaying David's reference to her as his girlfriend. Neither of them had agreed to be exclusive. Why did David act crazy like Candy? He used her to make Candy jealous. She thought to herself, *The only reason to attempt that maneuver would be if there were unresolved issues.* Thinking this may be the case, Jada hung her head. She made a mental note to be careful with her feelings for David because he seemed not to be over his ex-girlfriend.

On the ride up the elevator, David took the lead being the first to end the silence. As a man, he recognized the way he handled Candy might have been immature and not fair to Jada. "Jada, I'm sorry you had to be faced with that. Candy is a special kind of woman and a drama queen in search of every man's attention."

At that exact moment, Jada realized she cared deeply for David. If any of her previous friendships became a tad bit complicated, Jada ran away. Only now with David, she had to fight for him even though her red flags waved that David may not be ready for a relationship with her or any woman. He needed to close the book with his ex once and for all. A part of Jada did not care if he lacked certainty. Until David, there was not anyone she connected with on all levels like she did with him. Candy's reign was over, and she had to move out of the way because he was her man now. She needed him more than Candy wanted him, she thought.

"Jada, you aren't saying anything. Please forgive me. I should have prepared and alerted you to Candy working here, but I hoped I wouldn't run into her. I did not want you to waste an ounce of energy on Candy."

"David, I don't worry about ex-girlfriends. My concern is with you. Are you over her?"

David hesitated for several seconds. He shuffled his feet and took his time to think through his next reply. Spotting a chance to be alone with Jada and answer her question, he gently lead Jada into the intensive care waiting room. "Jada, have a seat." David pulled up a chair directly in front of her. Although David appeared nervous, he confidently told Jada, "I'm over Candy. She and I are akin to hot oil and water. I tried hard to make things work even though I knew she had her own agenda and it did not include me. I'm not going to kid you. I once believed I loved Candy. Now absolutely nothing between us exists."

Jada searched David's eyes. She thought they revealed a glimpse of pain that seemed to not matter much to Jada. She already persuaded herself to protect her heart. The way David eyed Candy screamed there was still some sort of connection between them. It was not important what his mouth said but rather how he acted.

"Well, David," she began speaking slowly, "why would you broadcast an obvious attempt to make her jealous by announcing to her and me that I am your girlfriend. For now, we are friends trying to decide if we want or will have more than friendship."

David let out a little laugh. "OK, you are right. That was extremely presumptuous on my part, and yes, I'll admit, I received pleasure from annoying Candy."

Not seeing the humor and not sure what David found amusing, Jada responded sarcastically, "I'm glad I provided help for your game."

David wished he could take it back, but he spoke the truth. He hated hurting Jada even though she tried to hide behind sarcasm. He pushed the chair out of his way and got down on one knee. "Jada Jordan, will you not make me a liar and do me the honor of being my girlfriend?"

Jada commended David's effort to break the tension between them. She sat upright in her chair and introduced her attempt at comedy: "Why, Mr. David Austin, I would love to, but I am too old to be anybody's girlfriend." She instantly relaxed and let out her own chuckle.

David wiped his forehead with the back of his hand, grateful that Jada allowed him to get off the hot seat. "OK, Miss Jordan, from this moment on, you are my lady. The next time I drop to one knee, it will be when I ask you to marry me. Jada, you need to fully comprehend that I've never met a woman that is more honest and pure. I prayed and asked God to send me someone that would appreciate and love me like I am willing to do for her. I want us to work, and I'll do whatever it takes." David pulled Jada towards him and placed his signature kiss on her forehead, lingering for several seconds. His hands slid down, touching her breast. An electrifying charge flowed from head to toe. The strong current caught him off guard. Although sexual stimulation ripped through him, David's heart jolted at the same time. His overwhelming desire inspired intimacy and not sex. Candy never lit a fire in him as Jada just did, he thought to himself.

The current Jada experienced from the inadvertent hair-raising grope emanated through her body, striking her proverbial wall and caused it to begin crumbling. She replayed in her head what David said about asking God for her. She considered telling him she, too, prayed for a man in her life that would not mistake her kindness as a sign of being weak, as Charles had done. A spark of confidence in herself and her future surfaced, one that was a long time coming. She smiled as she stood. She extended her hand as she said, "Shall we go check on Mom? I need to tell her you asked me to be your lady." She let out a hearty laugh, meant to relieve her pressure as if someone tickled her.

David smiled as he unclenched the heavy wooden door and stood back for Jada to exit before him.

Jada still laughing, caught a glimpse of Candy standing at the nurses' station. Her body came to attention as she regrouped, being sure to stand up straight and walk with her head high, as if competing in the Miss America pageant.

The stiffening of Jada's arms broadcasted tension to David and alerted him of nearby trouble. He followed her eyes, and they directed his to Candy. A sting of anger arose in him. Knowing Candy planned to work hard at causing problems between him and any woman signaled a difficult task for David. He would have to buffer Jada from Candy's shenanigans. Even though Candy, a resident physician, should be above drama, a bunch of ghetto lived inside of her. David understood from previous experience that her goal was to irritate Jada. He had the privilege of witnessing her work with another lady she suspected he was dating. This time, David's determination would protect Jada from anyone who ever tried to hurt her. He just needed God to keep him from blowing his stack. Although he hated making a spectacle in public, he resigned he had to do whatever necessary to preserve his relationship with Jada. He was not going to permit Candy to ruin another one. She no longer could control him with sex. However, David had to admit to himself that when he first saw Candy in the cafeteria, his mind drifted to the sexual relations they once shared. He always said having sex with Candy was the best of his life. However, this time he was better prepared because he instinctively knew from the electrifying charge he received by only kissing Jada that the story on who was the optimal sexual partner had not been written. He smiled to himself as he repositioned his pants to hide his carnal introspection of making love to Jada.

As they approached the nurses' station, Candy twirled around and produced another fake grin. She shot a dismissal glance towards Jada and stared deeply at David. She wondered to herself how she let a man as fine as Dave go. He seemed even more attractive to her now. She allowed her eyes to lustfully absorb his entire body, stopping to stare at his manhood. She followed up her scan with a sarcastic commented, "Dave, how did a girl get so lucky to run into you twice in the same hour?"

The nurses both stared at Jada to observe her response. They were acquainted with Candy and her flirtatious ways. One of them recognized David earlier but was unable to place him until that moment when she remember he dated Candy quite some time ago.

Jada stopped at the sight of her mother's doctor. Her priorities quickly shifted from entertaining Candy and the ladies to concern for her mother. She hastily walked towards Dr. Maxey, holding her breath, not sure that his report would be good or bad news.

David did not bother to respond. He brushed past Candy, in tow behind Jada, as if Candy were a ghost. His place was with Jada, and he wanted to hear the doctor's report firsthand.

The two health-care providers turned their attention to Candy. They were amused by David's lack of response or acknowledgment. Since Candy shared with them earlier that she was taking her man back, they chuckled when the fire in Candy's eyes flamed high because David showed no interest in her or her games. One mumbled, "Forget it, Candy. You lose."

Candy turned red and spouted obscenities. She was unable to control her temper tantrum and pushed a chart off the counter. She whipped back, placing her hands on her hips and did a head roll, causing her neck to snap and her shoulder length hair to fling around hitting her face. Being aware others watched her reactions, she tried to pull herself together and act as if nothing happened. Candy repositioned her body and headed to pick up the papers from the floor, while her eyes remained on David and the lady he presented as his girlfriend. She engaged in idle chitchat with the nurses. Pointing her index finger to her forehead, Candy tried but could not recall her rival's name. However, she did remember she told her why they were in the hospital. Trying to appear that she no longer was upset, Candy asked, "How is," as she pointed towards Jada, "her mother doing?"

Both of the nurses, familiar with the privacy and HIPAA laws knew better than to answer her inquiry. Neither of them bothered to respond. They gazed at each other as if to say, "We are not going to risk being fired or get caught up in her mess."

Candy walked away. She knew delving into a patient's condition, who was not her own, crossed the line. She hoped they would not report her.

Jada greeted Dr. Maxey. "How is Mom doing?" she asked, swallowing to avoid her question being filled with tears.

Just as he was about to answer, David joined their huddle and called him by his first name. The two shook hands, although perplexedly, as he greeted David. "Hi, Dave. I was not aware you knew my patient."

"Mrs. Smith is my lady, Jada's, mother."

Dr. Maxey covered his mouth to try to mask his grin and surprise. However, his nod signaled his approval of Jada, David's new choice. "Well, she's not out of the woods but cling to optimism as there has not been a change for the worse. She is still holding her own." He finished his sentence while looking at Candy as she approached them.

Candy bogarted, interrupting their conversation. She slid up to the doctor in her usual flirtatious way. She grabbed Dr. Maxey's arm, carefully placing her body against his.

Dr. Maxey stepped back and crammed his hands inside his white coat pockets, revealing his obvious embarrassment. He shot Jada an apologetic glance, then his eyebrows squeezed together, scolding Candy and televising his disapproval of her greeting. He turned to Jada and asked, "Shall we step back in your mother's room for privacy?"

Jada nodded her head in agreement while reaching for David's hands.

The three of them walked away again, ignoring Candy's obvious attempts to try to create her own movie for which she had the starring role.

Candy was now more furious than ever. Stomping her foot in disbelief, she murmured, "Who does that bitch think she is? I can have Dave if I want him, and I might have to show her." She fixed her scrubs and swung her hair around. "She has not heard the last from me," she said as she continued towards the elevator.

Jada strolled to her mother's bedside. "Mom, it's me, David, and your doctor. Can you squeeze my hand?"

Dr. Maxey walked closer to the bed to see if Nicke would respond to Jada's command.

Nicke did not make any movement, except a tear rolled down from her right eye.

"Why is she crying? Is she in pain?"

Pulling the chilled Littmann stethoscope from around his neck, he listened to Nicke's chest. He toggled between the bell and diaphragm by applying pressure to the chest piece. He reached for Nicke's arm and placed two fingers on her inner wrist to take her pulse. After that, he lifted Nicke's eyelids and shined his small flashlight onto her pupils. Next, he walked to the other side of the bed and checked her urine output.

Jada intently watched every movement he made.

Oblivious to Jada's guard-dog approach, Doctor Maxey appeared to zone in and stayed focus on his patient. He updated the detailed data he collected. Once he completed writing, he placed the chart back in its holder at the foot of Nicke's bed. He asked Jada to have a seat.

Jada did not bother to verbally respond. She shook her head, as if she was afraid to let her mother's hand go. She slid closer to Nicke and braced herself for what Dr. Maxey had to say.

Clearing the phlegm from his throat, he began with, "I'm concerned about the urine output Nicke is producing. I am going to consult with the kidney specialist to have him determine whether we may have to set Mrs. Smith up for dialysis. I need to start to wean her from the ventilator. When patients are on the machine too long, complications can occur, such as dependency or possible pneumonia. I would like to do a few trials of spontaneous breathing to see if she will tolerate being without the apparatus."

Jada's heart began to race. She clung to a miraculous recovery for her mother, but now she was beginning to have doubts.

David kept his eyes focused on Jada. Her positive spirit started to dissipate. Without speaking, he walked over to Jada and began to massage her shoulders as they both hung on to every word from Dr. Maxey.

The doctor noted fear in Jada's eyes. He wanted to give her hope, but he wasn't feeling too hopeful himself. He tried to walk a tightrope to avoid giving Jada false security; however, he also understood Jada's faith. He knew both he and Jada believed God was able to do anything but fail. So he attempted to try to explain Nicke's condition to her daughter by taking a neutral approach: "Jada many patients who experience a brain hemorrhage can and do survive. The good thing is the bleed was not very large and was not in the brainstem. On the other hand, if your mother does survive the intracranial bleeding, her treatment is going to be slow and may take months. I have had patients that over time, with extensive rehabilitation efforts, such as occupational, physical, and speech therapy, make a one hundred percent recovery." He paused and eyed Jada, then Nicke. "But, you should also know, sometimes others are left with sensory issues or perhaps persistent weakness. There is the possibility Mrs. Smith may experience residual seizures, severe headaches, or even memory problems. The worst case scenario," he swallowed and turned his attention from Nicke to David in order to avoid making eye contact with Jada as he continued, "is death."

The room was completely silent except for all the machines and equipment humming to keep Nicke alive.

Jada's knees buckled as she laid her body on David for support. She tried not to think about the death of her mother. Waves of guilt came crashing down on her pushing her further into David's arms. After a few seconds, she was able to collect herself. She slid close to the bed and softly whispered, "Mom, I guess you heard what Dr. Maxey said. You will have to fight harder to recover. It's not going to be easy, but you are strong. In addition, you have to hurry up and meet your future son-in-law." Jada watched as her mother's eyes started to rapidly flutter, as if she understood. She seemed to be trying desperately to open them and see David. Jada was so overjoyed at that moment. She sprang forward to be even closer to her mother. "Mom, I am sure you can hear me. Squeeze my hand."

Nicke responded this time to Jada's command, and she smiled as her eyes still continued to flutter.

Dr. Maxey stepped to Nicke's bedside, all the while monitoring the blood pressure machine. He prayed a silent, *Thank you, Jesus.* Nodding approval, he said, "All right, I see someone is ready to fight to get better. I guess she wants to attend a wedding." He beamed at both Jada and David as he turned, leaving Nicke's room happy about his patient's progress.

David was overjoyed at Jada planning a life with him. He figured they had a long way to go before they got there, but at least she was willing to try. He reached and took Nicke's hand that was tied to her bedrail. He leaned closer, "Mrs. Smith, I am David Darnel Austin. I'll be here for your daughter and grandson until you are well enough to help me. I care deeply about them both, and we want you to get better so you can witness the love I have for them." David kissed Nicke on her cheek. He then pulled his Bible out of his shirt pocket. He read the entire 23rd Psalms to Nicke. He ended with a prayer of protection for Nicke, Jada, Micah, and him. He approached Jada and kissed her tears as they rolled from her eyes. "Jada I'm going to give you some time alone with your mother. I'll be in the waiting room." He smiled, telling Jada not to rush.

Jada nodded and returned a smile straight from her heart. She watched him close the door before turning her attention back to Nicke. She explained to Nicke everything she knew about David, how they met, what a spiritual man he was, and that he stood by her when she gave a statement to Officer Nelson admitting that Charles was Micah's father. She said David treats her as if she was a queen. She ended with telling Nicke that she was falling in love with him. Then, she shared something that she had not even admitted to herself. She revealed that she and David were going to remain celibate until marriage. She was not sure how, but she wanted God to bless their union, so she would have to take plenty cold showers. She kissed Nicke good-bye and headed to join her man. Even though Jada's mother was fighting for her life, Jada appeared to be walking on soft, cushiony clouds as her heart sang a love song about a happiness she never felt before.

CHAPTER 8

Promises are Made to be Broken/Wishes are Made to Come True

Once You said You loved me
You said you'd always be there.
You promised me a future
Oh, how great it was supposed to be.
Once I said I'd always be there
I said no matter what.
I promised you forever.
Oh, how much I really cared

But today we avow we're sorry.
We express I wish you well.
We say I hope you have a good life
We pray each of us finds
The strength and courage of today
The resolve and contentment for tomorrow
And
The love and happiness of yesterday

L YRIC ROLLED OVER, being carefully not to awaken Micah. She gave thanks for being able to finally fall asleep. In her mind, she started to plan her day. The first thing she needed was a large hot cup of coffee, an instant pick-me-up to give her a burst of energy. Together with a clove cigar, both items guaranteed she would be ready for the new challenges of this day. She considered the unresolved issues remaining from the previous night. First were thoughts of Nicke? She hoped she endured through the twilight. She rested in the certainty that if her condition changed, Jada would have alerted her. Nonetheless, she said a prayer of thanksgiving for healing Nicke. Second, and a bit more unpleasant, remained what she planned to do about Johnny and his mistress, Donna. Next, she added placing a call to her attorney on her list. Lyric understood that even if she and Johnny's conversation did end on a good note, their marriage needed a resolution.

Lyric quietly slid out of bed and headed for the kitchen. She turned on the radio and tuned into Gospel Glory on the XM station. She considered the many flavored coffees that adorned her granite countertop. Deciding on the French Vanilla, she brewed a single cup. She headed towards the air-filtered sunroom but not before picking up the handset to the portable phone. She strategically laid everything needed nearby before placing the call. Just as Johnny's cell began ringing, she lit her cigar and took a deep inhale. Slowly, she blew out the smoke as Johnny answered the phone.

Johnny spoke in the identical whispered voice from the previous night, only this time he sounded sleepy, indicating Lyric had awaken him from his sleep. "Hello," he said with his eyes remaining shut.

"Good morning, Johnny" Lyric began. "I seem to keep waking you." Without waiting for a reply, she continued, "I thought you were at work," noticing the large clock on the wall as it gave a single chime indicating 9:30 a.m. CST. Lyric quickly computed in her head the east coast time.

After discerning the voice on the line as his wife's, Johnny woke completely as he slid out of the bed and headed to the front sitting area with a much louder, "Good morning. How are you?"

"Fine." Lyric waited for Johnny to address why he did not go to work.

"I slept in because my meeting is not until 1:00, so I decided to rest."

Lyric interpreted his remarks as Johnny's way of implying she bore responsibility for disturbing him. "Forgive me. I keep interrupting your sleep."

"No problem. There is a lot going on that you want to share. I'm also sorry for last night when I was too tired to hold an intelligent conversation."

With the apology coming from Johnny, Lyric decided she would take the opportunity to voice her concerns and insecurities. One of the things she loved about her husband was his communication skills. She recalled countless conversations where they talked through their problems and afterwards, they seemed to resolve most issues.

At first, Lyric, although hesitant, began by asking Johnny an open-ended question: "What is really going on?"

Johnny appeared taken by surprise. "What do you mean?"

"Johnny, you are acting strange and borderline cruel." Lyric started the ball rolling but was determined to get to the bottom of Johnny's recent behavior. Her instincts were so strong that they reminded Lyric of a time when Johnny previously participated in an affair. She forgave him but vowed if he was ever unfaithful again, she would end their marriage. Lyric decided to use the confrontation tactics the marriage counselor shared during the many sessions they attended. Three years has passed since Lyric's intuitions peaked to this level. Still, for her own sanity, Lyric had to address them. "I needed you last night, but you hung up the phone on me."

Johnny chose to listen and ascertain where Lyric was headed with her line of questioning. He thought the best defense would be to speak as little as possible. Unsure of what Lyric knew and what she suspected, Johnny told himself that he must only address the facts and not her ghosts. He also realized that he had to be extremely careful not to arouse Lyric's keen sixth sense. He tried to avoid her turning into a detective. Should that happen, Johnny feared being discovered.

Lyric continued her interrogation. "Johnny, are you aware it's been five weeks since you were home last, and you are always too busy for me to visit for the weekend? Every time I make the suggestion, you announce you'll come home instead. Why have you not made it yet?" Lyric took a deep breath and stopped to wait for Johnny to address her rambling concerns. For the most part, Lyric always detested nagging women and proclaimed she would never introduce that behavior into their marriage. But this time, she did not care. Her husband of 10 years needed to help her understand his inexplicable conduct. Although not sure of Johnny's excuses, she committed in her heart that if Johnny planned for them to remain together, his explanation better be good.

Johnny listened to the voice of silence echoing all around him. He grasped Lyric's expectation, and the hush represented the intended cue for his response. Waiting a few seconds more, Johnny considered how to address Lyric's concerns. Several options ran through his brain. One excuse after another rushed in and out before he decided to march down the path of least resistance. He realized he was not able to argue with the facts, knowing everything Lyric stated was true. The dilemma appeared to be if he cared enough to change anything. He was being forced to listen to Donna ranting that she wanted more of him and now at home his wife is complaining because she too wants his time.

He wondered if Lyric truly thought he was unaware of how long he had been on the road. He recalled perfectly well the last time he came home. A part of him wanted to tell Lyric, "I have not been home because I did not want to be there," but he decided to ignore that one and to agree.

"You're right, baby. I am working on a large project and had to stay focus. I have neglected you."

Lyric thought to herself, *No, sir, you are not getting away that easy.* She was armed with the knowledge that whenever Johnny wanted to avoid a conflict, he would agree with Lyric as an avoidance tactic. One of Johnny's favorite lines started resonating in Lyric's head. He often told her that agreements were his way to try to keep the peace. On many occasions, she recalled how she begged Johnny to tell the truth and attempt to work through their problems. However, Lyric did occasionally allow Johnny to manipulate her by either shutting down, cutting her off as she tried to speak, practice anger, or use the silent treatment as his forms of weaponry. He resorted to one of these tactics whenever he lied. Lyric resolved this time that she would not permit Johnny to retreat to his cave. She determined that her suspicions would be voiced and to let the chips fall where they may.

"Johnny, you say your job keeps you from returning where you live. Well, baby, I'm not buying that excuse. The real reason you are not home is because of another woman. I sense her presence deep in my soul." Lyric relented to no longer deny her existence. She decided to believe herself and refuse to be bullied out of her feelings. Johnny threw a fastball, and Lyric hit it in the outfield.

"Don't start, Lyric. I am working to take care of my family, and the last thing I need is you accusing me of having an affair. Besides, since you seem so certain, what is the woman's name I am supposedly cheating with?" Johnny came back as if an outfielder running and about to catch the fly ball Lyric hit.

"Johnny, last night you did not hang up the phone completely, and I listened to her talking."

Lyric turned her speed to high gear and now rounded third base. Johnny was still backpedaling, but would not catch the ball she hit. No longer could he continue to lie. Lyric had no intention of stopping on third base. With the speed and urgency of saving her life, she rounded the base and headed to home plate. This would be a home run one way or the other.

As expected, again Johnny pulled silence from his artillery. His mind racing as he headed towards the outfield wall. He hoped to avoid colliding with the wall, but Lyric's trajectory led him in that direction. He floundered, trying to develop an excuse to avoid smashing into the wall headfirst. He struggled to decide between his marriage or his two-year relationship with Donna. He languished over exposing his double life. He, too, recalled that when speaking with Lyric, Donna attempted to make her presence known. He tried to go into the bathroom, shutting the door to prevent her from using her catty ways to destroy what he took extra pains to preserve. She purposely spoke for Lyric to detect her voice. Johnny wrestled with thoughts of if he hung up quick enough to avoid Lyric from detecting his hidden secret. Donna constantly requested him to divorce his wife and join her teenaged daughter and their two-year-old love child. Johnny repeatedly tried to explain that he wanted his marriage and detested starting over. He instantly began to resent Donna for aiming to force his hand. He did not understand why things had to change from the way they were. He worked hard at balancing his indiscretion. Until now, Lyric failed to pressure him. She accepted that he travelled out of town often for his job. Johnny surmised if not for Donna's antics, Lyric's suspicions may not be raised. He recognized he needed to be careful with his response because he liked Donna, but he loved Lyric. Donna, her daughter, Marquise, and their son, John Jr., were getting rather expensive. It became increasingly difficult to manage both households. He weighed what Donna brought to the table to Lyric's qualities. Lyric won hands down. Donna, although she had a body and the thought of her many attributes caused him to rise, she was unemployed more then she worked, whereas Lyric offered him stability. She had been on her job for 30 plus years. Lyric made it possible for him to afford both families. Johnny did not discount Lyric's beauty either. She was beautiful inside and out, but she did not do all the things Donna did to him. Donna was his secret freak he did not want to dispose. He wanted them both because each of them served a purpose in his life. Taking deep breaths and as cool, collected, and controlled as possible, he trivialized Lyric's accusation.

"If you heard a woman, it was probably the television."

He became somewhat arrogant as, in his mind, he provided a plausible reason. He believed he caught the ball off the outfield fence and sailed it towards Lyric as she rounded third base on her way to score. He knew she would need to slide if she had a chance of being called safe.

Lyric put her head down and asked God for his help. She turned her speed up to the highest gear. She sensed victory and the umpire's call of safe. She took a few seconds to concentrate on her goal as peace and a calm feeling swept her over. The anger and her fastbeating heart dissipated. Never had she felt this type of certainty about her life. In her mind, she visualized scoring the winning run. *Game over*, she thought.

"Johnny, I want you to know that I thank you for everything being married to you for the last 5 years has taught me. It has given me so many life lessons."

Johnny was not sure where Lyric was headed, but he thought his explanation worked because she neglected to call him a liar. He intently continued listening, aware he had thrown the ball accurately to home plate.

Lyric continued, saying, "I love you, Johnny, and I'm not mad or upset with you." Tranquility overtook her speech. She continued without stopping to think about what she planned to say. It flowed out of her, as if someone else used her mouth to speak.

"But I have given my best and now realize it never was good enough for you. So, baby, I wish you well. I sincerely hope you find whatever you're searching for, but I am through with all the lies and deceit. I can no longer permit you to control my happiness. I love me too much to allow you or anyone else to destroy me, so good luck to you and Donna. I'll have my attorney contact your attorney." She gave a slight chuckle and hung up the phone.

For the first time in a long while, she felt empowered as she commandeered her life back. She failed to understand why she had no tears nor why instead of crying about the end of her marriage, she was relieved. She whispered to herself, *Home run. Game over.*

Johnny was still holding his cell to his ear. He was trying to process Lyric's speech. He studied a picture on the wall of Donna, trying to figure out how Lyric learned of her.

"What the hell just happened?" His mind was jumbled. He hung his head as he struggled to make sense out of his life. He feared he may have pushed Lyric a little too far, but he did not intend for her to end their marriage. He thought, *I'll go home next week and give Lyric some time to rethink her decision. As for Donna, it's all her fault. If she had not tried to make sure Lyric heard her in the background, I could have done this for another two years.* Johnny packed his things. He knew if he stood a chance at repairing his marriage, he had to move back to the hotel. A lump developed in his throat from guilt as he came to grips with the consequences of his decisions. A stinging pain also burnt in his chest—one he never experienced before. He even had to brush away a tear that managed to escape and run down his cheek. *I want an instant replay,* he thought. *I know I threw the ball before she scored. Lyric was thrown out!* At least, he hoped, she would be out in the game, but not out of his life.

CHAPTER 9

Be Careful Judging Me

Each and every day I tell myself to hold my peace
For I know I've got a goal within my reach.
My insides turn with frustration and pain
As my mind is my weapon that keeps me sane.
I smile for you as a tear rolls from my eye,
Hoping you'll see just how hard I try.
Your knowledge of me is based on your unfathomable view
Judging me on perception with no regards
for what I'm going through.
Looking through your limited eyes,
you've drawn an incorrect conclusion
Not supported by a shred of evidence, just your own illusion.
Still I struggle, fighting with my head held high,
proving you wrong
Hoping and praying for God's grace to keep me strong
So I can accept your feeble attempt to try to judge me
Knowing soon the truth will be revealed for the world to see

KJV Matthew: 7:1
Judge not, that ye be not judged

"**H**EY, CUZ, WAKE up and give me some love. How is my Auntie Nicke? Next, tell me who this fine man is you are laid up with?"

Jada sat up, rubbing her eyes and trying to focus in on her crazy and loud best friend and cousin, Tianna. They were raised as sisters, but they lovingly referred to each other as sister-cousins. Jada always counted on Tianna to have her back. As a teenager, she only shared that Charles fathered Micah with Tianna. She forced her to swear that she would never reveal his sin to anyone, not even her own mother, Lyric. Although Tianna held her secret, every time she happened to be in Charles's presence, she'd glare at him, as if wanting to hurt him. Jada recalled that once when they were younger, and Tianna spent the night at her house, Charles thought the two of them were asleep and crept into Jada's bedroom. Tianna sat up and pulled a bat from under the covers. She stared into Charles's eyes with the weapon raised, as if she planned on knocking off his head. Never saying a word, Tianna's rage seemed to imply, "If you touch her again, I'm going to kill you." Charles read her intent and walked out of Jada's bedroom. She gave Jada the bat and told her if Charles ever tried to touch her again, then she should flatten him like a pancake. Jada took her advice and slept with the bat. The next month, she found out Charles impregnated her. Since that time, he never touched her again. Jada credited the gift given to her from Tianna. She accepted the responsibility of protecting Jada. Even in high school, anyone that messed with Jada clearly understood the wrath of Tianna. They loved and took care of each other better than blood sisters. They claimed to be ride-or-die partners.

"Hey, sister-cousin, stop being so loud. Can't you tell people are sleeping?"

Jada flashed a huge smile as she jumped from David's lap, rushed towards Tianna, and flung her arms tightly around her neck.

"I'm sorry I didn't call you, but things are a little crazy. Besides, I figured your mom kept you updated on what's been happening."

Jada's voice began to crack as she faced her rock and confidant. Tears pooled as Jada fought to hold them in the wells of her lids. She appreciated Tianna for her unfailing support, understanding her every thought, and for her love.

Tianna, realizing Jada was about to break down, injected humor—what she did best was make Jada laugh and avoid crying. "Whoa, sister, before you tune up to cry, answer my previous question. I want some information on who you are snuggled up against." With a sly grin, she stood with her hands on her hips, looking at David in her demanding way. "This certainly is not David, the man you described to me. Give me David's phone number, so I can give him a heads-up that the finest brother in Texas has replaced him. I'll tell him no need for him to ever show up again. He has been thrown overboard for another muscular fish."

Jada giggled, beaming with pride. Knowing Tianna was armed with prior knowledge of a description of David's physical attributes made her laugh harder at Tianna's attempt to bait David. Also, she was certain her Aunt Lyric filled Tianna in on David's presence with her at the hospital.

David watched the two ladies' verbal and nonverbal exchange. With a perplexed look on his face, he tried to make sense out of their conversation. He figured out the striking, free-spirited young lady standing before him must be Lyric's daughter. From their exchange, it was obvious they cared a lot for each other, and their connection was bonded together by love. David stood up and extended his hand to the attractive woman.

"Hi, my name is George. Who is this David guy you are talking about?"

Tianna was unable to speak for a second. She hesitated before greeting him. She glanced at Jada with wonder in her eyes and observed Jada laughing. As she turned back to the fine man, he, too, started to laugh. She pushed David's hand out the way and reached up wrapping her arms around his neck.

"OK, you two got me. David, I guess you have jokes."

David shifted uncomfortably as Tianna's hug caught him off guard. He couldn't help but be mesmerized by her beauty. She was a light-skinned version of her mother, but her facial features were more keen and pronounced then Lyric's. Exhibiting a perfectly toned body, she dripped with confidence that said, "I know I got it going on," yet her poise was far from conceited.

Quite aware of her sister-cousin's beauty and its effect on both men and women, Jada acknowledged David's thoughts. "Isn't she beautiful, David?"

At first, David, a little unsure of how to respond, stopped to think. He did not know if he should acknowledge her allure or perhaps say something about Jada's appeal. He settled on what he hoped would make them both feel good and the truth. "I can't take any more gorgeous women; First you, your mom, your aunt, and now your sister-cousin. I need a gallon of the water you all drink."

They all laughed. As expected, Tianna used her quick wit to strike. "Good answer, David. I like you already. My name is Tianna." As she sat in the hard straight-back chair, again she showed her loyalty and protection of Jada. "But don't get it twisted. Jada has the whole package. Don't let the beauty fool you. I'll cut you if you hurt her."

"Tianna, you don't have to worry. I'm here, and I got her, but if I need some assistance, I'll call on you."

Jada turned red, hanging her head. "Thanks to both of you. How about Jada takes care of Jada, and if Jada needs help, she'll ask." She, too, sat down as she glanced at Tianna and David with a facial expression that read that she no longer was a child but a woman, capable and in control of her own life.

Laughing out loud, they nodded in agreement. Each quieted down and began thinking how Jada's struggles were only beginning. Even Jada had to secretly admitted to herself regardless of what her mouth said, she needed assistance from Tianna, David, Lyric, and what is more important, God's favor and blessings to make it through the trials yet to come.

Tianna broke the silence. "So, Jada, how is Auntie? What are the doctors saying?"

Jada swallowed as she tried to collect herself to prepare to give a positive response both verbally and through her body language. She lifted her eyes and directed them straight at Tianna but avoided making eye contact. "Mom's hanging in there. She rested well last night."

Tianna read Jada's nonverbal cues even though Jada tried hard to mask them. She decoded fear in her best friend's eyes despite her attempts to disguise the trepidation in her voice. *Jada never was any good at hiding anything from me. We have been friends too long. I recognize when she is happy, sad, or afraid,* Tianna thought. She positioned her arm around Jada's shoulder, giving her the kind of embrace that clearly indicated, "I'm here for you."

"Jada, why don't you and David go home, freshen up, and get some rest. I'll stay with Auntie Nicke. I promise to call you if anything happens. And anyway, Mom is coming up soon. I talked to her this morning, and she said she let Micah sleep in since he stayed up so late, but once they got up and got dressed, she would be coming to the hospital."

Jada looked to David as if she wanted him to make the decision for her.

David took charge and suggested Jada call Lyric to determine her arrival time. "We can take Micah back to my house with us."

Jada was so relieved because she did not want to be alone. She needed to be with him just in case her mother took a turn for the worse or she received a call that something bad happened.

She was certain Tianna and Lyric would take good care of Nicke because they, too, loved her. As Jada considered getting some rest, a sudden exhaustion took complete control as it occurred to her she had not slept well for the last 48 hours. Thanks to David, she did manage to get several small naps, but her body cried for some real sleep. Through her exhaustion, Jada elicited a nod in agreement with David and Tianna. She believed if she did not stop, she would instantly collapse. After a few seconds, Jada thanked both David and Tianna. "But first," she said as she slowly walked towards the recliner, "let me rest for a few minutes." Her body told her if she didn't lie down immediately, she would fall. "Tianna, why don't you check on Mom?"

David secured a folded blanket from a chair and carefully tucked the cover around Jada.

Tianna did not bother to respond. She turned and grabbed the handle, preparing to go visit her aunt. Just as she was about to pull the door open, two women bumped into her. They both aggressively pushed their way past her and into the waiting room. Tianna recognized them instantly, although they appeared to either not remember her or did not care enough to even acknowledge her presence.

The older lady was short and stocky. She carried her purse on her arm as most 70-to-80-year-old women do. Her facial expressions read, "I came to fight. Everybody get out of the way. I am only looking for my opponent. Just let me find her."

The other one was much younger and had a "Please mother don't embarrass me" expression on her face.

Tianna stepped back inside the waiting room. She identified the woman as being Charles's mother, Mrs. Viola Smith, and his sister, Jackie. Tianna flashed a glare towards David, signaling him to prepare for battle.

Without missing a beat and not sure why, David assumed his position. Getting up from his chair, he moved in one fluid motion to stand in front of the chaise where Jada lay. He posted himself as a strong, mighty protector and bodyguard for Jada. His demeanor resembled one of those English security guards protecting the queen's palace. The only things missing were his weapons and the furry hat with the chinstrap perched on his head. He took an erect stance where the only body parts moving were his eyes as they surveyed the strangers.

Jada, unaware of the intruders' entrance, collapsed in less than five seconds, succumbing to sleep. She probably set a Guinness world record for dozing off quicker than a lightning bolt flash before the thunder arrives.

Tianna brushed past the ladies and assumed her position next to David, shielding Jada. She was the first to speak. "Hello, Mrs. Smith," she said as softly as she could, in hopes of not waking Jada. "As I'm sure you can tell, we just got Jada to get some sleep, and we don't want her disturbed."

Tianna's tone, although low in volume, conveyed authority and conviction. It bordered on rude. Tianna thought if her mother heard her, she would lecture Tianna on respecting her elders.

"Quite frankly, I don't care about her sleeping. She needs to wake up and get my son out of jail because she knows she lied about him." Mrs. Smith did not attempt to speak softly. She intended to disrupt Jada as she headed towards her without regard to Jada's self-appointed bodyguards. She did not plan for them to stop her.

With perspiration forming on Tianna's forehead and a sudden increase in her heart rate, Tianna shook as if her blood surpassed 212 degrees Fahrenheit—beyond the boiling point. This lady's old age ceased to have any importance, which meant she would not mess with Tianna's friend. She always thought Charles's problems stemmed from his mother bullying everyone, including him. Mrs. Smith seemed to be more concerned about her family's reputation, which she was known to hide, cover up, or lie to protect, even when the family was wrong. Tianna recalled a number of verbal fights involving Aunt Nicke and this woman. She cussed out Nicke so many times, it ceased to be funny. She absolutely lacked class. She was a bitter old woman who lived her life vicariously through her children. Tianna stepped in front of her, cutting her off at the path.

"Mrs. Smith, I said Jada is sleep. This is neither the time nor the place. If you are here to start some trouble, you can turn yourself right around and leave. And another thing, as far as Charles being in jail, you may want to go to the trial before you confront Jada or try to defend him." Tianna's voice rose. She forgot about Jada sleeping. She unequivocally decided to lose control on her as she always despised the old lady for how she treated her aunt and her sister-cousin. Tianna readied herself to deliver some colorful words she would have to repent for later.

Mrs. Smith refused to be deterred or turned around. She thought, *I came to tell this tramp that she is the cause of my son going to jail.* Neither Jada nor her drunken mother were worth the time it took her to shit every day. *Who does this little girl think she's talking to?*

Mrs. Smith leaned around Tianna and David. She hollered, "Jada, Jada, wake your ass up! You better get your lying ass up and march it down to the police station. You go tell them people you told a lie about my son. You liar."

Jada jumped, startled by the noise. She focused and quickly identified Charles's mother and sister. Because she was weary, she lacked the desire or energy to fight with her step-grandmother. However, she decided their conversation was long overdue and past the time to address some of the things she should have said years ago. Jada sprung from her prone position and onto her feet.

David stopped her as she hurled towards Mrs. Smith. While David held Jada, Tianna stepped in between her and Mrs. Smith. She was almost nose-to-nose with her.

Although a caramel color, Tianna's face intensified to deep hue of red. Her anger exacerbated to a level of deranged. "I may go to jail, but you will not disrespect my family ever again." Tianna clenched her fingers tightly together, raised her fist, and swung at Mrs. Smith.

David grabbed her hand just in time before it could connect with Mrs. Smith's mouth. He pushed Jada on the chaise and wrapped his arms around Tianna as he repelled Jada, and now Tianna, from attacking Mrs. Smith. He endeavored to prevent a physical brawl in the hospital and determined no one would fight on his watch. David flipped to head referee because he and the sister seemed to be the only somewhat calm ones. He ordered Jackie, saying, "Take her out of here now."

The daughter halfheartedly tugged at her mother, attempting to remove her. Mrs. Smith snatched her arm loose and shouted, "Get off of me! I'm not going anywhere until both of those tramps admit they lied about my son." She steamed as if she was a wild bull. Digging her feet into the carpeted floor, she took aim towards Jada and Tianna. She was so loud that everyone in the hospital could hear her.

Jada lunged again. "My mother is not a tramp," she shouted back.

David struggled, holding Jada by the waist, and with his other arm wrapped around Tianna, fought to also control her.

Both women continued wrestling to get free. They tussled like chained pit bulls battling another enemy dog.

Mrs. Smith was firing them up more as she continued shouting obscenities to and about Jada and her mother.

At the last possible instance, the door to the waiting room flung open. Lyric rushed in with Officer Nelson behind her.

"What the hell is going on in here? Everyone in this hospital can hear you." She observed David trying to restrain both Tianna and Jada, then she locked in on Mrs. Smith. At the sight of her, she instantly figured the fire from Tianna and Jada was exploding from the grease thrown by Mrs. Smith. She possessed an uncanny way of provoking anyone and everyone she encountered.

Officer Nelson took in the scene and ruled in favor of allowing Lyric's attempts to bring order to the situation to prevail. Before interjecting, she needed to determine who the older woman was as well as who the other two young ladies were. However, she did recognize both Jada and David. She decided not to intervene yet with what appeared to be some sort of family issues.

Tianna was the first to acknowledge her mother and address her concerns. She shook from anger and was fuming, as saliva built in her mouth. Her nose flared, and the veins in her neck were bulging. She still struggled to break free from David's bear grip.

"Mom, this old woman came up here, waking up Jada. She started calling her and Aunt Nicke names. She cursed at us acting like she wanted to fight someone. Ain't anybody in here scared of her crazy ass. She should be up here apologizing to Jada for her child-molesting son's actions." Without stopping to take a breath, Tianna spouted out a thorough replay of Mrs. Smith's conversations.

Lyric, in a very soft but forceful voice, interrupted Tianna with a stern warning: "Young lady, you need to get yourself together. I don't care what she is saying. Let me see some respect from you just like I raised you to give. Do you hear me?"

Tianna rolled her eyes at Mrs. Smith as she pushed David's arm from around her waist. She calmed herself because her mother's wrath was much worse than Mrs. Smith could ever be. "You're right, Mom. I'm sorry. I should have never allowed this ignorant old bat, I mean Mrs. Smith, to upset me like this. I tried to tell her this was not the place or time for this, but she . . . "

Again, Lyric interrupted Tianna as she raised her index finger to her and headed towards Mrs. Smith. "Tianna is correct. This is neither the time nor is a hospital an area for this confusion. Nicke is laying down the hall, fighting for her life, and Jada," as she turned to Jada and noticed tears streaming down her face, "this child has been through so much and right now, she needs support."

Mrs. Smith turned to Jada, then back to Lyric. "She is gonna have something to cry for if she doesn't tell that judge she lied about my son."

"Oh, hell no!" Tianna shouted. "You got to get the hell out of here before I kick your ass," she continued, as she headed towards Mrs. Smith.

Officer Nelson decided it was now time for her to exert her police officer clout. She listened and learned how everyone's role fit in this puzzle. She cut Tianna off by stepping in front of her before she could enter Mrs. Smith's space.

She then turned to Mrs. Smith and said, "I am Officer Nelson. The family has asked you to leave the hospital, and now I am ordering you to go home." Turning to the other young woman that appeared to be making a halfhearted attempt to restrain Mrs. Smith, she said, "Are you with her?"

Mrs. Smith's daughter, Jackie, answered softly, "Yes, Officer Nelson, this is my mother, and we are just leaving. Come on, Mom, let's go," she said while gently tugging on her mother.

Mrs. Smith snapped her arm away from Jackie and made an about-face towards Officer Nelson. "I want this girl," she said, pointing to Jada. "I want her to march her little fast self to that police station and tell those people she lied about my son. He is in jail because she told them my son had sex with her and got her pregnant. I know him, and he wouldn't do that. Her nor her momma are any good." Mrs. Smith put her hands on her hips, as if she was waiting for Officer Nelson to do as she had been told.

"Look, Mrs. Smith," Lyric began. Her entire demeanor changed as Charles's mother managed to also push Lyric into losing her sophistication and cool. "Your son is in jail and will have his day in court. You should be careful saying what your son did and what he did not do. Now get your crazy butt the hell out of here and don't come back," said Lyric, as she pointed towards the door. Steam seemed to be rising from Lyric's head. She fought the urge to grab Mrs. Smith up by her collar and throw her out through the first opening available. It did not matter to Lyric if she sailed through a door or a window. She realized she would have to ask God for his forgiveness, but she felt like Popeye. She had all she could stand, and she couldn't stand any more.

Officer Nelson, noticing that Lyric, usually the voice of reason, was about to lose it, decided she needed to remove Mrs. Smith before things escalated any further, but not before David exercised his opportunity to lace into Mrs. Smith. He managed to contain both Jada and Tianna, and now it was his turn. Seeing Jada cry and feeling her pain triggered his rescue mode. David tried to swallow his thoughts, but they rolled from his mouth with the intent to slice the old woman to pieces. He hoped he would not regret this but could not resist knocking her off her high horse. She was not showing anyone any respect, so she deserved to have the tables turned on her. He chose a powerful armament designed to cut down to the white meat. He picked up his weapon of choice and walked towards Charles's mother and his sister. In a low voice, he asked Mrs. Smith, "Who do you think you are? God?" He went on to say to Mrs. Smith that James 4:12 says, "There is only one lawgiver and judge, he who is able to save and to destroy. But who are you to judge your neighbor?"

Mrs. Smith appeared stunned. She prepared for a physical or verbal attack, but she neglected to formulate a plan for a spiritual warfare. Hesitating, she wondered to herself, *Do I have the right to judge?*

The room was completely silent. Everyone but Mrs. Smith marveled at how David shut Mrs. Smith down by correcting her with the word of God.

Officer Nelson caught Mrs. Smith by the arm, but she snatched away from Officer Nelson.

Everyone gazed at Officer Nelson for her response to the obvious defiance.

Officer Nelson seized Mrs. Smith's arm again, telling her, "You can leave the hospital now or you can go to jail and join your son. You make the decision because it really doesn't matter to me." Officer Nelson squeezed harder, hoping to reinforce that she meant business.

The extra physical pressure obviously worked because Mrs. Smith gave them all one last dirty stare as she turned to exit. She threw her head in the air, as if trying to smell the clouds in the sky. Failing to say another word, she left, with Officer Nelson's help, of course.

As the door closed behind them, Jada released the most heartfelt, sobbing cry. She cried so hard and loud that her whole body shook as if she were convulsing. She stuttered, "I didn't lie. I didn't lie. He . . . He . . . He did molest me. I swear he sexually abused me. I didn't want him to touch me, but I . . . I . . . I was scared. I was too afraid to make him stop. He said he loved me and needed me to love him too. He said my mother didn't love me and all . . . all I . . . I . . . I had was him." Jada balled up in a fetal position in the chair and hid her head with her arms.

No one said anything. They all soaked in Jada's deep-rooted pain. The only sounds were those of Jada's years of buried truths as they surfaced and overflowed from her like a volcano.

David walked over to Jada and scooped her legs up lifting her in his arms. He held her like she was a baby. He lifted her limp arm and wrapped it around his neck. He pulled her closer to him. Jada buried her face in his shoulder. David closed his eyes as he rocked Jada. He attempted to shield her from the lava running from her soul, being released into the atmosphere.

Lyric marveled over the love scene playing out in front of her. Tears filled her eyes as she rapidly blinked to hide them. She wished for that type of love and support from Johnny. Lyric walked to her daughter. She hugged Tianna until she experienced the unconditional love flow from her to Tianna and from Tianna back to her. They spoke no words, but both connected at a place only a mother and daughter have the power to reach. Lyric felt completely drained. She held onto Tianna for dear life.

Jada calmed down but was still in David's arms. He held her without flinching or revealing that her 150 pounds were any heavier to him then a 10-pound sack of potatoes.

Everyone basked in the love felt for each other. The room was silenced by the whispers of love.

The door opened and disturbed the calm that settled in the room. Officer Nelson scanned from Jada and David to Lyric and Tianna. Everyone embraced, stomping out the pool of hurt with love, which permeated through the air. Officer Nelson stood for a moment, soaking in the ambience. She also wished at that moment that she had someone to hold her. She realized this case was forcing her to deal with the skeletons she buried a long time ago and prayed would stay covered in the ground. She became a police officer because she wanted to make anyone committing a crime pay through the justice system and not allow vigilantes to take the law into their own hands. Her mind could no longer fight back her own experiences of molestation. She sunk back to a place when she was nine years old, and her neighbor, who was 31 years old, molested her. She recalled the fear and the physical pain experienced after the despicable act, which forever changed her life. No matter how hard she tried, his body smell was never erased from her memory. It was a stench she never smelled before. Unlike Jada, she told her mother the same day the exploitation occurred. She visualized herself sitting on the front steps of their modest duplex, waiting on her mother to return home from work. The second her mother looked at her, she immediately discerned something was wrong with her baby girl. She approached carrying a bag of groceries. The moment her mother gazed at her face, she dropped the bags and started screaming and crying. She said, "Who touched you? Who was it?" Judith Nelson was only able to respond, "Mr. Steinberg." Mrs. Nelson left the groceries on the ground and pulled Judith into the house. She told her to go take a bath, and when she finished, to bring the clothes she was wearing to her. Judith closed her eyes as she pictured her mother's distraught face in her mind. She recalled how a part of her wished she had not confessed to her mother, as it added to the stress her mother already endured. Her mother was a single parent with two children, Judith and her 19-year-old brother, Brian. Brian was in and out of trouble from his early teenage years. He was sent to reform school twice until he finally dropped out and started hanging with the 69 crew. Judith's mother carried the guilt of a single parent, which failed her son, Brian. She always told Judith how she hoped and prayed Judith would do something constructive with her life.

Judith entered, took a seat, and continued reminiscing about her own life. She remembered she soaked for a long time. Her insides were hurting from the excruciating pain inflicted by Mr. Steinberg's member. She recollected that the water seemed to soothe her painful birth canal and slowed her trembling body to a mere twitch. Judith wanted to stay in the tub forever. She kept adding hot water to prolong her stay. When she did get out, she observed the traces of blood in her underpants.

She heard police sirens in the distance. They seemed to be getting closer and closer. There appeared to be a ruckus happening in front of her house. She thought about how she rushed to get dressed. She ran down the steps, taking them two at a time. She called for her mother, but there was no answer. Just as she opened the front door, she saw the police escorting her handcuffed brother. Brian looked at her and said he was sorry. He called her "baby girl" and told her, "He will never touch you again." Her mother pushed Judith in the house and made her go to bed. Later, she found out that her brother had shot and killed Mr. Steinberg after he found out what Mr. Steinberg had done. He served seven years in jail for voluntary manslaughter.

Lyric interrupted Officer Nelson's revisit to her past. "Officer Nelson."

"Lyric, call me Judith."

"All right, Judith. Thank you so much for your assistance. I tried to keep calm, but she provoked me. It has been a long time since I've wanted to punch someone. That old woman was about to get one across the mouth."

Everyone in the room took a seat and began to find the humor in their unwanted visitor, except for Jada.

"Mom, I had that," Tianna blurted out. "If you did not show up when you did, Officer Nelson would be picking the old bag and her daughter up off the floor." Tianna dispelled a hearty laugh. She turned to Jada and David. "David, you had my back right?"

"Yeah, Tianna, I did, but you didn't need me to do anything but clean up the mess you were about to leave behind. So instead, I shot her with my 66 chapters, King James version.

All laughed, including Jada.

"OK, cuz, back to what we were talking about before the crazy wicked witch and her daughter so rudely interrupted us. You two need to go get some sleep. I will hang here with my auntie to be sure no one else tries some unexpected crap. With everyone gone, there won't be any witnesses to me knocking them out." Tianna made a fist and punched her hand, simulating what she would do to anyone that bothered her family. "Officer Nelson, my mom will tell you, I'm not to be played with."

Judith cut her eyes at Tianna but decided not to comment. "Jada, I stopped by to let you know that Charles has his arraignment and bond hearing tomorrow morning. The judge will assign a future court date. He will be given the right to waive a speedy trial and to enter his plea of guilty, not guilty, or no contest. If he should plead not guilty, the judge will decide whether to release him on his own recognizance or to demand bail. If he enters a plea of no contest, which means he is not entering a plea at all but rather exercising his right to remain silent, his attorney will decide how much time he will need to prepare the case. The judge will then let Charles know whether bond is granted or not. If it is granted, Charles will be told when he will need to appear back in court. At that point, the arraignment will be concluded. You will receive a summons with the date to appear in court. For now, he has been charged with statutory rape." Officer Nelson paused a few seconds to give Jada a chance to absorb the courtroom procedures.

"Thanks, Officer Nelson," Jada said as she got up from the chair and walked towards the door. She did not have the strength or the desire to comment on anything. She just had one question she had to ask. Everyone could see she was visibly drained. "Cuz, I'm going to take you up on getting some rest. I am exhausted." She then turned to Officer Nelson and asked, "If he gets out on bond, can he contact me or my mom?"

"Jada, if you want no contact from him, you will need to file a restraining order. As for your mother, I am not sure about that. You should get some legal advice." Although Officer Nelson wanted to help and provide assistance to Jada, she had to be careful about what she told Jada and the family. The last thing she wanted was for someone to say there was some type of collusion.

"For now, Jada," Lyric began, "on your way out, stop by the nurses' station and limit her visitors to only those you want to allow access."

Jada grabbed David's arm to steady her. "I just don't have the energy to do anything right now. It's going to take all I have to just walk to the car and get in it."

"Well, don't be concerned about Micah. I dropped him off with Tasha and the kids. She wanted me to tell you he can stay as long as you like."

Tianna felt so sorry for her sister-cousin. She could tell Jada was about to collapse, explode, or erupt at any second. Her heart broke for Jada. She gave her a big hug. "Don't worry about it for now. No one that is not supposed to see my auntie will. You can take that to the bank and cash it. I promise to stand guard over her like I am the secret service for President Obama. For real."

Jada took solace, as she knew Tianna meant every word. She also appreciated the way Tianna loved her mother and did not doubt she would take good care of her. Like Allstate, her mother was in good hands. Jada forced a semi-smile as both she and David left.

Officer Nelson gave Lyric a courtesy hug. "I'll keep you informed on the arraignment. Expect a call or visit from me tomorrow. I hope you know if you need anything to please call." She handed Lyric her business card. "My personal cell number is on the back. You can phone day or night. Take care, my friend," she said as she left the waiting room. She wondered why she was so drawn to Lyric. She did not remember another case where she was so emotionally involved. All she knew is that Lyric's spirit and presence seemed to heal the brokenness in Judith. A light of genuine love radiated bright from her, perhaps because of Lyric's spirituality or maybe she held a gift in her placed by God. Officer Nelson envied Nicke for enjoying a friend such as Lyric. In her heart, she hoped when the case concluded, they could all be friends. Lyric was the type of friend she prayed for and wished she had in her life.

Lyric caught Tianna's hand as she led her towards Nicke's hospital bedside. She jokingly scolded her. "Tianna, you must maintain control of that temper. I've told you time and time again to respect your elders."

Tianna smiled, throwing her head back. "Right, Mom, just the way you did. I've told you time and time again to respect your elders." She laughed as she mocked her mother.

Lyric laughed too. She needed the laugh to release some of the pent-up tension and frustration. She pushed the hospital door open and stuck her tongue out at Tianna as a gesture to get even for her mocking. Just as she turned back around to face Nicke, she bumped into Dr. Maxey. "Oh, excuse me. I'm so sorry.

I wasn't paying attention," she nervously said. She tried to gather herself, but it was too late. She stumbled her words out, trying not to stare at who she considered to be the finest man on the planet.

Dr. Maxey did not make it any better. He grinned from ear to ear at the sight of Lyric. He read how fond of him she appeared. He enjoyed watching her flustered movements as she attempted to hide her feelings. "No problem," he said in his most flirtatious tone. "If I'm going to get run over, what better way than by two beautiful women. Come on in. I was just checking on our patient. Lyric who is this beauty accompanying you? Actually, I really don't have to ask. I think I can guess, as she appears to be the spitting image of her gorgeous mother. Did I get it right?"

"Yes, you did," she stuttered. "Dr. Maxey, this is my daughter, Tianna. Tianna, meet Nicke's doctor, Dr. Maxey." Lyric walked towards Nicke and left the two to greet each other. As she passed Dr. Maxey, she caught a whiff of his sandalwood cologne. She fought to compose herself. She inhaled deeply, as if she tried to savor his smell for a later time.

"Hi, Dr. Maxey. It's a pleasure to meet you. Thanks for the compliment." Her facial expression implied she did not intend to fall for his innocent compliments. She instantly discerned he was flirting with her mother. What Tianna found interesting, though, was that her mother seemed to enjoy his advances. She hoped she didn't have to remind her of being married. On the other hand, Tianna relished the thought of the fine doctor showing interest in her mother. Her parents' marriage seemed strained for the last several months, and her father neglected coming home and attempt to work on a solution. "So, how is my auntie doing?" Tianna asked as she turned her attention to the real reason she was in the room.

"Yes, doctor, how is she doing?" Lyric asked as she pulled herself together.

"I'm extremely pleased with her progress. It's still too early to tell, but her MRI shows the swelling is going down and her other vital signs are good. If she keeps this up, we may be able to do surgery in a day or two and identify the culprit." Dr. Maxey's tone seemed confident and, for the first time, hopeful.

"That is great news," Lyric replied, finding the courage to observe Dr. Maxey's big deep-set brown eyes.

"Lyric, why don't you let Tianna visit with her aunt and join me for a cup of coffee in the cafeteria?"

Dr. Maxey pushed the door and waited for Lyric. He did not give her a chance to reply.

Lyric kissed Nicke her on the cheek. "Nicke, I'm going to let Tianna sit with you while I go have coffee with your cute doctor. Girl, you better wake up soon so you can see this man." She winked at Tianna and strolled towards the open door. She accepted his invitation, while surprising him with her own attempt to cause embarrassment.

The confidence within Dr. Maxey faded as Lyric turned the tables. He wanted her to accompany him for coffee, but a part of him thought she was going to turn him down. He was delighted that she accepted. Together, they headed for the cafeteria. As they entered the elevator, both noticed they were the only ones in the elevator. Neither of them said a word. They listened to the creaking and strain of the elevator until the ding sound of the elevator announced their arrival on the floor of the cafeteria. They walked in silence. Doctor Maxey opened the door and ushered her to a two-seat table in the back of the room. "Lyric, how would you like your coffee, and is there anything else you like to have?"

Replying without looking up, Lyric told Dr. Maxey, "I would like a venti caramel macchiato with whipped cream and a slice of lemon pound cake from the Starbucks counter, please." She nervously pretended to be reading the Starbucks menu.

"Why certainly, Ms. Lyric. I will be happy to accommodate you. Your order sounds good so I think I will also get the same. I'll be right back."

Lyric sighed with relief. She required additional time to gather her nerves. She suspected they would discuss personal issues. The first thing she chose to reveal was her marital status. *No matter how handsome he is, I must be careful because I am extremely vulnerable. Between everything going on with Nicke and confirming Johnny is involved with another woman, the stress is unbearable; after all, I am only human.* Lyric thought, *It is a necessity to stay prayed up to fight this devil. Johnny may believe it is OK to break the vows he made to me in the sight of God, but I am aware that the wage of sin is death.* As the thoughts continued to flow through Lyric's mind, she gathered strength but admitted being around Doctor Maxey made her happy. He seemed kind and smart, a Christian with a job, and God knows he was definitely attractive. *Another place, another time,* she thought as Dr. Maxey joined her.

"Here you are, Lyric. I hope everything is to your liking," as Dr. Maxey pulled the chair beside Lyric. He glimpsed a wedding set on her left hand and second finger but hoped that it was used to scare men away. He decided he must find out. Never before was he so instantly attracted to a woman. After his divorce two years ago, he threw himself into his work. His ex-wife broke his heart, which resulted in his becoming gun-shy and distrustful of most women. He reminisced about her and her boyfriend in his house, sleeping in their marital bed, and how her boyfriend even drove his car. He wondered how he allowed them to make such a fool of him, but he swore it would never happen again. He asked God to send him a faithful helpmate. This time, he promised to wait on God, no matter how long it took. Dr. Maxey could not wait anymore. He had to find out if Lyric was married or not. He shuffled in his seat and took a deep breath. "So, Lyric, I have to ask. Are you married?"

Lyric sensed liberation. She could now admit to the doctor that because of her status, nothing more than friendship would exist between them. "Yes, Dr. Maxey, I am married and currently living with my husband. Although we are having issues, I am not divorced yet."

"Jim," Dr. Maxey said.

"Pardon me?" Lyric responded with a perplexed look on her face.

Again Dr. Maxey said, "Jim, please call me Jim." His pupils decreased in size as he lowered his head. His eyebrows rose. The sparkle that once enhanced his eyes faded away as his lips downturned.

"Oh, I'm sorry. Yes, Jim, I am married. Are you?"

Jim waited a second as he took a sip of his coffee. "No, unfortunately or fortunately, I am divorced. My marriage ended two years ago."

"Oh, that's why you sound sad, Jim."

"No, Lyric, I am unhappy because I wished you were also single. When I saw your wedding rings, I hoped against hope that you wore them to frighten men like me away."

Lyric chuckled. "No, but that is a wonderful idea, and one I will remember when I am divorced."

Jim glowed as he repeated, "When you are divorced? Are you in the process of a split?"

Lyric sipped her coffee as she stalled before answering. Glancing up she said, "Yes, I am. My husband should be served with papers in the next few days, although we still have to sort out some business."

Jim's eyebrows again rose as his eyes refused to focus. "I'm sorry to hear that, and I am also unhappy you are going through problems. The best advice I can give you is to lay it all on the altar. I'm not going to kid you, Lyric. From the moment I first saw you, there was an instant connection. Then when we prayed for Nicke together, I thought God was answering my prayers. I have been praying for a beautiful Christian woman." He hesitated before taking another sip. "I thought he sent you to me."

Lyric smiled while fixing her hair, straightening her clothing, and sitting up straight. She mentally left the conversation to check in with God. "God, are you doing this, or is this the devil tempting me?"

Before Lyric could get her answer, Jim interrupted her silent thoughts. "Well, Lyric, I wish you the best. Be sure you consult God before doing anything. He will reveal to you the road to follow. But thanks because you give me hope. I know he will answer my prayers."

"Thank you, Jim. I will, and I have. I'm just waiting on his answer, and yes, he will take care of you. Jim, my husband is having an affair. This is the second time our marriage has gone through this. I'm not that kind of woman. I forgave him once because I, too, stepped outside the marriage. I was so ashamed of myself, but I asked for forgiveness that I believe God granted. I will never make that mistake again. But similarly, I refuse to allow my husband to bring another person into our marriage. The first time was a mistake, but the second time means it is a pattern." Lyric stopped talking for a bit. She wondered why in the world she reveal so much to this man she just met. This was so out of character for her.

"I've been there. My ex-wife had an affair with another man, and neither she nor he had any boundaries. She had him in my house, in my bed, and in my car. I couldn't forgive that. Their affair lasted for at least two years. She played me for material and financial gains."

"Wow, I'm sorry. I'm sure that caused you a great deal of pain, but you make sure the next woman in your life comes from God, and you won't have to worry about that sort of thing ever happening to you again."

Jim enjoyed talking with Lyric. She understood his pain. He thought how other women he discussed his unfortunate circumstances with tried to seduce him into trusting them. They told him they were the chosen ones. But not Lyric—she sent him right back to the source. He secretly wished Lyric realized her own worth. He wondered what else her husband could be looking for when he already had a woman such as Lyric. She was attractive, intelligent, had a job, and loved God. He pondered, *Why would anyone risk losing all that for someone who probably did not boast half the characteristics of Lyric? I would wait for a woman comparable to Lyric.* "I know if I were married to you, I would never have to worry about you having an affair. That is comforting knowledge."

Lyric searched Jim's eyes. They revealed a flicker of hope. It was the same one that sparked inside of her. Because of the churning of her emotions, she thought it would be best if this were the last time they discussed their marital lives. She was already fighting the urge to ask him to hold her and protect her from the world. "Jim, I appreciate your concern for me, but I have to tell you something my grandmother shared with me a long time ago. She said, 'If something doesn't start out right, it won't end up right.' So for that reason, if we ever spend time alone again, I will be inviting you as a single woman with a single man."

Jim smiled. He examined not only her eyes but saw through them to her soul. He observed something he had not before noticed—years of pain and hurt. "I agree, Ms. Lyric, but you should know that I've changed my prayer from 'God, send me the woman you want for me' to 'God, I've found the woman you want me to have. Help me to be patient and wait.'" Jim stood up and pulled Lyric's chair from under the table. He buried his nose in her locks and sniffed the sage and ginger oil emanating from her hair. He thought, *I will keep this scent locked away until I can officially take this woman into my life.*

Lyric felt his nose against her hair. She stood still as she did not want to lean into his body. One touch would not be good for her or him. "Jesus, this isn't funny," she said, as she fought the overpowering urge to lie into his arms.

Jim filed the scent of Lyric away in his memory bank. He carefully stepped back so Lyric could get out of her chair without their bodies touching. He understood what Lyric meant.

"You are so right. It is not funny. Now let's go before I embarrass myself."

They headed for the elevator. Jim hoped someone else would be on the elevator other than the two of them. The door opened, and it was empty. Jim hesitated before entering. He thought, *I am going to take the opportunity to kiss Lyric on her cheek.* Just as the doors were closing, someone pushed the button, and they reopened. Standing there was Resident Candy. She appeared shocked to see Dr. Maxey. She cut her eyes at the striking woman standing next to him. She quickly deduced she must be with him as both were holding Starbuck cups. "Hey, Doc, what's up?"

"Hello, Candy." Dr. Maxey kept his greeting short and sweet as he watched Lyric's response. He noticed her trying to ignore everyone by studying the floor numbers as the elevator rushed to the seventh floor.

Candy softened her tone to a childlike whine as she extended her back and poked out her breast. "So, Doc, how is your patient that Dave and his new flavor of the month are visiting?"

Dr. Maxey responded in a perturbed manner. "Candy, I don't discuss my patients and their health, particularly not in a public elevator with someone who has no business learning that knowledge."

"Well, isn't she with you?" Candy asked, pointing to Lyric.

Lyric ignored the comment, continuing to stare at the elevator pad as it approaches the third floor. She concentrated on the lights as they each lit up, thinking, *Please hurry up and get me away from this dingbat.*

Deciding he would not permit Candy to disrespect someone he was hoping and praying would be his wife one day, Doctor

Maxey reprimanded her. "Look, Candy, you are very disrespectful, and I don't appreciate it. You need to take your antics somewhere else. You were Dave's flavor of the month. From what I can see, he has a real woman now, and they seem to be in love with each other, so get out of his business and mine."

The door opened to the seventh floor, and Lyric stepped out with Dr. Maxey's hand gently placed around her waist.

"Lyric, I am sorry. Someone forgot to raise that young woman."

Lyric remained quiet as they walked to Nicke's room. She gathered from the conversation that the disrespectful flirtatious lady had ties to David. She hoped David's intentions towards Jada were honorable, but she remained uncertain. *Jada is much more refined then that ghetto broad*, she thought.

Dr. Maxey stepped in front of Lyric and held the door. "Tianna, your mom is back safe. How is Nicke doing?"

"She's doing great, Doc. When I told her you and my mom went for coffee, she lifted her hand. I'm not sure if that is a good or a bad sign."

"I am sure it was positive, Tianna. She likes me."

Everyone laughed.

Without opening her eyes, Nicke raised her arm again.

Dr. Maxey went to her bedside. "Nicke, it is Dr. Maxey. If you can hear me, squeeze my hand."

Nicke squeezed his hand.

"Good job! Now I want you to work hard on waking up. Your friends and family have a lot to share with you."

Nicke did not respond.

Dr. Maxey clutched Lyric's hand. She flinched as she looked to see if Tianna was watching.

He then grabbed Tianna's hand. "Let's have a quick word of prayer so I can check on a few other patients."

After the prayer, Dr. Maxey said good-bye to Nicke, Tianna, and Lyric.

"Thank you, Jim, I mean, Dr. Maxey."

He smiled. "It's just Jim, Lyric." He shut the door to Nicke's room.

Tianna waited to confront her mother's behavior with Dr. Maxey. "Auntie, did you hear Mom calling your doctor by his first name? I told you she seems to be smitten by him. You better hurry up and wake up before she divorces my dad and marries Jim."

Embarrassed by her daughter's comments, Lyric lowered her head. She thought she should not bother to directly respond. "Hi, Nicke. How are you today?" She continued giving Nicke a synopsis of the day. She mentioned David and Jada. She also relayed Mrs. Smith's visit to the hospital and how Officer Nelson escorted them out of the hospital. She continued rambling for fear that Tianna would mention Jim again. She decided to try to figure out the situation before she commented to anyone but Nicke. She missed her friend and wanted help to sort out her life. Although Lyric clearly knew Nicke's stance, there remained little doubt she would encourage divorcing Johnny and dating Jim, she still required her input. Nicke did not care much for Johnny. She would say, "He was as full of shit-stuffing as a Christmas turkey." Lyric laughed to herself as her mind replayed Nicke saying those words. She decided when they were alone again, she would share with Nicke her thoughts about both men.

"Mom, so what's up with you and the doc?" Tianna faced her mother and waited for a response. She noticed how her mother blushed when Dr. Maxey paid her a compliment. Although beautiful, Tianna noted how her mother took extra steps to ensure her attire, makeup, and hair were all flawless. *She prepared for a date rather than coming to the hospital to sit with her friend,* Tianna thought.

"Tianna, what do you mean what's up with me and Dr. Jim?" Lyric got tongue-tied and confused as to whether she should refer to her new doctor friend by his first name or his professional name. Her speech jumbled together as a combination of the two.

Tianna turned to her Auntie lying in the bed. "See, I told you. You have to wake up and talk to your sister-friend. She is flirting with your doctor." Tianna looked at her mother. She comprehended that her mother tried to live a Christian life, but she also recognized she was a woman first. To her knowledge, her mother never participated in an affair, but the doctor was cute and seemed very interested. She recalled how devastated her mother became when she learned of her stepfather's infidelity. Tianna hurt also. They conducted a family conference where he promised never to disrupt the family again. At the time, Tianna had her doubts he would remain faithful, but her mother refused her opinion, stating their marriage belonged to her and Johnny. She prohibited Tianna or her sister's involvement. She reminded them that a grown woman makes her own decisions. She also told them that as long as their stepfather treated them with respect, that should be their only concern. Tianna thought about the differences between her parents. Her mom practiced Christianity, and her stepdad, although he believed in God, never attended church with them, stating churches were scams to take hard working people's money. Tianna loved him, but she secretly wished they both would find other loves.

"Nicke, Tianna is right. You do need to wake up 'cause I'm gonna hurt your niece. She is too grown. You know how you would always say you really birthed her? Well, it's time to take your child back. She thinks I can't admire beauty. Girl, your doctor is fine, and all I've done is appreciate his beauty, in a Christian way, that is." Lyric laughed as she spoke to Nicke as if she was conscience and fully capable of understanding everything going on around her. Lyric tried to deflect Tianna's inquisition. She understood the importance of not being a hypocrite because she had to be a living example to her daughters. She must ensure her lesson was right and godly. As a woman, Lyric comprehended one day that Tianna may find herself in the same situation and would remember the decisions Lyric made.

Tianna decided she should stay out of that part of her mother's life. She wanted so much for her to be happy, and her gut told her she was going through the motions. Her mother taught her happiness was a fleeting moment, and that it was far better to be thankful then happy. "OK, Mom, I'm going to leave you alone about the good doctor." Tianna snickered. "Mom, why don't you go home and get some rest? I'll stay here tonight."

"No, baby, you go home. I did sleep last night and besides, I need to be here. That crazy woman may try to come back again, and you will end up in jail, whereas I'll just call security and have her removed."

Tianna laughed, as she could not avoid getting in one more jab. "You mean you'll call Dr. Jim to come save you." She enjoyed watching her mother squirm.

"No, girl. I'm gonna kick your butt. Keep messing with me." She leaned down as close as she could to Nicke, saying, "I'm telling you, Nicke, you better hurry up and wake up because you are going to be minus a niece or daughter, whatever she is to you." Lyric turned her attention to Tianna as she said, "She's got plenty of jokes."

They both heartily laughed as the tension dissipated from the room.

Tianna decided to take her mother up on leaving the hospital. She figured she would be needed at some point to cover for both Jada and her mother. They all cared deeply for Nicke. Tianna really considered Nicke as her second mother. She was proud of her aunt, as she appeared to have had a hard life. There remained no doubt that Charles molested Jada. Now Tianna wished she had told someone. But the fear of betraying Jada would not allow her to. Looking back, Tianna realized her mother was the source she should have chosen. She thought that perhaps if she did defy her agreement, her auntie may not now be fighting for her life.

Tianna kissed her mother good-bye. "Mom, call me if you need me. I don't care what time. I'll come back. I love you." She kissed Nicke good-bye too.

"Okay, baby. Mommy loves you also. Be careful going home." Lyric watched as her daughter left the room. She thought how thankful she was to have a daughter like Tianna. She might have a fiery temper, but she was also so loving, caring, and compassionate. She smiled at her thoughts.

Lyric turned her attention back to the patient. She wished it were possible to will Nicke to open her eyes, although she believed her friend heard everything. Once she read that if a person was unconscious, you should talk to him or her. The article acknowledged how people who were once in a coma recovered, reporting their awareness even though they could not speak. Believing that, Lyric poured her heart out to her sister-friend. She finally confessed her overhearing Johnny and his girlfriend talking. She admitted being tired of Johnny's trickeries. As she spoke, sadness erupted when laboring about the decision to divorce Johnny. He left her no other choice as Lyric determined not to accept him being with another woman, and she told Nicke so. She also discussed Jim and how she had an attraction to him, but lacked a clear stance. She also admitted he was merely her fantasy. Lyric expressed her fears of being hurt again. While digressing, Lyric studied all the tubes, IVs, and the respirator. She then apologized for selfishly mentioning her problems and ignoring Nicke's battles. She asked Nicke to forgive her for being inconsiderate.

As a peace offering, armed with the joy Nicke received from hearing her sing, Lyric decided to indulge her again. Sometimes Nicke would call and say, "I don't want to talk. I just want you to sing a song for me." She would request every gospel song from Yolanda Adams to Paul Morton. Lyric would comply, even though she was usually too shy to perform in front of people. Nicke would tell her, "Girl, God gave you the voice of an angel. If you don't use your finely tuned instrument he's gonna take your talent back. So I am keeping him from snatching it back."

"Nicke, since you love this song so much, I'm going to sing it for you." Lyric pulled her chair close to Nicke. She laid her forehead on the edge of the bed. Looking at the floor, she cleared her throat in preparation. Her hands were folded, and it appeared she was about to pray rather than sing. Lyric elected a song by Tamala Mann that burned in her soul. Closing her eyes and opening her mouth, she belted out, "Take me to the king. I don't have much to bring. My heart is torn in pieces. It's my offering." Lyric tried to sing softly, but the words resonated so deep inside her that she couldn't help herself. The melodious notes flowed from her, as if she had written the song and was performing for an audience of thousands. Lyric began the verse: "Truth is, I'm tired. Options are few. I'm trying to pray, but where are you? I'm all churched out. Hurt and abused. I can't fake. What's left to do? Truth is, I'm weak. No strength to fly. No tears to cry, even if I try. But still my soul refuses to die. One touch will change my life." Lyric banged her fist on Nicke's bed, fighting to keep her tears from overflowing. She continued to pour every ounce of herself into singing at the top of her voice. As she neared the end of the song, she stood and extended her arms. Her head laid back towards the heavens. Her eyes were shut tight but unable to create a holding place for her tears. The dam broke, and they flowed carefree down her face. "Take me to the king, take me to the king, take me to the king." Each time Lyric repeated, she soared higher to another octave until she reached the top of her range. She started stamping her feet and flinging her arms until ending the song. When she finished, there was a thunderous round of applause. To Lyric's surprise, as she opened her eyes, several nurses, patients, and doctors, including Dr. Maxey, were enjoying her testimony in song. Many had tears running down their faces, as her heartfelt rendition touched them. No one seemed to be concerned that it was 1:00 a.m.

and Lyric's singing woke every patient on the wing. Lyric took a modest bow. An older black woman and obvious patient held on to her IV pole and began to shout. She repeated, "Thank you, Jesus!" Over and over again. One of the nurses acted as if she was a church usher and helped the patient back to her room. Under normal circumstances, Lyric would have been embarrassed as she only sang in front of family and friends, but this time was different. She was humbled that God used her scraps and talent to reach doctors, nurses, and patients. She turned her focus to Nicke. Lyric's heart jumped for joy as she pointed in amazement to Nicke's opened eyes. Lyric shouted, "Dr. Maxey, she's out of her coma!"

Dr. Maxey, still stunned by Lyric's singing, snapped back into his job. He motioned for everyone but Lyric to leave the room. He closed the door and headed towards his patient. He then pulled his stethoscope out and listened to her heart. Nicke began wiggling and thrashing around in the bed. She tried to pull the respirator tube out, but her hands were tied. Dr. Maxey pushed the call button for a nurse. She quickly ran to his side. While continuing to work on Nicke, Dr. Maxey took her blood pressure. He told her to administer 2 ccs of something Lyric couldn't pronounce. He spoke softly to Nicke, telling her he was going to give her something to calm her down. He pleaded with her to try to lay still and assured her when she relaxed, he would remove the tubing.

Lyric sat quietly and observed the hustle and bustle as one nurse would enter, then another. She prayed she did not make things worse. The nurse shot a needle with a clear liquid substance into the IV bag. Nicke's squirming slowed, and she appeared to rest as her eyes began to close. Lyric guessed the doctor ordered some type of sedative. She thought it must be extremely strong because it quickly took effect. Two nurses continued to assist Dr. Maxey, one changing the urine bag and recording the amount of urine, while the other checked all the attached tubes. Dr. Maxey wrote in Nicke's chart. One of the assistants asked the doctor if he needed anything else. Dr. Maxey asked if she would check to see when Nicke could be scheduled to have the respirator removed. He stated that he needed to test if Nicke could breathe on her own with the aid of an oxygen tube in her nose. He ordered the nurse to schedule the procedure at the first available time. Both nurses left the room to complete their assignments.

Lyric remained out of the way, awaiting results of the change in Nicke's condition. She sensed a different vibe coming from Dr. Maxey. He seemed more professional. Lyric admitted she, too, was experiencing a different sensation. Her nerves did not jump at the sight of the doctor as they once did. However, she tried to deny her attraction, but found it difficult to lie to herself.

Dr. Maxey completed his assessment. He sat in the chair beside Lyric and began to discuss his treatment plans and strategies.

Lyric noticed the sparkle vanished. His lips were turned down, and he avoided making eye contact with her.

He said he hoped to have her in surgery by tomorrow morning to remove her tube. "If she tolerates the first surgery, I would then like to prepare her for an additional surgery. We will need to get inside her head and see if there is any neurological damage or any more bleeding vessels. It's a good sign that she is out of the coma. Now we can assess what, if any, damage occurred because of the stroke. So continue praying." He took Lyric's hand, bowing his head, and said another short prayer. He stood to leave. Just before he got to the door, Dr. Maxey turned to face Lyric. "I just want to say you have a beautiful voice. I had no idea. I felt your pain, and I wanted to apologize to both you and God. I'm sorry. You are still a married woman, and I should have respected you nuptials. Please forgive me."

Before Lyric could accept his apology, Dr. Maxey left the room. Lyric knew in her heart that he was right. She thanked God for intervening on her behalf. She, too, asked God for forgiveness. Looking at the clock, she read 2:05 a.m. She thought the hour was too late to phone Jada with the good news. She figured she should let her sleep and call when the time of the surgery was determined. She kissed Nicke on the cheek. Taking a blanket, Lyric crawled up on the hard hospital chair. She leaned it back and propped her feet on the ottoman. It was time to get some rest. She was drained after her performance. She smiled when she thought about how she had an audience and didn't even know it. She made a mental note that when Nicke got well enough, she was going to tell her. Lyric drifted off to sleep.

CHAPTER 10

Journey to Destination

Although life has its own way of beginning and ending,
We control how it is lived.
If we will love or be loved is within our control.
All we must do is let go of our heads and let
our hearts lead the way.
Your pilgrimage may be riddled with
uncertainties and insecurities
But trust what you feel and believe what you see.
Betwixt peaks and valleys
Up mountains and down hills
Expected roadblocks, caution lights,
and even stop signs as your heart steers forward to your destiny,
Continue heading towards that prevailing place.
The pursuit where your head leads is your destination.
How you get there is your journey
Where you will find what your body craves and desires,
Peace of mind reigning supreme.

ARRIVING HOME, DAVID pulled into the garage. While Jada slept, he silently prayed that God would help him to uphold his vow. He struggled to keep his thoughts pure, but something inside of him wanted to take Jada to another place where they could become one. Passion was consuming his mind and body, but he determined he would not curse their relationship. He realized he fell in love with Jada, and if they held out on the sexual part until marriage, God would give them each the desires of their heart. "Jada, baby, wake up. We are home."

Jada stumbled as she exited the car. She liked the sound of David referring to his house as their home. She smiled as she walked into the house but was too tired to respond.

"Would you like something to eat?" David asked.

"No, thanks." Jada surveyed the kitchen and family room. Everything was so neat and decorated with expensive furnishings and accessories. Jada marveled at the similarity of their taste. The only items out of place were toy cars on the oak end tables. She guessed Micah played with them while visiting. "If you don't mind, I need to shower and then go to sleep."

David led Jada to the master bedroom and handed her a set of towels. He returned to the family room to give Jada some privacy. He fought the pictures in his head of Jada's unclothed body as he listened to the water running.

"David," Jada shouted. "Do you have a clean razor?"

David entered the bathroom. He gazed at the silhouette of Jada's body as she took a shower. It almost drove him crazy. He struggled with the urge to join her. He was certain if he did though, their pledge of celibacy would be broken. "Sorry, baby, I broke it while shaving my legs." He nervously chuckled.

"Funny, David," Jada said as she stepped out of the shower.

She wrapped a towel around her body, but not before David took advantage of the opportunity to inspect every inch. He wanted her so badly. He thought, *This is the first person I've ever turned down.* His mind drifted to the night Jada invited him over and she wore a red see-through negligee. Her large, rounded breast filled the cups, overflowing from the top and sides. He visualized everything. He recalled how shocked she appeared when he refused to make love to her. David, using his amateur psychology skills, deducted that because of what Charles did to her at such an early age, Jada thought having sex meant the same as making love. He decided he would show her there is a difference. "Would you mind if I lotion your back?" He asked, then regretted the suggestion immediately.

Jada smiled. "Of course not, sir," she said, laying on her stomach across David's king-sized bed. She unloosened her towel and allowed it to rest under her breasts.

David closed his eyes as he performed an erotic massage to Jada's back, buttocks, legs, and feet. Her skin reminded him of his Kumi Kookoon fine silk shirt. He couldn't help but to admire her beauty as his hands caressed her body. He wanted to make love to her so much he ached. After a moment of reaching anticipated pleasure, he moaned as he handed a large T-shirt to Jada, hence again torturing himself as he stared at Jada's perfectly toned body being engulfed and covered. He again prayed for strength that he would not succumb to his weakened flesh. He kissed Jada goodnight.

Jada rattled from the sensual massage, almost unable to control the dam from breaking. Aware of her purposeful attempt to arouse David, she forgot to consider the impact to her. She closed her eyes, rushing to enter a dream world where she would determine the outcome of their evening spent together. When her head hit the pillow, she entered her dream state.

David lay on top of the comforter, while Jada remained bundled under the covers and peacefully slept. He wrestled to calm down until he gave in to emotional and physical exhaustion and fell asleep.

After awakening, David slowly slid to the edge of the bed. He sat quietly for several minutes, studying Jada as she slept. He wanted to kiss her and hold her tight, but instead, he decided to get up and fix her breakfast.

David washed his face and brushed his teeth. He headed for the kitchen. He put a pot of coffee on and began making grits, eggs, and turkey sausages. Turning the radio to a gospel station, Christian music flowed out and aided him to shake the picture of Jada's body from his memory. While cooking, David drew a comparison between Jada and Candy. Although unable to deny Candy being attractive and sexy, David thought about how her ways, how she acted, and her treatment of other people made her ugly. Jada was indeed the whole package, just as Tianna said. She was beautiful, sexy, and caring. She was a rough but gentle spirit. His only concern with Jada remained her inability to trust him, or any other man for that matter. David wondered how they would climb that mountain. If Candy ever saw just a little bit of Jada's insecurities, she would attempt to capitalize on them. *Candy is reckless*, he thought. *She will lie, steal, or cheat to get what she wants*. The problem is Candy didn't ever want him unless she thought someone else wanted him. She already destroyed two of his past relationships. The first one, David accepted the responsibility of destroying. He fell prey to her ploys to get him back. Once she did, she decided she wanted someone else. The second time, David managed to be better equipped and prepared for her games. She tried everything in the book, until she lied and told Keisha that they were still sleeping together. At first, Keisha did not believe her, but Candy tricked him into coming to her house under the pretense that someone had broken in and she was afraid. When David arrived, the lights were low, soft music played in the background, and Candy greeted him almost naked. She called Keisha, telling her David loved her and was going to break up with her. The next thing he knew, Keisha showed up at Candy's house. Candy answered the door, inviting her in to observe the prearranged love nest. Nothing David said or did convinced Keisha that Candy played them both. David recalled how angry he became with Keisha because she wouldn't believe him. Candy took advantage of the mood and successfully seduced him. Partially because of guilt and because Keisha did not trust him, David broke up with Keisha the next day. This is when he decided to allow God to send him the next woman in his life and promised to remain celibate until he did.

David longed to be a father and a husband and to settle down with one woman. Although Candy provided him entertainment, she clearly did not represent the marrying kind.

David pulled the bed tray from the cupboard. He placed Jada's plate and coffee on it. He searched around for a trinket to adorn the tray. He found a sterling silver cup holder given to him by a coworker. It read: "Today is a new day full of promise and opportunity. Don't be blinded by your past broken promises and missed opportunities. Live in the present." (JJS.) David smiled as he read the inspirational message. He thought how perfect for Jada and how it also served as a reminder to him.

He carried the food into the bedroom. He stopped suddenly. Jada kicked the covers off and her T-shirt was raised, revealing her very round and plump bottom. Her legs were full and beautiful. He loved the way the small tattoo on her upper inner thigh curved around to the back of her leg. Whoever put the tattoo on her body was truly an artist. The vine had one single apple hanging. David cleared his throat, as he thought, *Not today. I will not eat the forbidden fruit.* He sat the tray on the bedside table. Kissing Jada, he said, "Wake up, love. Breakfast is served."

Jada opened her eyes and smiled at David. "Thank you so much." She pulled her T-shirt down, covering the body David had admired. She sat up in the bed and looked the tray over completely. "How sweet of you. How long have you been up? You should have woken me up so I could help. Give me a few. Let me use the restroom, wash my face, and brush my teeth."

David smiled from the pleasure of making Jada smile. "OK, but you better hurry up before your food gets cold."

On her way to the bathroom, Jada asked, "Have you eaten yet?"

"No, I only have one bed tray, so I'm going to eat in the kitchen."

Jada flushed and turned on the water in the sink. "No, sir. Let's eat together. Will you take my tray in the kitchen so I can join you when I complete my business in here? By the time you fix your plate, I will be finished."

David took the tray in the kitchen as Jada's cell phone, which was on the table, rang. He yelled to Jada, "Do you want me to get it or bring it to you?"

Jada yelled back, "Please answer the call. It might be about my mother."

David answered the phone. A recording said, "You have a collect call from an inmate in the Dallas County Correction Center. Will you accept the charges?" David froze for a second. He tried to decide if he should accept it or not. He had no doubt the call came from Charles. He made a hasty decision and decided to accept. "No, Charles, we will not ever accept your calls and don't call Jada again." He immediately ended the call. After hanging up, he wondered if he did the right thing or not. He held the phone in his hand and hoped his decision was correct. Just then, the phone rang again. He didn't even wait for Jada's permission to answer. He answered with a loud, pissed-off voice, "Hello!"

Jada entered the kitchen as he had completed his rude greeting. She gave him a perplexed look. "Who is it?"

"David is that you?" he heard Lyric say.

David, glad to hear Lyric's voice, responded, "Yes, it's me, Lyric. Is everything all right?"

Lyric, still trying to figure out why David answered so mean, said "Yes, everything is fine here. But what's going on there? Things don't sound OK."

David replied, "Oh, I'll tell you later. Let me let you speak to Jada. I know she wants to know how her mom is doing." He handed the phone to Jada, avoiding her confused stare.

"Hey, Auntie. How is Mom?" Jada let out a joyous, "Wow, that's great! What did she say to you? What did Dr. Maxey say?" Jada fired questions at Lyric and did not allow her an opportunity to respond before asking something else.

Jada listened while Lyric told her everything. She added an occasional OK to the conversation. She intently took in Lyric's report. "So what time is her surgery? OK, I am going to get there when I can. I was going to Charles's arraignment today at 9:00. OK. We will come after court is over, and I change clothes. Thanks, Auntie. I love you too. Good-bye."

David understood by the sound of Jada's voice that she had good news. He still considered if he should tell Jada Charles called. David placed his plate on the table and sat down to eat.

Jada said grace. She told David that her mother had regained consciousness and would be going to surgery to take out the breathing tube. She seemed so excited. Her face beamed, and her eyes flickered as she related her mother's progress. She said, "Thank you, Jesus" several times.

David listened to Jada but got caught deep in his own thoughts, so he remained quiet. He wanted to attend the arraignment, but he did not want to bring up Charles's name for fear that Jada would remember she received two calls. He hoped that when Jada found out what he did, she would not be upset with him and understand that he tried to protect her.

"David, do you have any plans for the day?" Jada asked. She wanted him to go with her but did not want to impose because he had supported her for the last couple of days and probably needed to handle his own business. She thought, "*If he can't go, I'll ask Tianna.*"

"In fact I do," David replied. The gleam in Jada's eyes seemed to disappear as he concentrated on the flicker as it dimmed.

"Oh, OK. I understand. I just hope you are aware of how much I appreciate all the time you shared with me. You helped me through some tough times. I am sure I will never be able to repay you."

"Why do you want to know if I have plans?" David enjoyed playing the cat-and-mouse game with Jada. She seemed to always be on guard and so serious most of the time.

"No problem. I'm sure Tianna can go with me."

David put his fork down. He kneeled in front of her and held Jada's face in his hands as his eyes penetrated deep into hers. "She can go with us you mean."

Jada, confused at first, replayed his comments. Unable to hide her excitement, she sprang up, jumping into David's arms. She grabbed his neck, squeezing with all her might. "Thank you, baby. Why are you playing with me?" She was so glad he consented to go. Having him by her side assured her protection, which she understood she needed. She kissed him on his neck.

David's temperature rose, among other things. He lifted her and stood up with Jada's legs wrapped around his waist.

Jada ran her fingers through his hair. David could not control himself any longer. He gave Jada a passionate tongue kiss, causing his knees to buckle as he walked with her and leaned her against the wall.

David glided Jada down his legs to the floor. With all the sincerity he could muster up, he lifted her chin. "Miss Jada, I am in love with you. Don't you get it? *I love you.* Now I need you to understand that I want you so much, so please don't say another word. I have to go take a cold shower. It's getting harder and harder, no pun intended, to resist you. I want you to be clear on my decision. I am not having sex or making love to you not because I don't want you. I choose not to make love to you because I need all of you, and I want God to bless our union." He kissed her on her forehead and headed for the shower, leaving his uneaten food. He realized if he waited another second, they would both be in trouble.

Jada wondered how she got blessed enough to meet David. Never once did she consider she deserved a man that phenomenal. She thought about the tremendous reasons he gave her for fighting to remain celibate. A tinge of guilt jumped out as she considered her attempts to tempt him to change his mind. Now she comprehended the importance of her supporting his decision and electing celibacy also as her choice to preserve their relationship. Although a part of her still failed to trust David completely, she decided to hold back some until Candy dropped out of his heart and life. Nonetheless, she gave thanks to God for his son, Jesus. Through it all, he had never left her. She also offered praise that even if David changed his mind, she knew God would still remain.

Jada continued to read the cup holder David placed on her breakfast tray. She held it to her chest, as if trying to ingrain the words and their meaning deep inside her heart. She grabbed the inspiring cup holder and entered the bedroom to ask David if he intended for her to keep the silver container. It was now her turn. She gasped as she took in David, standing before her naked. She couldn't resist checking him out from head to toe. His body was chiseled to perfection. She believed him to be perfect, but she had no clue just how perfect.

"I am the one that needs a cold shower right now. She rushed past him and shut the dressing room door." She leaned back with her head against the door. "My, my, my," she mumbled to herself, wiping the sweat from her forehead. "David, I love you too," she shouted. *Now I understand and can appreciate what I'm waiting on*, she thought. She giggled as she turned the shower on cool and sensuously washed each part of her body.

David smiled to himself at Jada's reaction. He rushed to get dressed because he did not want to be in the bedroom when Jada finished showering. He opened the dressing room door without even sneaking a peek. He threw Jada's overnight bag in the room, as he was not strong enough for Jada to step out unclothed again. He finished dressing. Stopping, he took a final once-over at himself in the mirror. David studied his black pleated pants, black shoes, and initialed baby blue starched shirt, all created by the designer Giorgio Armani's black label line. He pulled his black blazer over his shoulders. Next, he brushed his jet-black, short, thick, and curly hair until every wave lay in place, creating a water wave pattern he selected. To match his clothing selection, he sprayed on his expensive special occasion Armani Prive Eau de Jade cologne. After taking one final glance, he headed for the kitchen to wait for Jada.

Shortly after, Jada made her grand entrance. She was completely dressed and with every hair in place. David's eyes bucked as he inhaled her beauty. Although he never doubted Jada's body symmetry, today the way her 26-inch waistline accented her wide hips, and the stilettos presented her legs sleek as a gazelle, she enticed him in such a way he wished they were going to court to get married and not to Charles's arraignment. Her body popped in the dark blue A-line dress that molded to every curve. The low cut V-neck line, although revealing was covered with a mesh material that made her breasts seem to play peekaboo. Her face was radiant through the flawless makeup. Her hair was pulled up and combed to the side, with a few ringlet curls hanging. David found it next to impossible to stop gloating. He got up and slowly twirled her around. His eyes soaked in every drop of her exquisite elegance.

"You are beautiful, baby! I'm sorry. I cannot stop staring. I do not want to touch any other water but the one you drink." He spun her around again. His eyes began to water as he realized Jada lacked the awareness of her own beauty. He remembered how quickly she recognized Tianna as being beautiful, but neither Tianna, Lyric, or for that matter, Candy came close to the gorgeous woman standing before him. David blamed Charles for killing her spirit and because of that, his heart ached for her. "Maybe we need to rethink this celibate thing, and go make love, and stay in the bed for the rest of the day."

Jada gave him a playful punch. "Get out of here, man. By the way, you're quite handsome yourself, not to mention the scent of your cologne has me climbing the walls." She noticed his muscular arms, which refused to stay hidden under his shirt. They bulged through despite the shirt's attempt to stand out and say, "look at me. I'm all starched and pressed."

The two of them complemented each other and made for a handsome pair. They exemplified the Will and Jada Pinkett-Smith among couples.

Jada prepared for the women to be envious of the eye candy on her arm. She still did not believe she deserved this man she managed to snag. She thought David's compliments of her were only given as a cursory homage. "We probably should take a change of clothes with us. I also need to stop by my apartment and pick up Micah a few things. We can drop them off after we leave the courthouse."

In David's playful way, he said, "I don't need any clothes." He stuck his chest out and flexed his muscles. "Before we go to the hospital, I can slip into my birthday suit." He laughed as he caught the daggers Jada threw at him with her eyes.

Being quick on her toes, Jada fired at David with what was supposed to be a joke. "I bet Candy would love that."

"Aw, now that is a low blow. You win this round." He dropped his head to avoid Jada's glare. "Hold on, let me get my clothes. I'll be back." Although David understood Jada intended to tease him, he disliked thinking about Candy. He once had much love for her, and if the truth must be told, he finally got over her. Candy sexually whooped him. All she had to do was take him to bed and lay it on him, and he would do whatever she wanted. He despised her ability to control him with sex. He acted so addicted and too weak to resist. He hoped the first time Jada and he made love, she would take him past the moon where Candy left him standing.

"OK, let's go. Your chariot awaits you my lady."

David drove his spotless blue BMW with white interior. The car integrated the couple's attire. As the sleek automobile raced to the courthouse, cutting in and out, it screamed, "I'm bad and my occupants are tougher than me. Look at us." David pulled to the front entrance. He asked Jada, "Do you want to get out, and I'll park?"

"No, I'd better stay with you, so I don't have to beat any of these women off of you." Jada smiled.

"Don't worry, baby. I am all yours." He reached across her to let her out. "I'll be back."

Jada gracefully swung her legs out the car. She winked at David and shut the door. As she exited, an unknown lawyer-type gentlemen going in the building glanced at her. He turned completely around and walked backwards as he fixated on Jada. He stared so hard, he stumbled into the revolving door, almost falling.

Jada giggled at the sight of David watching a man captivated by her appearance. His attention did wonders for her confidence.

He parked his car and headed towards Jada. A woman yelled his name. Turning, he determined that it was Officer Nelson that signaled, as she rushed to catch up to him. They exchanged greetings.

"Is Jada here?" Officer Nelson asked.

David replied, "Yes. She is waiting for me by the front entrance. However, Officer Nelson, before we reach Jada, I want to let you know that Charles called Jada this morning."

She stopped in her tracks. "He did what?"

"You heard me. Jada isn't aware he tried to reach her because I answered her phone. I did accept the collect call from the inmate at Dallas County, but I told him not to call again. I didn't let on he called."

"Good. David, I'm worried about Jada. Charles fits the profile of a deranged man. I think he has lost touch with reality. He believes he is in love with Jada and that she loves him. Please be sure Jada secures a restraining order on him. I'm hoping he won't get bail. If he does, I'm afraid there are going to be some problems."

David mulled over what Officer Nelson told him. He received the same vibe the night he first met Charles. He seemed irate because Jada had male company. He gave him a dirty look that if looks could kill, David would be dead. He realized his mission would be to protect Jada. *Charles will never hurt her again,* he thought.

Officer Nelson and David approached Jada. She appeared surprised by Judith Nelson's presence. She hadn't given any thought as to who might be at the proceedings. All she wanted was to look Charles in his face and hear him plead guilty. Jada noticed from her peripheral vision a sight she had to avoid. She grabbed David by the arm and pulled him away. She gave a quick greeting to Officer Nelson as she hurried to escape from one of her approaching nightmares.

Her sudden exit surprised Officer Nelson. She hoped Jada did not get upset with her for walking with David, but it soon became clear why Jada quickly left. Walking up behind her was Charles's mother and sister. Officer Nelson gave her a stare down, suggesting she better not start anything in here.

Jada and David found courtroom number five. David escorted her to the third row behind the District Attorney. He sat on the end seat with Jada to his right sitting so close to him, they looked like conjoined twins.

Jada surveyed the courtroom, scanning for Charles. Suddenly, her body began to tremble and her stomach decided to perform somersaults as she waited for the proceedings to begin. But even though she was nervous, Jada experienced a sense of safety having David beside her. She squeezed David's hand as he placed his arm around her neck. She held on tight. As she continued to study the room, she zoomed in on Mrs. Smith's eyes. She closed her eyes and rolled them while slowly turning her head away from Jada. She then threw her head up in the air so hard, Jada thought it might snap.

Officer Nelson sat behind Jada and David. She scanned the room as Charles's family took their seats behind the Defense Attorney. She also witnessed the evil eye flashed at Jada. Officer Nelson smiled to herself as she thought how that short, old, prune-faced woman was going to act when she found out her son did indeed impregnate a 14-year-old child, not to mention, his stepdaughter.

The courtroom door on the right of Jada opened. In walked a police officer pulling on the arm of handcuffed and shackled Charles. His long narrow face appeared scruffy and in need of a shave. He was pale as a ghost. His once deep blue eyes appeared almost gray. Jada never noticed how white his skin looked before now. She guessed it was because he had not been able to get his weekly dose from the tanning booth. His straight blonde hair was pulled back in a short ponytail clearly revealing his German descent.

Charles immediately spotted Jada. He stared at her as he walked across the courtroom until he made it to his seat. His glare seemed to penetrate through Jada, as if they were performing an x-ray to visualize the organs under her skin.

Jada turned away to avoid his stare.

David pulled her closer to him. He kept his eyes fixed on Charles, observing the way he watched Jada. He hoped Charles noticed him as he fixated on Jada. He wanted to show Charles that he was not afraid of him. What was more important, he wanted to let Charles know that Jada was his lady. He grit his teeth at Charles, attempting to signal that if he came near Jada, he would have to deal with him.

Officer Nelson monitored everyone. She glimpsed Jada look away to avoid the mean eye David gave Charles and Charles's visual undressing of Jada. The way he gawked at Jada even made her uncomfortable. He seemed as if Jada was his prey, and he considered pouncing on her at any second. Officer Nelson placed her hand on her gun just in case.

Charles's mother left her seat and attempted to approach Charles. The officer intercepted her and told her to immediately return to her seat.

What is he doing with Jada? Charles recognized the man with the woman he loved as being the one that left her apartment when he went to her house to declare his love. He speculated that they were sleeping together. He declared to himself that no other man would have Jada. She belonged to him. First, he needed to get out of jail so he could convince her of the love he held for her and Micah. They were family, and no one would change that.

The bailiff announced, "All rise. The honorable Judge Johnson presides." Everyone stood when the judge entered.

Charles ignored the judge and turned his attention back to Jada. His eyes met David's. The two men exchanged grimace scowls, which required no words. Fortunately for both men, neither of them had guns. They shot "dead man" stares at each other without either of them flinching.

Judge Johnson told all to be seated. He called the *State of Texas vs. Charles Rome Smith*. Charles stood. The judge verified his identity. Charles responded affirmatively. He asked Charles if he had retained counsel. Charles responded that he was not represented. The judge advised him he had a right to an attorney, and if he could not afford one, one would be provided free of charge.

Charles shocked the courtroom when he relayed that he would be representing himself.

Judge Johnson silently read the charges, then asked Charles if he realized there were serious charges being filed against him.

Charles told the judge he was aware of the charges.

The judge, seeking to be sure Charles understood, expressed he could expound on his charges one by one if necessary.

Before answering, Charles turned back to look at Jada again. He said, "Yes, please do," as he continued watching Jada.

Judge Johnson read each charge and its definition.

Officer Nelson quietly exited out the rear door, then reappeared at the same side door Charles had entered from. She handed a note to the bailiff. The bailiff walked the note to Judge Johnson.

Judge Johnson pulled his horn-rimmed glasses down on his nose. He peered over them, frowning as he glanced at the defendant. He then asked Charles to reconsider his request to represent himself. He told him he would appoint an attorney to be sure he understood the consequences of his decision. Judge Johnson again read the charges one at a time. "For the charge of statutory rape, how do you plead?"

Charles cleared his throat and said, "Not guilty."

Judge Johnson then asked, "For the Charge of third degree rape, what is your plea?"

Charles responded, "Not guilty."

Judge Johnson asked, "For the charge of third degree sexual assault, what is your plea?"

Charles looked at Jada as he said, "Not guilty."

Judge Johnson began again. "I have reviewed Mr. Smith's record, and this is the first time he has been in trouble with the law. I also see he works in the United States and owns property in this county. Therefore, I do not see Mr. Smith as being a flight risk. Considering the charges, I am invoking a $50,000 bond. I also am ordering a Full Order of Protection for one Jada Jordan, Micah Jordan, and Nicke Smith, effective immediately. Mr. Smith, this means you are not permitted to have any form of contact with those I previously named. You also are to stay away from the home, business, school, hospital, or any other place these witnesses are known to frequent. There is to be no attempt at contacting them by phone, text, email, or letter. If the order is violated, Texas Police will arrest you and the defendant will be charged with criminal contempt in the first degree, which is an E. Felony for your knowing failure to abide by the rules of this court."

Jada was shocked that her name, Micah, and her mother's name were mentioned by the judge. She had no idea how he learned of her mother being in the hospital, but she was so thankful the order was issued. She recalled the last time Charles attempted to see her and totally lost control because David had been visiting her. She didn't tell Officer Nelson, David, or for that matter, admit to herself until now, but if her mother and Lyric had not come in her apartment when they had, she feared Charles would have raped her. Somewhere inside Jada, she doubted Charles would abide by the Protection Order. She expected, when given the opportunity, he would come looking for her and Micah.

David now understood why Officer Nelson left the courtroom. She requested that the judge issue the Protection Order. He took great delight over the order, but did not believe it would stop Charles. Perhaps it would provide Jada a sense of relief. However, he just could not shake the way Charles looked at Jada. Knowing that Officer Nelson also shared his fears and concerns, to the point she passed the judge a note requesting the Protection Order, left him doubtful. Either way, he resolved he would protect Jada and Micah no matter what.

"Mr. Smith, do you understand the terms of the Protection Order?"

"Judge, I pleaded not guilty, and that's my family."

"Mr. Smith, this is not debatable." In a stern voice, the judge repeated, *"Do you understand* absolutely *no* contact?"

Charles again looked back at Jada with a sly grin, then turned back to the judge. Reluctantly, he said in a low voice, "Yes."

Just like that, the arraignment was over in all of 10 minutes.

Jada and David stood up as Judge Johnson left the courtroom.

David kept his arm around Jada and pulled her closer to him. He did not take his eyes off Charles. Charles appeared possessed by demonic forces. It reminded David of a sharpshooter skilled in precision, aiming his projectile weapon and lining up his target while he waited on the perfect time to fire a shot intended to kill.

He grabbed Jada's hand and pushed his way past Mrs. Smith. He moved quickly because he wanted to get her out of that courtroom before she cried. He read the way she kept blinking; she was fighting to hold the tears back while still trying to keep her head held high. As they brushed past Mrs. Smith, David overheard her say, "I'm going to pay that $50,000 bond right now and get my son out of here. They are treating him like he's some caged animal. They have him shackled like he is a criminal."

At that point, David realized with certainty that he and Jada would have contact with Charles despite the Protection Order. As they walked down the steps, Officer Nelson stood below, obviously waiting on them.

Jada hugged Officer Nelson. "Thank you so much for getting to the Judge."

Officer Nelson carefully addressed Jada's statement, as she considered she may have overstepped her authority. "I did what you and Lyric asked me to do last night." She hesitated before continuing trying to cover herself. In case anyone would ever question why she had the judge place the order versus having Jada go to the police station and file the necessary paperwork, she would say the family requested her intervention. She didn't want to tell Jada it was clear he would be getting out on bond, and if she waited for him to be served with the order, two or three days would have passed. "You all said last night when Charles's mother came to the hospital that you wanted to limit visits with Nicke. So I carried out your request by adding you and Micah to the protection order. I thought I heard you make the request."

David knew immediately what Officer Nelson was trying to say. He attempted to help her out. "Jada, when Officer Nelson and I met in the parking lot, I told her the family requested a no-contact order." He looked at Judith as if to say, "Don't worry. I'll tell everyone the family requested protection."

She sighed a sense of relief for the assistance David offered. She did not want to alarm Jada but felt she had to do all she could to prepare her. In her career, she was exposed to many people like Charles, and most of them had no respect for a restraining order. Several of the cases did not turn out well for the victims. "Jada, listen, I've been doing my job for over 20 years. I have seen many similar cases to yours. Please be very careful. Under no circumstances should you ever allow Charles near you. It's my opinion he has some serious mental issues and cannot be trusted. Please be extremely careful and avoid him at all costs."

Jada soaked in everything she said. She realized Officer Nelson was correct, but did not want to alarm her or David by telling them just how scared she really was of Charles. "Thank you. I will be careful." She tried not to exhibit her fear.

Wanting to be certain Jada understood how dangerous she considered Charles, she continued her instructions. "I would recommend you not go anywhere alone, check in often with someone to let the person know where you are, and if you can, you should consider sending Micah out of town."

David felt Jada buckle as she almost collapsed when Officer Nelson spoke of Micah. Her body shook, and no matter how hard she tried to act brave, he held her fears in his arms.

Officer Nelson continued. "I see you have an iPhone, so be sure to turn your location finder button on and share your iTunes password with someone. I apologize. I don't mean to scare you. I hope Charles will follow the order, but in case he doesn't, I don't want you to be tricked or deceived by him. Besides, I promised Lyric I would watch out for you." Officer Nelson handed both Jada and David her business card. "Call me anytime."

David gave her his contact information. "If you need me or Jada, also feel free to call me no matter the time, day or night."

Officer Nelson nodded in agreement. Slowly, she walked away from the couple, hoping they would be careful as instructed.

David opened the car door for Jada and helped her inside. As he walked around to his side of the car, he made a life-changing decision. He got in the car and sorted out how he would execute his plan. Both he and Jada were quiet all the way to her apartment. David parked the car and guided Jada inside her apartment.

"Hey, pack enough clothes for both you and Micah. I want you to stay at my house. Don't worry, I'll sleep in the guest room." He pinched her butt, trying to lighten her mood.

A half smile came across Jada's face. She thought her staying with David would be a great idea, but she didn't want Micah to be there. Charles knew the location of his day care program, and she was more fearful for Micah than herself. "I think I'm going to ask Tasha if Micah can continue to stay with her. She's a teacher and is home for the summer with her children. Between her mom, Lyric, and Tianna, they will also help out to keep him from being a burden. Charles does not know where she lives."

David sighed without commenting because he hoped they would all be together as a family, but he had to agree that sounded like a better suggestion. They packed three suitcases for Jada and one large bag for Micah. David took the bags to the car.

"You got everything, baby? The suitcases are in my trunk. David searched around Jada's apartment to be sure she had everything. He slipped in her bedroom, opening the top drawer of her jewelry box. He secretly secured the item he wanted and slid it in his pocket.

"David I'll be right there I am getting my laptop and iPad, as I plan on doing some work while at the hospital."

They headed down the stairs. "Jada, why don't you go over to Tasha's and visit with Micah? I'm sure he has missed you. I have several errands to run. We can meet at my house in a few hours.

I've got to stop by the office and pick up some work. I'll hurry to finish. You should drive my car so you will be able to use the garage door opener to enter the house. The security code is 6131. I'll call you when I'm on my way. Don't change clothes because as fine as you are, I would be honored to take you out for a late lunch. After that, we can go to the hospital to visit your mom."

"Sounds like a plan to me." Jada handed David the keys to her 2012 Nissan Maxima. She laughed as she said, "A new BMW for an old Nissan. Hell yeah." She kissed David and pulled away. Jada found it hard to believe the amount of support David gave her. She thought about how he held her in the courtroom and the security and safety his presence provided. She realized the last time she had a real boyfriend happened at 12 years old. After Charles, Jada did not consider herself worthy of having any steady relationship. She participated, however, in many one, two, or sometimes three night stands. She avoided commitment because of being unable to trust men, but somehow David seemed different. He wanted her for her. She smiled thinking about him and reached for her cell phone. She noticed two voicemails. She listened to the first message. Her Aunt Lyric relayed Nicke's surgery for her mom had been moved up to 8:00 a.m. and only lasted 30 minutes. The removal of the respirator proved successful and her mother did tolerate the nose oxygen tube. Lyric also told her Dr. Maxey expressed being pleased with her progress. She said Nicke was fading in and out of consciousness, but only because of the anesthesia and not the coma. Jada praised Jesus repeatedly. She next listened to the second voicemail. No one said anything. The person held the phone line without speaking until the line finally disconnected. Jada wondered who called and failed to leave a message but dismissed it as a possible wrong number. She pulled into Tasha's driveway. She could not wait to hug Micah. She missed him so much.

Pleased Jada had not suspected anything and agreed with how he planned to steal away from her, David started to lay out everything he needed to accomplish. He had a lot to do, and a short time to complete it all. He strategized. First, he would go to the hardware store and have the key to his house copied. He would have it gift wrapped in a small box with a bow. The second stop was the jewelry store to buy an engagement ring and a memento for Micah. He determined that the engagement ring set for Jada must be beautiful and whatever he got Micah needed to symbolize them becoming a family. He borrowed a piece of jewelry from Jada's apartment so the jeweler would be able to determine her ring size. Next, he would head to the florist and buy two-dozen roses for Nicke. He would then stop by the liquor store and purchase a bottle of Dom Perignon champagne. His final place would be the bookstore. He wanted to buy matching Bibles for the three of them, symbolizing God as the head of their family. As David continued planning the necessary stops, he expressed thanks for meeting Jada. He had no doubt about her being his gift from God. He refused to allow anyone to interfere in his or her relationship, including Candy and Charles. He thought about how quickly they fell in love. Although their dating time consisted of only six months, David found the only woman meant for him.

Finally, he completed all his errands. He checked the clock and realized that instead of two hours, it had taken him four. He spent most of his time trying to pick out the perfect ring. He had a surfeit of styles to choose from. He narrowed them down to two; a three-caret princess cut with a platinum band or a unique 2.5-caret Asher cut brilliant pink diamond also with a platinum band. David chose the pink stone ring because it seemed to represent Jada as different and a beauty he never witnessed before. He hoped Jada would approve. He found one silver and one gold pendent, which he decided to have both engraved and placed on chains. One said, "God made you for me" and the other one for Micah read, "God made me out of love." David paid extra to have the engraved pendants ready later that day by 8:00 p.m., which meant he would have to leave the hospital early and must arrive before store closing time of 9:00 p.m.

Knowing he missed lunch because of the time, he had to make another plan on how to ask Jada's hand in marriage. He settled on waiting until they found themselves home alone. He planned to take Jada's Bible, the small wrapped box with the house key, and Nicke's roses into the hospital. He would leave the necklaces, Micah's Bible, and Jada's engagement ring in the car.

After completing his shopping, David dialed Jada's phone. "Hey, babe. I'm sorry about lunch. I tried to catch up on some things, and time slipped away from me.

"That's OK,. I'm leaving your house now. I ran in to get my phone's wall charger and thought I would head straight to the hospital. Aunt Lyric called and says mom is talking. I'm trying to make my way soon."

"OK, I am at the exit for Baylor hospital, so I'll just meet you there. Do you want me to wait in the parking lot for you?"

"No, babe. Go on in, and I'll call you when I arrive." Jada's excitement about her mother's ability to speak hindered her concerns about Charles's whereabouts. All her thoughts centered on getting to her mother.

As David drove, he rehearsed proposing to Jada. His heart raced as he planned his speech. He pictured Jada accepting and her happy tears falling. But first, he decided to practice how to secure Nicke's permission and blessings. He hoped she would not think they rushed their relationship. He pulled in the parking space and headed, almost skipping for joy, to visit Nicke.

Lyric had stayed with Nicke. She thought that when Jada arrived, she would step outside and call Johnny. He did not call her all day nor had she phoned him. She figured they needed to talk. She surmised that by now, he had received the divorce papers.

Dr. Maxey entered his favorite patient's room and interrupted her thoughts. She smiled as her form of greeting him.

He returned her acknowledgement in a similar fashion. He struggled with trying to get Lyric off his mind, particularly after they shared coffee together. He tried to stop thinking about her singing and how her rendition rattled his bones. Her hurt flooded through her testimony, making him want to save her. He continually prayed all night, asking God to remove the thoughts of her. His knowledge of the Bible assured him that thou shall not desire his neighbor's wife nor covet thy neighbor's house. After last night, he wanted both. He always fought to walk a Christian life. But Lyric caused him to continually ask God's assistance. Taking a deep breath, he walked closer to Lyric and asked her how his patient was doing.

Lyric avoided eye contact with him as she answered, "Nicke's progress is a miracle."

Deciding to find out for himself, Dr. Maxey stepped to Nicke's bedside. "Nicke, how are you doing today?"

Nicke opened her eyes and whispered, "I'm doing well, Doc." She looked at Lyric, and in the way only Nicke could do, she threw wood in the fire. "Girl, he is fine. Lyric don't be a fool and let him get away."

Both Dr. Maxey and Lyric blushed. Neither of them said anything for a few seconds. Lyric gave Nicke the evil eye, showing her embarrassment.

Dr. Maxey leaned down to Nicke's ear and, in a low voice, announced, "I wish I had met her a long time ago. If she sung to me like she did for you, we would be married with ten babies." He chuckled as if joking, but he meant every word he said.

Nicke whispered back, "She's a good woman and there is no better friend in the world." Nicke closed her eyes and went back to sleep.

The door opened and in walked David. He carried a beautiful bouquet of two-dozen red long-stemmed roses. They appeared slightly open but stood strong and mighty in the green ceramic vase. He greeted Lyric and Dr. Maxey. He approached Nicke's bedside, setting the flowers on the windowsill and a gift bag by her closet. He sat on the side of the bed.

Lyric and Dr. Maxey stepped out of the room to allow David some one-on-one time with Nicke.

Nicke opened her eyes and looked deeply into David's. She flashed a glance to the vase of roses decorating her windowsill. Even though she had never seen David before, she seemed to recognize him. She reached for his hand and smiled. Whispering, she managed to say, "Thank you for the roses and for helping my family." Nicke confirmed by her response that even though she had been in a coma, she had an awareness of both David and Jada's presence.

She must have heard me pray for her, or perhaps talking to Jada, and recognized my voice, David thought. Although not sure how, his heart sang a song of thanks. "No, thank you, Mrs. Smith, for having such a wonderful daughter. I love her and Micah very much."

Nicke smiled. "Please take good care of them. Jada has been through a lot." Nicke forced the words out. Her throat hurt from the respirator tube. She could not speak above a whisper.

"I plan to support them for the rest of our lives. David took a deep breath, then continued. "May I have your permission to ask your daughter to marry me? I know it's only been a short while since we've known each other, but I love them both." David fought the tears back as he had made his intentions official by asking Jada's mother. Although certain he loved Jada and wanted to be with her, his nerves reminded him marriage is forever.

Nicke's heart danced. She nodded, affirming to both her and David; the time had come for her to turn her daughter over to a man who professed to love her. Something inside told her that Jada and David would be happy. She wished her eyes would remain open, and she could continue talking to David, but her eyelids felt like someone placed a ton of bricks on them. She could no longer fight the weight.

David thanked God for his blessings. Candy never made his heart jump as Jada, without trying, did. He pegged Candy as a self-centered person and a taker. Only one concern remained with him when he thought of Candy: the way his mind would drift back to them making love. It seemed as if she haunted him with her body. Even now as he sat in the hospital room with Jada's mother, having just asked her permission to marry her daughter, he failed to shake the memories of Candy. He asked God to remove this picture from his life. He secretly hoped once he and Jada were married and made love for the first time, these thoughts would flee, never to return again. David snapped out of his trance. *Get thee behind me, Satan. I am sure this is you. I will remain celibate*, he thought. David retrieved his phone and called Jada. He thought she should have made it to the hospital by now.

"Hi, baby, I'm sure you are wondering where I am. I hope to be there in about five minutes," he heard Jada say, even though she exaggerated and was at least twenty minutes away.

"I'm glad because I started to worry."

"David, I appreciate your concern, but I am fine. I decided to change my clothes, and then I had to stop back by my apartment because I left all my makeup. From there, I went by your house and retrieved my phone wall charger. I'll be there in a few. How's mom doing?"

"Jada, she talked to me. Don't ask me how but she recognized me," he said excitedly.

"That is wonderful. I will be there soon. Got to run, so I can hurry up. I can't wait."

"Be careful, baby. I love you." David ended their call.

Smiling and looking forward to hearing her mother speak, Jada longed to introduce her to David. She would love David as she did, she thought. Jada's excitement rose as she entered the freeway. She exceeded the speed limit, attempting to cut down on the time it took to reach the hospital parking lot. As she finally turned in, a blue pickup truck sped through the lot in front of her and cut her off, causing Jada to apply her brakes and squeal to a sudden stop. Her hands shook as she realized she just missed hitting the truck. She turned her head left then right repeatedly, as fear of almost having an accident combined with the blue pickup truck, which resembled Charles's, caused her to experience a panic attack. The dark black window tint in the truck made it impossible to identify the driver. Jada began to shake violently and sat frozen, stopped in the middle of the street. Someone behind her started blaring his or her horn for her to move. Jada glanced in the rearview mirror and noticed an old woman in a white Cadillac making hand gestures for her to move out of her way. Jada continued and pulled forward into a parking space near the hospital entrance door. She celebrated the space for being close to her destination. Jada sat in the car to try to collect her nerves. She surveyed the area, looking for the blue truck. She strained her head trying to search as much of the lot as possible. Jada's body still would not stop trembling. She tried to calm herself down. She took deep breaths; inhaling deeply in and exhaling slowly out. As she gathered control, she picked her phone up to call David. Just as the phone dialed, it disconnected. "Damn, my battery is dead. I forgot to charge my phone," she said out loud. Jada sat in the car, looking at every vehicle entering or exiting the parking lot. Talking to herself, she said, "OK, Jada, get it together, and go see your mom. You are in Texas. How many fools here have blue Ford pickup trucks?" She answered herself. "Too many. Besides, you are in David's car. Even if it were Charles, he would not be familiar with his car." Jada quickly exited. She hit the lock on the remote while continuing to search her surroundings, looking for Charles. She put her power walk on that amounted to almost a gallop. Once reaching the automatic hospital door, it opened, inviting her in and provided her a sense of safety. Jada relaxed as she stepped into the elevator and pushed her floor's button. After all, she was about to have a conversation with her mother—the first one in what seemed like years, she thought. Her excitement coupled with her fear caused her emotions to make their entrance as a rapid heartbeat and a perspiring forehead. She attempted to freshen herself up with her hands as she caught a glimpse of her reflection in the bronze elevator door. As Jada tried to make herself presentable, the door slowly reopened. Jada took a deep breath as she waited to see who was going to enter. She had an uneasy feeling. She clutched her purse close. Her eyes darted left then right, trying to identify who would be joining her. She waited, but no one entered the elevator. The door slowly began to close again when suddenly a white male's arm entered the door, causing them to reopen. Jada backed into the rear corner. She began to hyperventilate. As the doors opened, standing before Jada was a tall, stocky white man. Jada exhaled a sigh of relieve when she realized he was a stranger. What is more important, the man was not Charles. She guessed the reason for him spooking her came from the sight of the blue truck in the parking lot. "Get yourself together, Jada," she said to herself. She arrived at her floor and almost ran out. She rushed to make it to her mother. She knew on the other side of the door in hospital room 7-623 would be the security of her mother and her number one man, David.

"Hey," David greeted her as he rushed towards her. I tried to call you, but your phone kept going to voicemail.

Jada fell into his arms. Out of breath, she said, "Hi, baby. I'm sorry. My phone is just about dead."

David felt her shaking in his arms. He pushed her back so he could see her face. "Are you OK? You're trembling."

"I'm fine. I rushed to get in to see mom." She glanced at her mother sleeping. She broke loose from David's grip and ran to her mother. "Mom, it's me, Jada."

Nicke opened her eyes, and the sight of Jada caused her to beam, lighting her entire face. The glow brightened the room. She smiled and pulled Jada down on her. Jada's face laid next to hers. "Hi, my baby girl," she whispered in Jada's ear. "Mommy loves you. I always have and I always will." Her body wiggled and jumped in the bed from the excitement of Jada's presence, as if she were a child at Christmas overwhelmed by their gifts under the tree.

Jada did not move off her mother. Her tears soaked the sheets of Nicke's bed. Her prayer was that God would allow her to again hear her mother call her "baby girl." Jada's prayers were answered. She cried so hard she began to choke on gratitude. Her mother adding that she loved her always had and always would put the icing on the cake. Afraid her mother might die and she would never hear those words again caused Jada to loudly bawl. The sobs penetrated into every cell of her body. Only one task remained for Jada. "Mom, I'm sorry for all the hurtful things I said and did. Please forgive me."

With the last ounce of remaining strength, Nicke whispered, "Nothing to forgive. Just be happy, baby girl. Please forgive me for hurting you," she said, before falling asleep.

Jada lay there for several minutes. She then walked over to David and kissed him ever so slightly on his lips while using her fingers to wipe the tear from his face. "Who are the roses from?"

Through all the emotional pain David witnessed, nothing moved him more than the scene of the mother and daughter's love he witnessed. For the first time in many years, David wished for his mother. To avoid the pain of his absent mother, David shut the door on his pain to answer Jada's question. "I guess a secret admirer of your mother's brought her flowers."

Jada's face changed from happy and relaxed to tense and scared.

David immediately knew what she thought and quickly added, "The admirer of your mother also loves her daughter."

Jada melted with a sense of relief. "Would my mom's admirer be named David?"

"I'll never tell," David jokingly said.

"I guess Aunt Lyric went home, huh? Jada asked.

"No. She and the good doctor stepped out of the room to allow me and your mom some time alone."

"Oh yeah. So what did you and my mom talk about?"

"Just some things between her and me." David grinned like a fox as his eyebrows arched upward.

As Jada continued to needle David for additional information on his conversation with her mother, in walked jovial Tianna.

"What's up, lovebirds? You two need to get a room and stop this X-rated stuff in front of my auntie." Tianna wore black leggings and a multicolored scoop-necked top. She portrayed a sexy woman every man had trouble resisting. Her personality shined bright as the sun. "Guess I missed my mom," Tianna said as she hugged Jada.

"Hey, sister-cuz. Calm yourself. Your mom is still here. She stepped out the room for a few." Jada looked at David as if being careful to cover for her auntie.

David smiled, recognizing how Jada failed to mention Lyric left with Dr. Maxey. "Hey, Tianna."

Tianna acknowledged David with a nod as she made her way to Nicke. She kissed Nicke on the cheek.

"Auntie, your real daughter is here now," she joked. They enjoyed playing the "your mother is my mother" game.

David glanced at his watch and verified the time as 7:30. His heart rate increased as he remembered he had to pick up Jada and Micah's gift by 8:00, but definitely before the store closed at 9:00 p.m. "Baby, I think I'll leave you two ladies to battle over who belongs to Nicke. I have a few errands remaining, plus I need to rest up for tomorrow. I'm going back to work and must prepare."

Jada studied David. She hoped he would spend one more night, but she understood he had a job. She needed to protect her mother in case Charles showed up. She reluctantly agreed. "I understand, baby, but I want to stay with Mom tonight."

David hesitated because he had planned to ask her to marry him over a romantic dinner since their lunch date did not work. "OK, baby. I thought I would rush home to make you a late night meal. Maybe you can come home early tomorrow, and we eat breakfast together before I go to work."

Aware of the disappointment in David's eyes, Jada weighed her decision. She thought of how commendable it was for him to be so understanding and accommodating.

"Jada, I can stay with Aunt Nicke. I brought my laptop with me, planning to work from here. Why don't you go home with David? Both you and my mom need some rest."

Jada thought about Tianna's offer, but the instinct to protect her mother weighed heavy on her heart. She just couldn't shake the feeling. "Cuz, thanks, but I want to be here at least tonight."

Tianna sensed Jada already made her mind up, so to argue the point would be futile. She, too, understood Jada wanting to be with her mother since Nicke's recovery from the coma. "All right, I'll prepare to stay tomorrow night."

Before Jada responded, the door opened, and Lyric and Dr. Maxey appeared. Jada's interest changed to viewing Tianna's expression. She seemed to show disapproval of the doctor spending so much time with her mother.

"Oh, there you are. I thought you went home, but I guess you and the good doctor had things to talk about." She glared at Dr. Maxey.

Lyric, not quite impressed with Tianna's sarcasm, thought she disrespected both her and Dr. Maxey. She did not appreciate the way she assumed that something existed between them other than friendship, especially since both she and Dr. Maxey discussed how their belief in God would not allow either of them to cross the line. "The last time I checked, my birth certificate read grown woman. I'm married, and Jim is well aware of the fact. He respects me and my marriage, which is more than I can say for my daughter."

Tianna, embarrassed by her mother scolding her in front of everyone, had to admit she got what she deserved. She realized her mother would not permit another man to cause her to break her vows to God. This included her father and all his shenanigans he pulled on her throughout the years. She secretly hoped her mother would get tired of him and find her own happiness. "Mom, you're right. I'm sorry to both you and Dr. Maxey. I was trying to be a comedian, but I guess I crossed the line." She kissed Lyric. "Do you forgive me?"

Lyric felt a little guilty for making such a big deal of Tianna's comments. She understood what Tianna really wanted to know was why she and Jim spent so much time together. She wished she did not make her comments in front of Jim and David. "I accept your apology and your concern." She smiled at Tianna.

Dr. Maxey seemed impressed by Lyric protecting both his and her own reputation. He, too, did not like the assumption that he was some type of player. He loved God and wanted his light to shine so all knew and respected that. "Tianna, no need to apologize to me. Lyric is beautiful, and I understand you protecting your father's interest. You were just being a daughter, but your mom is right. We have to live by example so we can bring others to God." He turned to Jada. "How do you think my patient is doing?"

Jada turned to her mother, relieved Doctor Maxey broke the tension in the room. Looking at David, she threw her sly comment directed to him and their prior conversation: "She's doing wonderful! She shared with me and separately discussed some unknown things with David."

David smiled. "Hey, everyone, I'm going to go now. I have some other important things that also need my attention," he fired at Jada, as he threw the curve ball back. He held his hand out as he headed towards the door. "Baby, walk me to the elevator, please. I might give you a hint about my conversation with your mother."

Jada, without saying a word, obliged him. "So give me a hint."

"Sorry, baby, I don't have time. I may tell you in the morning."

He seems to be in a hurry, she thought. She headed to the elevator and kissed him. "Stay out of trouble."

"OK, I will, but be sure to call me before you come home. I'll see you in the morning." David hastily stepped on the elevator.

Jada waited until the door closed. She headed back to her mother's room. Letting out a deep sigh, she wished she could go home with him, but her place was with her mother. An uneasy thought would not allow her to relax, as there seemed as if David had something else going on. She was not sure if David's secret was good or bad, but she realized it was something. Jada learned to read him in their short time together, and he obviously was hiding more than his conversation with her mother.

CHAPTER 11

Delusions of Love

Delusions of love
Plague my mind
I need you
I want you
I got to have you
No one can take you
I'm the one for you
These thoughts attack me

Delusions of love
Plague my mind
You want me
You need me
You got to have me
You're the one for me
These thoughts consume me

Delusions of love
Plague my mind
Please need me
Please want me
Please don't go

Please be the one for me
These thoughts destroy me

Delusions of love
Plague my mind
A belief that is not true
A false idea
A persistent psychotic belief
A belief caused by mental illness
An abnormal state marked by such beliefs
These thoughts are reality
Realities of love
Love is kind
Love is good
Love protects
Love gives
Love does not purposely hurt
Realities of love
Come from the heart not your mind.

DRIVING DOWN THE road at a high rate of speed in his blue Ford pickup truck, thoughts jetted in and out of his mind. Charles gloated about being released from jail. He vowed to never return to that zoo again. He faulted Nicke for him being in jail. She called the police on him. *She's mad because I didn't want her. I love Jada and my son. She is mine, and I am sure with her mother out of our lives, she will also want me. Nicke is standing in the way of our happiness,* he thought. *Jada does not want that man she brought to court. He couldn't love her the way I can and do. I'm making a beeline to the hospital and waiting for Jada. Ain't a judge in this world going to tell me I can't be with my family. Besides, I will die before I allow them to put me back in that hellhole. Those men are all gay. They tried to do to me what* *my uncle did, but I swore to kill any man before I let one take me again. I'm gonna make Nicke pay because she is trying to ruin my life. She is jealous. She probably introduced her to that man so we would not be together. How could Jada allow anyone else to touch her? I am her first, and the only one for her.* Charles picked up his phone and dialed Jada. After the first ring, her melodious voice sang through.

"I love you, David. My phone is about to die again, so talk quickly."

Charles, stunned by Jada's comments, refused to believe Jada said she loved someone named David. He pictured all the times they made love. He reminisced how she laid quietly and enjoyed him as much as he delighted in her. He recalled her tight insides and her crying tears of pleasure. Now some other person was getting off with her. Oh no. He will never allow him to touch her again. "Jada, if I can't have you, *no one* will!" he shouted.

Charles listened to the dial tone, angered that Jada would hang up on him. Infuriated, he punched the gas pedal and sped through a red light. He hit his brakes, skidding to avoid an oncoming car. "Get out of my way fool!" he hollered as he laid on his horn. *I'll get Jada and Nicke. They are responsible for putting me in jail. So both of them are going to pay,* he thought. While banging his hands on the steering wheel, he looked at the clock and estimated he would arrive at the hospital in less than thirty minutes. *They will not treat me like I am some old dog. After all I did for them, and this is the way they repay me,* he thought.

***

David, thinking of his surprise for Jada, laughed. He realized she suspected something and probably thought he was up to no good. *She will be surprised when she finds out what I've planned,* he thought.

The elevator stopped on the fourth floor and interrupted his thoughts.

In walked his past. Standing before him was Candy. She had scrubs on, with a stethoscope hanging around her neck, an overnight bag in one hand, and her keys in the other.

When she recognized David, she grinned. "Hello, Dave. You were the last person I expected to meet in the elevator," she said, as she glanced around, noticing his sidekick was missing. She hoped for an opportunity to catch him by himself, convinced that if they had a conversation, the realization of how much he loved her would sink in, and he'd come back to her.

David slid to the rear corner, uncomfortable being alone with Candy. He worried about the constant tricks she enjoyed playing on him. He recalled once when she pushed up on him, how weak and hopeless he felt to her advances. He decided this time to be strong and resist any temptation she threw his way. "Hello, Candy," he said, implementing his nonchalant attitude and voice.

"Where's your lady friend?" Candy asked, trying to mask the joy of seeing him without her.

"She's spending the night here at the hospital with her mother. Why?"

"Because, Dave, I need to talk to you. Can we go around the corner to the Coffee House? I want to discuss something with you."

David sighed a sense of relief, knowing his tight schedule would preclude him from joining her. "Sorry, there is no time. I must get to the mall before closing."

Trying to think fast and offer David a solution, she decided, "No problem. I don't mind following you, and we can grab something from the food court." Candy pushed diligently to prevent this chance from slipping through her fingers. She stepped closer to David, making sure her breasts rested on his arm. Aware that Dave found resisting her impossible, she pushed her body closer to him. Candy checked his crotch for a response from his nature, as she noticed her secret powers over him. Just as she thought, her friend disconnected from his brain and gave her a hearty welcome back.

David tried hard to avoid Candy, but somehow she always managed to arouse something in him no other woman could successfully awaken. He pictured Jada in his mind to fight her attacks as he moved away from her body, which she strategically placed on him.

Perceptive of David's attempts to negate her advances, Candy realized a more aggressive approach was necessary. She rubbed his nature in her hand, as she rubbed her body against him. She was aware David was desperately fighting the sexual effect she had on him and now became more determined to win the battle.

David jumped, pushing her away. "Get off of me!" he shouted as the door opened to the lobby.

Still, Candy was adamant. She meant to not be deterred. Dave was her man and always would be. She thought about his whimpers of ecstasy and her self-assurance in having this type of control over him.

"Please, Candy, I can't deny how satisfying you once seemed to me, but there is more to life and me than sex. Jada is the entire package. She understands and respects me for the man God created me to become. I will do nothing to hurt her or destroy the faith she has emotionally invested in me, including sleeping with you. I love her, so no, you cannot go to the mall with me. I'm picking up her engagement ring and plan to ask for her hand in marriage." David, aware he lied about the reason he had to go to the store, excused himself as he partially told the truth. He tried to avoid telling her he needed to pickup pendants for fear Candy might not understand the magnitude of his love for Jada. So instead, he embellished, changing an engagement ring for pendants.

The marriage bomb thrown by David dropped and landed square on Candy. She stopped walking and stood dead in her tracks. She gasped for air and fell against the wall as she battled to absorb her Dave marrying another woman. After all, he'd only known her for a few months, and she had been with him off and on for several years. Never once did he consider matrimony with her. Candy battled the defeatist attitude, which tried to sneak in her head because something inside of her heart rejected the spirit of surrender. She rushed to catch up to David, who appeared to be leaving her behind. She realized that if she did not move fast, her Dave would vanish out of sight and reach. She snatched his shoulder, forcing him to stop walking, and said, "Dave, I'm in love with you. I'm sorry I didn't know the correct way to treat you. I played games with you, trying to make you jealous so you would realize how much you loved me. I hoped you would fight to prove my importance in your life. To me, I became your pleasure toy; otherwise, why did you take me back no matter how I hurt you?" Candy hung her head as tears rolled down her face. "I wanted you for *my* husband!" She spoke with conviction. Her gut hollered that she must do all she could now or never. She was not sure how, but she had to fight to get the only man that ever truly loved her back. She waited, staring into his eyes as her tears continued to roll.

David, shocked by Candy's confession, admitted he wanted her to be this real with him before now. He thought about the number of times he begged Candy to stop hiding from him. No matter how he tried to pull out her feelings, she never said she loved him. David's anger overflowed. "Why, Candy. Why now? Do you have any idea how long I waited for you to say you loved me? Are you just trying to get me to break up with Jada so you can play your crazy games again?"

"No, Dave, this is not about her. When we were together, all I ever thought you wanted or expected from me was sex. You allowed me to treat you bad as long as I continued our sexual escapades." Candy realized this was probably the first time she was being honest with Dave or herself. She placed her hand on her forehead to keep her brain from exploding. Her truth shocked even her.

David decided at that moment that he might not be ready to ask Jada to spend her life with him. He needed time to be sure his love for Candy did indeed die. The doubts about his and Jada's relationship crept inside of him. He worried because he already asked Nicke's permission to marry her daughter, and she gave him her blessing. Confusion set in, confirming his desire to immediately get away from Candy. Without additional pressure, he needed to sort his emotions out and pray for guidance. Jada deserved a man certain of his love for her, and right now he lacked good judgment. He turned and literally sprinted to the parking lot to get away from Candy. He jumped into Jada's car and sat for a few seconds. He contemplated his options. After starting the car, he saw the time was 8:30. The store was at least twenty minutes from the hospital. He wondered if he might get there before they closed. He decided to try, but if he failed, he thought it might be a sign, and he may have found his answer to the dilemma between Jada and Candy.

Candy tried to fathom why David ran from her. She realized if David proposed to that girl, Jada, she did not stand a chance of reconnecting with Dave. She discerned a scheme of marriage prevention would be necessary, and she had to develop and implement the plan quickly before it was too late. As she walked to her candy red Mercedes SLK sports car, inspiration struck— one she was certain Dave would not be able to resist. He would not be able to deny his love for her and would have no choice but to admit that girl, Jada, was not his Candy. She believed her plan guaranteed the results she sought and thought to be foolproof. Words of wisdom from her mother came to her remembrance. She told Candy, "Work what you got to get what you want." Candy slowly wiggled her curvaceous body while gliding her hand from her breast to her knees. Happy, she successfully devised a strategy to steal Dave back, Candy thumped the hood of her car as she set out to implement her plan. She smiled as she slid into her car preparing to recapture her man.

David, relieved he had gotten away from Candy, stopped at the light exiting the hospital when a blue Ford pickup squealed around the corner, almost hitting him. The truck made a U-turn. David thought that fool must be drunk as he sped, heading towards the mall. He entered the entrance ramp to highway 635, hoping neither construction nor traffic caused him any delays. David's journey to the mall and his new life began. He wanted with all his heart to arrive at the store before closing. He drove seventy miles per hour down the freeway until he approached his exit to the Galleria. Glancing at the time, David realized he had ten minutes to park and get inside. To accomplish this task, was going to be close to impossible. To save precious moments, he chose valet parking. Handing the attendant a fresh 20-dollar bill, he yelled, "I'll be right back." He ran around the rear of the car and almost got hit by a pickup truck, which pulled in behind him. David jumped out of the way, but did not bother to look up at the driver. He raced down the hall to the jewelry store. Just as he approached, the clerk slid the bars closed.

"Sir," he shouted, out of breath. "I need to pick up an item that I had engraved earlier."

The sales representative recognized David. "You just got here before I locked down for the night." He let David in the store and closed the security doors behind them. He told David the cash register had been tallied out.

Still panting, David managed to get out, "I already paid for them," while pulling out the receipt.

The man went to the rear office and returned with David's package. He opened them for David to inspect.

David smiled. The necklaces and pendants turned out better than he expected. He thanked him and started back to the car. Swinging his bag, a sense of pride caused him to strut, anticipating Jada's response and seeing the joy in her eyes. He took being able to pick up the gifts as his confirmation of his love for Jada. He decided to give her the necklace but would wait until he was certain he was ready before he asked for her hand in marriage. However, David maintained that Jada excited his heart and his mind, while Candy never conquered those parts of him. She had to scheme and plan to seduce him. Deciding to stop thinking of Candy, he thought about making his next stop to the grocery store to purchase food for Jada's romantic breakfast.

***

Charles, banging his hands on the dashboard, was angered because he thought he had followed Jada, only to realize he tracked her boy toy instead. At first, he considered waiting for him, but decided to locate Jada. He remembered that he followed Jada earlier that day. She drove a blue BMW. He also recalled how she raised the garage door to an unknown home. She only stayed for a few minutes, then left before he had an opportunity to park and approach her. *That must be where this man lives*, he thought. Charles followed her to the hospital, and if that stupid car had not caused him to almost wreck, he would have caught her in the parking lot. I bet she is at his house, waiting on him. He rehearsed in his head how he would take Jada and Micah far away. He thought once he told her how much he loved her, she would leave with him, and he would avoid going back to jail. He opened his glove box and secured his concealed .44 that waited to be used. Charles's mind was cluttered with thoughts of Jada making love to another man. His hands started shaking with sweat, soaking his shirt, as he sped down the highway and prepared to be with Jada forever. *I will have her one way or the other*, he thought.

***

Trembling, Jada still tried to process the words Charles spoke. She repeated, "If I can't have you no one will." They frightened her. Not sure if she should call Officer Nelson, tell David, or maybe alert her Aunt Lyric, she struggled trying to decide. She was so confused. A part of her wanted Charles to pay, but another part hated for him to go to jail. After all, he was still Micah's father, and she had no doubts about his love for him. However, after Charles' call she feared his physical threat to cause her bodily harm. She reached her mother's room and before entering, she hesitated, as she wanted to make a decision about whether to tell of Charles's call. As she pushed the door, all eyes focused on her. She tried to hide her confusion, but they must have shown through like water in a clear plastic bottle.

"Jada, what's wrong? Are you OK? You look like you saw a ghost," Lyric said as both her and Tianna rushed over.

"What happened, Jada?" Tianna yelled, shaking her. "Tell me."

Lyric tried to quiet her. "Shh, not so loud. We don't want to wake Nicke."

Jada felt as if her legs were rubber. She still found difficulty in speaking. She slid down in the seat next to her mother's bedside, and her legs straddled open as she held her head in her hands.

Lyric and Tianna exchanged glances at each other, wondering what in the world happened between the time she left the room to walk David to the elevator and the time to walk back. When she left, she had smiles and a bounce in her step, but returned dejected and about to cry, as if someone died.

No one spoke for several minutes as everyone became caught up in his or her own thoughts, with Jada as their focal point.

Jada spotted a gift bag beside her mother's bed. She reached down and pulled the bag on her lap. "Whose is this?" she asked, trying to sound as if she had not hit rock bottom

"David brought the bag in with the roses," Lyric announced.

Jada riffled through the bag and discovered a gift wrapped box. A flowered tag hung from the perfectly tied red bow, which read, "To my wife-to-be, Love David." At first, Jada wondered about the meaning, then smiled as she thought David would one day ask for her hand. She put the box back in the bag and pulled out another small box, also wrapped and tied with a red bow. The package appeared to be the same size as a ring box. This one said, "The key to my heart and happiness begins with you." David's suspicious behavior began to make sense to Jada. David tried to get her to come home with him so they could have a romantic dinner. *He was going to ask me to marry him*, she thought. *That's what him and mom talked about.* Jada had an immediate urge to get to David's house. She needed him to advise her on what to do about Charles phoning her, particularly since he was planning to be her husband. "Tianna, would you mind staying with Mom tonight? I think I need to go to David's house. Things seem as if he had plans for me," she said as she showed her the small box.

"You go girl! Looks like a ring to me. Sure, I'll stay with my mom," Tianna joked. "In fact, Mom, call your good doctor friend and have him walk both you and Tianna to your cars."

Lyric rolled her eyes at Tianna. "Come on, my real daughter," she said, grabbing Jada's arm.

Everyone laughed.

Tianna kissed her mother good-bye. "I love you, Mom. I'll be back in the morning."

Lyric kissed both Nicke and Tianna. "See you later, smarty pants," she said jokingly to Tianna.

The two women headed towards the door. As they walked down the hall, Lyric asked Jada if she wanted to talk about what was bothering her.

Jada shook her head no.

They pushed the button for the elevator. The moving platform seemed to be taking an inordinate amount of time to arrive, but they both continued to patiently wait. After about five minutes, Jada said she was going to the nurses' station to find out if they were out of service.

While Jada headed to find the cause of the delay, Dr. Maxey swaggered around the corner.

Shocked and pleased by his good fortune, he said, "Ms. Lyric the elevator is down, and you will have to walk through the west tower to exit the building. Where is your car parked?"

"It's parked on the east side of course."

"Well, can you wait until I check out at the nurses' station? I can escort you to your car. I am finished working for the night."

Lyric gave him a look that seemed to ask, "What are you up to?" Nonetheless she agreed. "Sure, but we also have to walk Jada to her car."

"Why, of course we will. Then you and I can go around the corner to the coffee shop." He smiled at Lyric while his eyes begged for her to join him.

They walked to the nurses' station. Lyric stood back against the wall. She told Jada that Jim was going to walk them to their cars because they needed to exit through the opposite side of the building. Jada was relieved that a man would be joining them because she did not know what to expect from Charles. "So, Auntie, Dr. Maxey is sweet on you."

Lyric tried to downplay her statement. "He's just walking us to our cars."

Jada gave her a questioning glance, and asked, "Then what?"

"What do you mean 'then what?'" She tried to duck Jada's interrogation, but somehow she couldn't. "Well, he asked me to have a cup of coffee with him, but I haven't decided."

"Look, Auntie, go have coffee with him. He's a great guy and is very into you."

"I'm a married woman."

"Yeah, Auntie, but is your husband a married man?"

"Jada, he will have to answer for that. I'm not going to hell for Johnny."

"Auntie, he asked you out for coffee, not a motel room."

Lyric blushed, then laughed as the doctor approached. "Let's go, ladies. I trust I didn't take too long." He grabbed them both, tucking his arm through theirs. "How often do I get the opportunity to walk two beautiful women to their cars?"

Jim winked at Lyric. "I hope you have your walking shoes on because we have to go all the way around the building. If you want, you two can wait in the emergency room area, and I can get my car and drive you to your cars?"

Lyric looked at Jada for her response. Jada shifted the gift bag from one hand to the other. "Auntie, you decide. I just want to get to David's house as soon as possible. I'm sure by now he has gone to bed."

"Maybe so, but I don't think you will have a problem waking him up." Lyric got tickled at her own statement. She was trying to break through the funk Jada seemed to have fallen into. Although Jada was endeavoring to hide whatever was bothering her, Lyric saw through her façade. Clearly, something was distracting her, and judging by how nervous she seemed, her burden appeared to be too heavy for her to carry alone. Lyric hoped her troubles did not involve David. She believed he would be the perfect man for her.

"Well, ladies, we're here and I need a decision. What's it going to be? Are you going to walk with me or wait for me to come back?"

Lyric decided for both her and Jada. "We'll wait for you, unless you're scared of the dark?"

"No, I'm not afraid. I like the dark." As his eyebrows raised, Jim directed his comment to Lyric. "Be right back. Don't worry. I shall return in about 10 minutes."

Lyric was glad Jim had left to get his car. She decided to try another shot at figuring out what had Jada so upset. She eyed two chairs in the corner that provided a clear view to the exit door and also allowed for her and Jada to have some privacy. She led

Jada to the seats and decided to be forthright. "OK, what's wrong with you? And don't tell me nothing."

Jada hesitated telling her aunt because she didn't want to worry her, but something said she had to confess because she did not know what Charles planned on doing. "Auntie, I'll let you in, but you have to promise me you won't tell anybody until I can figure out what my next move will be."

Lyric hated to make deals like this. She always tried to keep her word. She hoped whatever Jada told her, she would be able to keep. "Jada, to hold a promise depends on what you have to say. I don't want to make a commitment when I may have to break our contract later. I can say I will try."

Jada thought for a moment, but decided she must disclose to someone, and she might as well choose her Auntie Lyric. "Charles called me," she blurted out.

Lyric was stunned. "Didn't the judge place a no-contact order?"

"He did," Jada said, as she tried to determine whether she would tell her aunt what he said.

"What did he want? What did he say? Is he still in jail?" Lyric fired her questions at Jada.

Jada knew she couldn't tell Lyric what he said because she definitely would cause her to panic. She had to avoid the question. "My phone died before he finished talking."

"You have to let Officer Nelson know. He has a no-contact order, and he violated the mandate."

"I plan to head to the police station in the morning. David will probably go with me."

"OK, good. Just be careful and call me once you get to David's house."

"I will, Auntie." Jada was relieved Lyric accepted her answer without pressing her to find out what Charles said. If David became aware, she did not doubt he'd immediately accompany her to the police station.

"Let's go, Jada. I see Jim is outside."

The two ladies jumped in Jim's sleek Jaguar.

"Wow, Dr. Jim. Slick car," Lyric said as she admired the cream leather interior and the brightly lit dashboard.

Being his quick-witted self, Jim responded in a teasing way. "My car is OK, but for some reason, not as pleasing to the eye as you are."

Lyric rolled her eyes at him, but inside she loved the attention he showered on her. Johnny didn't have time to devote to her anymore. He was so busy with his other woman. She wondered if he had received the divorce papers. She was tired of all the women he constantly brought into their marriage. She figured he must really want the one he was with now because he no longer bothered to come home, wouldn't allow her to come to New York, and he even stopped calling. This assured her the marriage was over. She promised herself she would not open the door to the doctor until she first shut her current one on Johnny conclusively. Though she had to admit Jim did make closing the door easier to do but, her real motivation was watching Nicke fighting for her life. Nicke made her realize life was too short and too precious to waste time on someone who obviously did not want her. Watching her struggle forced Lyric to examine her own life as she realized how quickly life changes. She concluded the time was now to walk in her God-given purpose. She decided the night she spent at the hospital with Nicke to write a book and to work on her nonprofit organization, CAPS. (C-hildren A-re P-rotected against S-exual abuse). She started the book that night and had already completed three chapters. She felt inspired to use the scraps from her own molestation to try to help others. She also resolved to start a movement to save children from predators. This would be followed by her next major move, which was to retire from her job. She had the necessary time and was almost retirement age. Lyric committed to devote the rest of her life to bringing attention to children that were sexually abused as well as those who tried to pretend the assault never happened. By bringing attention to child abuse, she hoped to lessen the frequency of it through education. She solidified her dedication to God and to fulfill her purpose in life. For the first time in a long time, Lyric realized she was happy in spite of all of the external pressures of life.

"Dr. Jim, the blue BMW on the right is David's car." Jada reached from the backseat and put her arms around Lyric's neck. "I love you, Auntie, and I thank God for having you in my life. Be happy. God would want you to be. Thanks Dr. Jim." Jada hopped out the car before Lyric could comment. She searched her surroundings to be sure she did not see Charles's pickup truck.

Jim backed up to allow Jada to maneuver out of the parking space. He waited until she got in her car and pulled in front of him. She made a left turn onto Stemon's Freeway. Jim kept straight, heading to the coffee shop. Jada's parting words to Lyric were ringing in his head. "Be happy. God would want you to be." He knew no matter how much he wished he could have Lyric, he was going to respect her marriage. He realized he had to be careful not to pressure Lyric. He was resigned to the fact that if he and she were meant to be, their relationship would happen. He prepared himself to wait for the appropriate time. Once arriving at the coffee shop, he parked his car. When he glanced at Lyric, her blank stare confirmed something heavy weighed on her mind. Jim walked around to the passenger door and held it open for Lyric. He enjoyed watching the graceful way she stepped out of his vehicle. Her beauty could not be denied. He wondered if he would ever have a chance to be with her. Never before had a woman pierced his soul like Lyric. He pitied her husband for not seeing Lyric's real beauty, although he understood how a man could be crazy enough to let a real woman go and exchange her for a want-to-be girl. He made this mistake once or twice in his life, but after the last time he had a fake one who was stuck on prestige, he promised God he would only accept quality, no matter how long he had to wait. In his mind, there was no doubt Lyric represented the virtue he searched to find. However, since she was married, he chose to be content with friendship. However, he admittedly wanted more.

"Sorry, they don't have Starbucks coffee, but their drink is always freshly brewed. What may I get for you?"

Lyric snapped out of her daze. "I'd like coffee and a tea cake since I can't eat anything heavy this late."

"OK. I'll order it for you. After 10:00 p.m., you have to order from the counter. I'll place our order, and if you will excuse me, I also need to stop by the restroom."

"Sure." Lyric stared as Jim stepped away. She noticed the way he seemed to prance when he walked. Several other women patrons also admired him. She shook her head as she admitted he surely exemplified a handsome man, inside and out. She retrieved her phone and noticed three voicemails. She listened to the first one. A lady's voice said, "Lyric, you don't know me, but I am with your husband. Thank you for setting him free. We are in love with each other and we have a two-year-old son." Lyric gasped in disbelief. She held the phone down, perplexed. Checking the call log, she determined the caller used Johnny's phone. Holding her chest, she felt the pangs of hurt. She wondered how he disrespectfully allowed another woman to call her. Lyric's anger rose. She continued to listen and could hear Johnny in the background saying, "Donna, hang up the phone. You shouldn't have called Lyric. You got what you wanted. You read the divorce papers. There's no need to rub her face in our mess." Then the phone disconnected. Lyric pushed the end button. She lacked the strength to listen right then to the other voicemails. She was right about Johnny having an affair but had secretly hoped when he received the legal documents, he would come running home, begging her not to divorce him. She wasn't sure what she would do if he had, but at least she would have thought he cared about her. A part of her wanted to cry and another part of her wanted to kick somebody's butt. *How could he get another woman pregnant at his old age, and then hide his child from me? Oh well,* she thought, *I guess I need to be careful what I pray for. I asked God to reveal it to me, and he did.* This realization caused Lyric to relax some, but the pain in her heart remained. She repeatedly asked herself how could he do this. She hurt so bad that she needed to find a way to release her suffering. *God forgive me,* she thought.

Again, Lyric picked her phone off the table. She decided she would listen to the other two voicemails. This time, she decided to check who the calls were from before she listened. One was from Johnny's phone and the other from Officer Nelson. She chose to skip Johnny's message and listen to Judith's.

"Lyric, this is Officer Nelson. I called Jada but got her voicemail. I wanted you and her to know Charles posted bond this evening and he is out of jail. Tell Jada to be careful and to call me immediately if Charles tries to contact her in any way." Lyric's mouth fell open as she thought about Jada asking Lyric to keep her secret. She first assumed Charles called Jada from jail, but to know he called after his release caused her to panic. An uneasy feeling of danger crept through her body.

As she replayed the message, Jim walked up and placed her coffee in front of her. Lyric visibly shook.

He wasn't sure whether he should walk away to give her some privacy or try to console her. He decided not to interrupt. As he attempted to leave, Lyric grabbed his arm. He came back and sat down. He waited until she ended the call.

"Is everything all right?" he asked as he checked his phone to be sure the hospital had not called him about Nicke. He left strict instructions with the nurses' station that if any changes occurred, then they were to call him immediately. He had no messages. He turned his attention back to Lyric, searching for an answer as to why she appeared flustered and angered.

"Jim, I'm scared."

He reached across the table and held her hands in his. "Lyric, scared of what?"

"I think I made a mistake." Lyric was talking in riddles. She would not come right out with what was bothering her.

Jim started to get frustrated. "Lyric, tell me what's wrong. I want to hear everything."

Lyric began rapidly speaking telling Jim how Jada said Charles had contacted her. "Charles is out of jail. Jada was going to wait until in the morning to go to the police station. I didn't call Officer Nelson to tell her Charles called Jada. I hope he doesn't hurt that girl."

Jim interrupted Lyric. "Lyric, calm down. Call Officer Nelson now and tell her."

Lyric was thankful Jim forced her to get control of herself. She called Officer Nelson. "Hi, Judith. This is Lyric. I got your message. Charles has already contacted Jada. No, she didn't tell me what he said. I know she was extremely upset. No, she left the hospital about 10 minutes ago and headed to David's house. I told her to call me when she got there, but she hasn't called yet. He lives about 10 minutes from the hospital. Do you have David's address? All right, I'll call you when Jada calls me. OK, thanks. Call me when you get to David's house. Yes, I will." Lyric hung up the phone. Her eyebrows squinted together and her lips tightened to a pucker, revealing her concern to Jim.

Jim tried to reassure Lyric that everything would be fine, but he, too, had uneasy thoughts. "I'm going to stay with you until we hear something. I won't let you be alone. Why don't you call Jada and find out if she made it to David's house?"

Lyric dialed Jada's number, but the call went to voicemail. She then tried David. His phone rang and rang until he finally answered. "David, this is Lyric. Is Jada with you?"

David told Lyric to hold on a second as he was putting groceries in the trunk and couldn't hear her that well. "OK, Lyric, what did you say?"

"Is Jada with you?"

"No, she was going to stay at the hospital with her mom tonight. I just picked up some groceries. I'm about 20 minutes away from my house."

"David, Jada left about fifteen minutes ago. She was on her way to your house."

"Oh, good. I have a surprise for her. She is probably already there. She has the garage door opener, so she can get in. She thinks I'm at work or running errands."

Lyric tried to remain calm. "I called her but her phone went straight to voicemail."

David sighed a sense of relief. "Oh, don't worry. Her phone was dead. We'll call you when I get to the house."

Lyric was unable to remain calm. Her nerves got the best of her. She had to make David understand her fears. She blurted out. "Charles is out of jail, and he called Jada. Jada wouldn't tell me what he said, but whatever it was really scared her."

David got the picture. He understood Lyric's concern. "Lyric, I'll call you shortly. I'm on my way home." He hung the phone up and sped as fast as he could to get to his house. He felt Jada was OK, but he wasn't sure. He remembered how Charles looked at her. He wondered if he would risk calling Jada, what else would he do? David slammed on his brakes to avoid running a red light.

Lyric did not know what to do next. She wanted to hear from Jada or David to make sure everything was OK. She then realized she forgot to tell David that Officer Nelson was en route to his house. She didn't care who called her. She just wanted someone to call her and soon.

Jim was cognizant of the terror in her eyes. Neither of them had touched their coffee. Jim pulled out a five-dollar bill and left it on the table. He pulled Lyric out of her seat. "Come on, let's go. Do you know where David lives? Let's get our own answers."

"No, not exactly. I know he lives in the Valley Ranch area somewhere off of Cowboy's Parkway, but there are only a few other streets that intercept with that street, so it should not be hard to find."

"Well, that's good enough. We can head towards the area so when David, Jada, or Officer Nelson calls, we'll be close and you can see for yourself that Jada is fine." Jim hoped this would be the case, but somehow he had doubts. He shared Lyric's fear but kept it hidden from her.

***

Officer Nelson pulled in front of David's house. A red sports car, a tan minivan, and a blue truck were parked on the street in proximity to David's house. Her gut told her the pickup directly in front of the home did not belong there. She radioed in and asked the dispatcher to run the tags. She stayed in her squad car, attempting to detect any movement inside David's home. She could tell low lights or a candle flickered in the front room. The dispatcher soon confirmed what she suspected—the pickup belonged to Charles and Nicole Smith. She told the dispatcher to immediately send backup. According to her department guidelines, she had to wait until her fellow officers arrived before attempting to enter the house. She considered ignoring the rules but decided she better wait. She thought about calling Lyric but quickly decided to call David instead. She searched her car for the business card, which David had provided her. Before she could locate his number, a police car with red and blue lights flashing parked behind her. Officer Nelson quickly exited her car telling her fellow officer to cover her. Officer Nelson drew her gun and was about to head for the front door when the dispatcher radioed advising receipt of a 911 call from David's home. The operator reported a call was received from a woman stating that two people were shot inside the house, a man and a woman. Judith froze in her tracks. She was too late to save Jada, she thought. The first thing that came to her mind was how she was going to tell Lyric and Nicke. Two more police cars showed up. She waved two officers to the front of the house, while the other officers moved to the rear of the house. All the officers had their guns blazing and would be ready for whatever awaited them. At that moment, the front door opened and someone let two of the police officers inside the house. Officer Nelson took a deep breath as she prepared to enter. As she headed for the door, she heard a familiar woman's voice frantically hollering and calling her name. She turned to identify the person and saw Lyric sprinting towards her. She grabbed Lyric and pulled her back towards the squad car.

"Officer Nelson, is Jada all right? Did something happen to Jada? Please tell me she is safe." Tears were streaming down her face and desperation engulfed her entire being. She constantly jumped up and down, begging for answers.

Jim tried to restrain Lyric as she continued to lunge towards David's house. He fought to hold her while repeating, "Calm down, Lyric, calm down." His heart broke for her. He felt so helpless and did not know how to assist. He did manage to whisper a prayer to himself.

Officer Nelson appeared stunned. She tried to steady herself for Lyric. Finally, she conveyed to Lyric the 911 operator's report of a shooting. "I'm on my way inside to find out the details. Lyric, please remain calm until I have a full report." As Officer Nelson made sure Jim was holding Lyric tight, she attempted to step away when her fellow Officer approached.

"There is a young black female that appears to have been shot by an older white man. A young black female visitor to the home discovered the homicide. At this point, she is much too distraught to give a statement. Looks like a murder-suicide."

David skidded to a sudden stop in front of his house. He saw the police and all the commotion, As he attempted to run inside, an officer grabbed him. He noticed Lyric and Jim. He ran towards them hollering, "What happened? Tell me, please!"

Hearing the officer's account of what happened inside, Lyric began screaming, "We failed to protect another child! The police, her family, her friends, and the courts failed her. When will it ever stop? Can anybody protect our babies?"

There was absolutely no fight left in her. Her shield and her armor had been stolen. She no longer was a victorious woman. All she could do was muster up enough strength to fall on her knees and cry, "Lord, have mercy. Please father have mercy on us! Dear God, have mercy." Lyric collapsed into Jim's arms, trying to find shelter from all the torment flooding her soul.

Someone Save Our Children

Will someone save our children from the abuse that lies within?
Within the debts of darkness
That's covenant and sin
Our children are being raped, molested, and killed
Sometimes by folks they call kin
23% of sexual assaults occur under the age of 18.
Adults were the offenders in 60% of the sexual assaults
Adults were the offenders of children
under the age of 12 years old
89% of children being sexually assaulted involved persons known
to that child.
I taught my child to be accountable
No sex before marriage;
Use a condom
And how it's better to practice abstinence.
Then comes my family, friend, stranger, or acquaintance and
They teach my child
No matter what age they are
They are never too young to be sexually mountable.
Will someone save our children
From the abuse that lies within?
Within the depths of darkness
That's covenant and sin
No more covering up.
Trying to protect your so-called name.
Save our babies.
Make every perpetrator pay

Then our children will know that they are not to blame
They'll grow up and learn to trust
And won't be afraid to love
They'll feel protected
It's not an option

It's a **MUST!**

i-CAPS

PLEASE SUPPORT I-CAPS. Lyric is starting a nonprofit organization to help educate and protect children. We must openly have discussions on this subject, which is difficult for people to acknowledge. Sexual abuse occurs every day to children of all ages, including infants. We must stand up to the truth and stop perpetrators from using children for their own selfish gratification. Our children need to be educated at early ages on what is proper touching and what is not. They also need to be provided with several avenues where they can comfortably report assaults. Moreover, we must believe our children.

Adults should create safer environments for children. So many trust others without bothering to know the person; they babysit our children and can be boyfriends, girlfriends, spouses, and other family members.

Child sexual abuse has long reaching tentacles for adult survivors. Children are robbed of their childhoods. The results carry into their adult life and are manifested through lack of trust, self-mutilation, depression, unhealthy relationships, masking pain through the use of alcohol or drugs, and many more. Researchers suggest many victims become offenders, and the cycle continues.

Please save our children!
Children

Are
Protected against
Sexual abuse
If a child is being abused, please contact:
Churches
Adults (trusted)
Parents or Police
Schools (teachers or administrators)
To report child abuse cases, please contact your Department of Social Services. The contact number for local child welfare agencies can be found at http://www.childwelfare.gov/

References and Citations

The National Center for Victims of Crime/Child Sexual Abuse Statistics

U.S. Department of Health and Human Services 'Children's Bureau report Child Maltreatment 2010

Finkelhor, David & Emily M Douglas, Crimes Against Children Research Center.

U.S. Department of Health and Human Services, Administration for Children and

Families, Administration on Children, Youth and Families, Children's Bureau. (2013). Child Maltreatment 2012

Rape, Abuse & Incest National Network (RAINN.org); Statistics

National Children's Alliance 2012 and 2013 national statistics collected from Children's Advocacy Center members

Barack Obama, Presidential Proclamation—National Child Abuse Prevention Month, 2014

Yolanda Adams, 'Open My Heart' released 1999. Album 'Mountain High . . . Valley Low.' Label; Electra. Writer, James Harris; James "Big Jim" Wright; Terry Lewis; Yolanda Adams.

Tamela Mann, 'Take Me To The King' released June 12, 2012. Album, 'Best Days.' Label; Tilyman Music Group. Writer and Producer, Kirk Franklin

Bishop T. D. Jakes, "Save Your Scraps", TD Jakes Ministries Published 2012, The Potter's House

About the Author

J. J. began her writing career long before she realized she would become an author. At the time, writing poetry became a necessity, which was dictated by her emotions. She kept her writings secret and only shared them with a very few close friends and family. Many of the poems listed in her book were written twenty plus years ago. Although *Deflowered Lyric* is her first published book, she is far from a novice. She has written numerous reports, articles, business plans and the like for a 35-year corporate career job. She recalls a manager expressing to her that her writings were like reading a book. This was preparing her for this moment in time. She credits God for revealing her purpose. She believes everything that happened in her life was designed and orchestrated to manifest itself at this particular time. Stepping out on faith, she retired from her job to walk in her purpose as ordered by her heavenly father. When asked, why she would give up the security of permanent employment for the uncertainty of self employment. She smiles and replies, "God said so." She further explains her purpose is more than writing. "This is a movement to save our children from sexual abuse. I want to educate children and adults about this once forbidden subject that seems to be continually swept under the rug.

Please feel free to contact J. J. for speaking engagements, book signings, child sexual abuse insight, the many different ways you can assist her with 'saving our children' or just to share your thoughts about 'Deflowered Lyric'. She would love for you to be an integral part of her life's journey to fulfilling her purpose and also perhaps yours. God bless you.

J. J. Staples
P.O. Box 631184
Irving, TX. 75063

P. 469-708-6613
Web- defloweredlyric.com
Email- mailto:defloweredlyric@gmail.com
F.B.-facebook.com/defloweredlyric
Twitter Follow me @CapsJackie

Photographer:
bookings@shootwithgary.com
www.shootwithgary.com
Make-up : Glossbylkatrea@gmail.com
www.stylesat.com/lkatrea